BACK TOGETHER AGAIN

Also by Shawn McGuire

WHISPERING PINES Mystery Series

THE WITCHES OF BLACKWOOD GROVE Mystery Series

GEMI KITTREDGE Mystery Series

THE WISH MAKERS Fantasy Series

BACK TOGETHER AGAIN

The Wish Makers, Book 5

Shawn McGuire

Chapter 1

Ainsley

Not many people could play a ghost fiddle. That was my talent for the Holly Lake High Talent Show tryouts. I hadn't expected to want a spot in the show as badly as I did. All of the kids who'd tried out wanted spots, I knew that, and I hoped they all got in. The thing was, chances were slim-to-none that I'd be around to try out again next year, so for me, it was now or never.

"Ainsley!"

I spun to see Bryce Dalton, the cutest boy in school, coming my way. That boosted my spirits.

"Hey, Bryce." I adjusted my grip on the bulky box I was carrying and walked backward down the sidewalk, until he caught up with me. "What's up?"

"Oh, um . . ." He turned sunburn red before my eyes. How could such a popular guy also be shy? An enigma. "I wanted to tell you how great your audition was."

He reached for the box to carry it for me. I handed it over and shook out my arms.

"You think? That was my first time ever on a stage. I nearly puked from nerves, and I messed up at least six notes."

"I didn't notice." He was being gracious. He had to have noticed. "I've never heard anyone play wine glasses before."

"Ghost fiddle."

"What?"

"Some people call it a glass harmonica or glass harp. Some call it wine glass music. I prefer ghost fiddle because it sounds more mysterious." I waggled my eyebrows at him. "Also, it makes people say 'What?' and starts a conversation."

He smiled, dimples piercing the corners of his full mouth.

"How did you learn how to do that?"

"See? Conversation started. I taught myself."

"So you put water in a bunch of glasses until you had all the notes on a scale?"

"Pretty much. It started when I was ten. We stopped for dinner at this place in New Mexico. I was waiting for Mum to come back from the bathroom and traced a water drop around the top of my glass. This pretty humming sound came out." I closed my eyes, remembering the sound. "I did the same thing to Mum's glass and a different tone came out. It took me about two seconds to realize why."

"The amount of water in her glass was different."

I tapped the tip of his nose with the tip of my finger. "Right you are. Next thing I knew, I was chugging down what was left of the water and sticking those glasses in my backpack."

"You stole them?" He looked around, like maybe the police were just now catching up to me.

I held my left hand in the air and placed my right one over my heart. "I swear, that's the only thing I ever stole. I felt so guilty about it the second I did it, I took an extra five dollars out of Mum's wallet to leave for a tip."

Bryce looked sideways at me. "So you stole from your mom's purse to pay for the stolen glasses."

I'd never thought of it that way before and hung my head in shame. "I'm a serial stealer. I haven't stolen anything since, I swear. I'm going to sneak five dollars back into Mum's purse when I get home."

He grinned at me, amused. "You're a little different, aren't you?"

I analyzed the question for a moment then asked seriously, "Aren't we all a little different in our own ways? And doesn't all of us being different actually give us something in common and, therefore, make us all the same?"

Bryce raised his hand. "Question."

I held my hand over my eyes like a visor and squinted, like he was at the back of a large classroom, then pointed at him with my non-visor hand. "You, the cute boy with the dark curly hair."

And gorgeous blue eyes and shy dimpled smile. He really was cute. Especially when he blushed the way he was right then.

He looked at his feet as he spoke. "I've been wondering, why do you call your mom *mum*?"

"First," I began, holding up a finger, "always ask a question as soon as you have it. You might not get the chance to ask again, and then you'll have to go through life with an unanswered question. Not good."

"Yes, ma'am." He gave a little salute.

"The answer to your question is, I've always called her that. She says *mum* sounds worldly and more exotic than *mom*." I shrugged. "That's it. No one's ever asked me that before. Guess I should come up with a more exciting story."

Bryce shook his head. "Always tell the truth. I want to know the real you."

I'd been rendered speechless. And that didn't happen often. Over the last couple of months, Bryce and I had been getting to know each other. We were at the point where we could say things like *I want to know the real* you and not feel stupid. I realized, for the first time ever, that by traveling as much as Mum and I did, I'd been missing out on something important— true friendships and connections.

I blinked, my eyes stinging suddenly. "I want to know the real you, too."

"Ainsley, Bryce, wait up."

I turned to see Gabrielle Fernandez, my best friend, running towards us across the school lawn. Well, what used to be lawn. The grass had turned crispy months ago. Maybe it was because of Bryce's *real you* comment, but the impact of the label *best friend* also hit me. Until Gabrielle, I had never, not once in the fifteen years of my life, had a friend I could call a best friend. We moved too often for me to get to know anyone well enough for that to happen.

Bryce and I stopped walking and waited for Gabrielle to catch up. When she got to us, she hung on to my shoulder and bent over to catch her breath.

"What's the emergency?" I asked.

"I had to tell you," she gasped.

"Tell me what? Wait. Catch your breath first, or you'll pass out."

Thirty seconds later, she was ready.

"You're in." Gabrielle twisted her straight, deep-brown hair into a bun and wrapped the elastic from her wrist around it. "It's hot today. Isn't it hot today?"

"It's a little warm," Bryce replied. "But you were running."

"That could be it. It rained earlier, too. Feels a little muggy."

I waited for them to finish discussing the weather and then asked, "I'm in what? Wait. You don't mean the talent show, do you?"

"Um, yeah. You killed it at your tryout."

"I did?"

"Told you," Bryce said.

Gabrielle fanned the back of her neck with her hand. "Before we even started discussing anyone else, we unanimously voted you to be the closing act. That's the most coveted spot. Actually, I was forced to abstain, because we have a personal connection, but you know I would've cast my vote for you if I could have."

There was the C word again . . . connection.

This whole thing started when Gabrielle stopped by our apartment one day last spring and saw my ghost fiddle. I had the glasses set out on the coffee table and was playing "Hedwig's Theme" from *Harry Potter*. I'm not sure how long she'd been listening before she started squealing.

"Ohmigod," Gabrielle had said. "You have got to be in the talent show next year. You have to!"

"Next year?" My heart sank as she snapped a picture with her phone of me with my fiddle.

"Yeah. Gives you all summer to practice your act."

"True. Practice is a good thing."

What I hadn't told her was that the chances of me seeing a second school year in Holly Lake, Colorado were astronomically low. We'd been there for almost six months at that point. I'd never lived anywhere for that long.

Now, Gabrielle was standing in front of me, still fanning her neck, and waiting for me to respond to the news that I'd made it. "Aren't you excited?"

"Of course I am. Have to admit, I'm a little nervous, though." Also, my mind was boggled by the fact that five or six months ago I'd made a plan, and the plan happened. My life never worked this way. I didn't trust it.

"You? Nervous?"

"Well, sure. Now that I'm in the show, I'll have to be competitive. I'm not used to that." I closed my eyes. "I have to wear this information for a minute and decide how I feel about it."

"She's so weird," Gabrielle said.

"That's what I love about her," Bryce added.

Something in my belly fluttered at his words. I opened one eye to see his sunburned-embarrassed look turn third-degree-burn embarrassed and worried that he'd burst into flames.

Gabrielle's dark eyebrows arched high and she mouthed

wow. "I'm gonna go." She gave me a hug. "I'll call you later and let you know how things will go with the show."

She headed back to the school, where her mom was probably waiting in front of the building to take her home. Bryce and I walked along in silence, cutting through the football field.

"Sorry," Bryce said, after we'd gone from one end zone to the other. "I didn't mean to embarrass you."

I bumped my shoulder against his. The red on his face had faded to pink. "I'm not embarrassed. I'm sorry if you are."

"I am a little. And since I already am, can I ask you another question?"

"You just did." I grinned at him.

"Can I ask you many other questions?"

"Go ahead. Lay them on me." I threw my shoulders back and lifted my chin, ready for whatever he had to ask.

"I've been wondering about your hair."

"You mean why my bangs are white?" The rest of my hair was red, smack in between auburn and copper penny.

He nodded.

"I'm a mutant."

He laughed. "No, seriously."

"Seriously. It's a genetic mutation. I'm not like Rogue from the X-Men. I can't kill people with the touch of my hand." I opened my hand wide and reached for him. "At least, I don't think I can."

He took my hand and held it as we walked. The little fluttery feeling in my belly from before got bigger. It traveled up into my chest, warming me and making me feel super-charged. Another entry for my Journal of Firsts. *A boy held my hand today.*

"It's called piebaldism. I've also got patches of white skin." I lifted my bangs to show him the spot at the center of my forehead at the hairline. "This is my triangle of power. That's what Mum always called it. There are splotches on my elbows." I showed him, but didn't mention the ones on my butt cheeks.

"There are some on my back, too. My father must have it, because I guess that's usually how a person gets it. From a parent. Mum is one-hundred-percent blonde."

Bryce looked confused. "You don't know if your dad has it?"

"Never met him," I said. "He took off before I was born. Mum says I'm not missing out on anything." We got to the town's unadorned main road of old single-story, sun-bleached shops. I pointed right. "I live three blocks up."

He pointed at a bench sitting in a gravel patch twenty yards away. Technically, the bench and the gravel patch were a city park. A small bronze plaque on the bench dedicated the spot: *To Jorge Romero, in loving memory from his partner and children.*

"Do you want to sit for a while?" Bryce asked.

"Sure."

It was Thursday, which meant Mum was working the nightshift. I was on my own for dinner, and I couldn't think of anything I'd rather do than sit in the tiniest park ever with Bryce Dalton. He set the box filled with my glasses safely on the ground next to the bench. We sat there for probably two hours and talked. I can't say how much getting to know him filled me with happiness. He was especially curious about all of the places I'd lived.

"Where haven't I lived? The first place I can remember is Florida. Or maybe it was Georgia." I waved toward the southeast. "One of those states down there. Then we started the *westward expansion*, as Mum called it, going as far north as Missouri, then into Kansas, down to Oklahoma and Texas. Over to New Mexico."

"That's where you started your ghost fiddle collection."

"Right." I smiled. Not because he remembered, but because it felt good to have someone know about my life. "Then Arizona, Utah, and now here."

"I'm glad you're here." He brushed my white bangs out of my eyes.

"Me, too." My heart was pounding like I didn't know it could. I'd never felt this way before.

"One more question."

"Okay."

"Is it alright if I kiss you?"

All I could do was nod.

He leaned left, and I leaned right, so we bumped noses. We laughed. Then he leaned right, and I leaned left. Again we bumped. Again we laughed. He put a hand beneath my chin, and a little shiver, like when you touch your tongue to a 9-volt battery, shot through me. Then he tilted my head to the side a little and placed his lips on mine. I closed my eyes so nothing would disturb the moment.

A boy kissed me today.

My first ever boy-kiss was soft, gentle, and ever-so-slightly moist. It felt like the world had stopped to allow us to hold that kiss forever. It felt like we'd barely kissed at all.

He pulled away, and I sat there with my eyes closed. Maybe he'd do it again. If not, I'd live in the moment for a little longer.

"Ainsley?"

"Right here," I said dreamily, eyes still closed.

His voice was as soft as his kiss. "Everything okay?"

"Yup. I'm imprinting that kiss on my brain."

He kissed me again. Just as soft. Just as sweet. Just as perfect.

When I opened my eyes, he was sitting back and grinning at me.

"That was nice."

"It was," he agreed and then frowned. "I have to get going, though."

"Okay. Should I walk you?"

He pointed toward the other end of town. "I live way that way."

"I could still walk you."

"You're almost home. You can walk me tomorrow."

Tomorrow. What a beautiful word. Especially when Bryce was attached to it. *Tomorrow* was my new favorite word.

"Okay. It's a date."

"Tomorrow is Friday," he reminded. "We could go get burgers then head out to the reservoir. I guess there's a meteor shower going on. It's good and dark there so it's a perfect spot to watch."

"You mean a real date?"

"Do burgers and a meteor shower count as a date?"

"Will we be doing those things together?"

"That's the plan," he said.

"Then it's a date. I've never seen a meteor shower before." Or been on a date. My journal was going to get a lot of entries.

We exchanged numbers, I picked up the box with my ghost fiddle inside, and Bryce walked across the street with me. He gave me one more kiss before saying, "See you tomorrow."

Then he headed west, and I went east.

I walked the last three blocks to my apartment in a happy daze. What a day this had been. One of my best ever, and I wanted it to last forever.

"Ainsley!"

I blinked, my brain foggy and my lips still tingly from Bryce's kisses. Mum? She ran up to me and grabbed my hand, yanking me not only down the block but out of my happiness bubble.

"Where have you been? School was done hours ago."

What was she so upset about? And why wasn't she at work? Something bad must've happened. The happy flutter in my belly turned to a hard, acidic lump.

"I tried out for the talent show." I nodded at the box in my arms as proof. "Remember?"

She grabbed my elbow and dragged me down the sidewalk.

"Mum, stop it. I'm going to drop my fiddle. What's going on?"

I walked into our ground floor apartment and stopped dead as my whole body went numb. There were boxes sitting by the back door, which was open, giving me a clear view to the garage. Our ancient, red Volvo wagon was in the driveway, our tiny trailer attached to the hitch.

No. Not again. Not *now*. "Mum—"

"Pack your stuff."

"What? No. Why?"

"They used your picture. He's coming."

Chapter 2

Desiree

S orting wishes was a total high. Sorting wishes was a total drag.

I'd learned that, oddly enough, wishes came in themes. Today, for example, most of the two hundred that had come in were from kids wishing they didn't have to keep going to school. I dismissed half of them immediately. I felt for them. Few people *wanted* to be trapped listening to someone yammer on about stuff they'd never use in actual life. Knowledge is power, though, and I was all in favor of them becoming as powerful as possible.

The other half I took a little more time with. These were more legitimate reasons for not wanting to go to school. A few of the kids couldn't read and were afraid to tell anyone. Pressure to achieve was about to shatter others. Teachers were making inappropriate advances on some. (I had a special plan for those candy asses. The kids were afraid to tell, so someone else would have to expose them. Overstepping my magical authority? Maybe. Could not care less.) Far too many kids were being bullied. Those hit close to home, especially after Robin's wish, one I'd recently granted that had almost ended in disaster.

There were the standard *I wish I had a pile of money*. The wish was genuine, but like my mom told me long ago, "Throwing money at a problem doesn't fix it. You have to figure out what caused the problem to begin with." In a few rare cases, I did place a charge on the path to *earn* a pile of money during my time as a Guide. What they did with that chance was on them.

There were the *please let my dad/son/best friend/fill-in-the-blank survive this illness/injury* wishes. Some of those I could help with. For those I couldn't, I did what I could to make the passing as peaceful as possible. Often, it was the wisher who needed to find acceptance of the inevitable.

For every wish I had to deny, I let some good little thing happen for the person. Like winning back what they'd spent on lottery tickets that day.

When an IW (Incoming Wish) came to me, it arrived as a swirling light that looked like a tiny aurora borealis. It would hover around me like an eager pet, waiting to either be assigned to a Guide or returned to the wisher. I'd reduced today's aurora cloud by a good three-quarters when a new wish came in.

Usually the little auroras were soft, muted pastel shades. Now and then, a brighter jewel-toned one, indicating a time-sensitive wish, would arrive. The one that had just come in, well, I'd never seen an aurora like this one. It was a rainbow of intensely-bright neon shades. It pulsed and swirled and floated in front of my face.

"You seem to want my attention." I captured it in my hand and tossed it at the window that covered an entire wall of my little cabin office.

Usually, the window looked out at a sparkling mountain lake surrounded by majestic Ponderosa pine trees and snow-covered mountain peaks. When I tossed the auroras at it, the window became a monitor. The image of a guy appeared there. He was lying next to a dumpster in an alley. I couldn't tell how old he was because his face was swollen and bloody. He'd been beaten. As always, the wish words had been captured as they were spoken.

"I want to live." His voice got weaker with each word. "I want a home."

He stopped me cold. Not only had he been beaten, he was dying. The universe populated the screen with the fact that he was seventeen and that his name was Clay. That's all I got, not even a last name. Normally, I received tons of information that would help guide a wish. Clay's was simple, though. He wanted to live. No need to dig into his background to guide that one.

As the leader of the genies, I was the only one with powers strong enough to save a life on the brink like this. An unexpected thrill rushed through me.

"Indira!"

Wait. My second-in-command was off helping with another wish. Someone needed to be in charge while I went to him, though. There was only one Guide I knew could handle that responsibility.

I looked at Rasta, my dreadlocked Hungarian Puli that I'd dyed in the colors of the Jamaican flag. "She'll be so smug about this."

She will, Rasta thought telepathically at me in his matching Jamaican accent, *but you must do what you must do.*

"Can't I leave you in charge?"

Sure you can. I'll grant every wish that comes in, because I'm not mean like you.

"Fine." I inhaled and called, "Olanna!"

A tall, beautiful Nigerian woman appeared in my cabin a few seconds later. Her freakishly long neck always gave her a poised, regal appearance. She had an attitude that matched, but not in a good way.

"You called?" she asked, bored.

"You're in charge. There's an emergency, I have to go. I'll explain when I get back."

"Desiree—"

Before she could finish what I'm sure was an objection, I'd arrived at Clay's side. He was lying beneath the dim light of a flickering streetlamp at the center of an otherwise dark alley. He'd curled himself into a fetal position, one arm clenched to his stomach, the other covering his head as if he'd been fending off blows.

"Clay." I knelt at his side and touched him gently on one knee. He startled and scooted away, wedging himself into the corner made by a dumpster and the brick wall of a building. "I'm not going to hurt you. I'm here to help."

The process of moving that way seemed to zap the last of his energy. He went limp and his arm fell away from his stomach. A blood stain on his shirt made me guess he'd been stabbed. A flashback to the night when my friend Dara almost died from a stab wound skittered through my head.

"Can you hear me?" I leaned in close and spoke softly into his ear. He smelled like he hadn't bathed in a week and was so caked with grime I honestly couldn't tell what color his skin was. The tufts of hair poking out from beneath his slouchy cap were black. "Clay?"

"Help me," he whispered.

When I was a Guide, my powers were limited to performing any magic necessary to bring a granted wish to its conclusion. Saving a life was a power that only the Wish Master or Mistress, the leader of the genie world, could perform. That unlimited power was now mine, but rules still applied.

He was growing weaker by the second. Sure hoped I could do this magic right. I closed my eyes and focused all of my thoughts on healing his wounds. Then, when nothing but a fully-cured Clay filled my mind, I tapped my pointer finger and thumb together.

Instantly his pain was gone. The blood stopped flowing from his stomach as well as the cuts and scrapes on the rest of his body. His eyes opened and focused on me.

Those eyes. Lined with thick black lashes and canopied by heavy black eyebrows, they were the darkest brown I'd ever seen. For an instant, I saw the true soft, gentle, and compassionate Clay. His soul was right there for me to see in those gorgeous, dark eyes.

We all have different personas we wear at different times. In my life, I'd been a daughter, a granddaughter, a sister, a friend, a girlfriend, a hippie, a Guide, and now the Wish Mistress. Each version was me but unique from the others. When I was alone, I was different still from any of those. That's true for everyone, I think. Nothing wrong with it.

An instant after showing me his true self, a different Clay emerged. The gentle compassion was gone. Fear, exhaustion, loneliness, and desperation like I'd never seen before moved in.

"What did you do to me?" His voice was strong now, street-smart, breathy, and tinted with a Latino accent. "Who're you?"

"I'm Desiree. I can help you if you want to live."

Cosmos, please, let me do this right.

Clay sat up cautiously and pulled his hand away from his stomach. When he lifted his shirt, not only could I see every one of his ribs—this boy hadn't been eating much—but a gaping knife wound, too.

He raised his empty, dark eyes to me. "It's not bleeding."

"I stopped the blood," I said. "I halted your pain, too."

Distrust clouded his face, more a mask of self-protection than defiance. What had happened to make him this way?

He laid his head back against the dumpster. "Leave me alone, lady. I can't deal with no more right now."

"You made a wish. I'm here to grant that wish. My name is Desiree. I'm a . . . I'm a genie."

It was easier to say genie than to explain what a Wish Mistress was.

Clay turned his face away. A gesture that clearly said, *beat it.*

"You said, 'I want to live. I want a home.'"

He turned back to me then. Confusion. Fear. Hope?

"How do you know that?"

"That you want to live? I don't know exactly what happened to you, but obviously someone stabbed you and beat you up pretty badly. Do you know how close you were to dying?"

He looked away again. "Don't take no genie skills to see I got beat up. Anyone would wanna live." He turned partway back to me. "What makes you think I need a home?"

Oh, how he wanted to believe me. If he didn't, he would have tried to leave already. I'd seen it before. When people got this far down, they couldn't even believe in wishing anymore. Clay reminded me of many of the people who ate their meals at Rita's soup kitchen in San Antonio. I'd learned from my too-short time working there that shit happened, and people ended up with lives they never imagined they'd have. What happened to get Clay to this point?

I gestured from his head to his toes and back. "You're filthy. You look like you've been camping for a week. Since there aren't any campgrounds in downtown Denver, I'm assuming you've been living on the streets. I'm also assuming that you didn't choose this situation. So there's that, and I heard you. You wished for a home."

He stood. "Thanks for whatever you did to me. I'm going now."

"There are conditions," I said to his retreating back.

He continued to walk away, ignoring me. So I followed.

"The healing is only temporary. I can save your life, but there are conditions."

"Of course there are." He laughed humorlessly and spun on me. Anger now filled those dark eyes. "For the last eighteen months, every time somebody offered to do something for me, I had to do something for them first. Some of it was easy. Walk a dog, earn ten bucks. Clean the patio furniture at a restaurant, earn a meal. Some wasn't so easy. Want a place to live for a week? Sleep in my bed."

His bitter tone made it clear that sleeping wasn't the only thing going on in the bed.

"I can make you magical." I tried hard to keep the

desperation out of my voice. If I couldn't get Clay to agree, I'd have to let him die. That was a rule straight from the universe, and I had no choice but to follow it.

"Haven't heard that one yet," Clay said. "What drug do I gotta take to become *magical*? And what do I gotta do to you to get it?"

"You have to serve me." Immediately, I knew that was the wrong way to put it.

"Sorry, lady. Not that into you."

I needed a different approach. What had Kaf done when he rescued me from dying in that roadside ditch? I stared into Clay's eyes and then touched my fingers together.

"What was that?" He mimicked me, tapping his own fingers together over and over.

"I told you, I can make you magical." I held my hand palm up and nodded at him to do the same. Reluctantly he did. "Wish for something."

He laughed, humoring me. "If I do, will you go away?"

With my palm still up, I manifested my blue granny glasses and plugged them onto my face. His eyes went wide, and his jaw dropped.

"If this doesn't convince you, yes, I will leave." I nodded at his open hand. "Wish for something. In your head, not out loud."

He focused on his own hand, and a second later, the sloppiest triple-bacon-cheeseburger I'd ever seen appeared there. He took a huge bite and moaned with pleasure. Next, he held up his empty hand. A container of onion rings appeared, which he shoved into the crook of his arm, and then he manifested an enormous soft drink.

I hoped his enthusiasm meant I'd get him to agree with what was coming next. Even if he didn't, I wasn't about to take that meal away from him.

"How'd you do that?" he asked once he'd eaten the last bite.

"*You* did it. How could I have known that's what you wanted?"

He pointed at his still-bloody shirt. "How'd you stop the bleeding?"

"Magic."

He narrowed his eyes. "What's going on?"

"Like I said, you made a wish. The universe deemed it grantable and sent it to me." As I said the words, a longing I couldn't quite identify tugged at my heart. Maybe a few more details about me would help him believe.

"I became a genie back in 1970." I held up a hand to stop the obvious next statement. "I've been a teenager this whole time. I made a stupid mistake back then. Well, I made many stupid mistakes. One in particular ended in a car accident where I nearly died in a roadside ditch. As I lay there dying, I wished for a second chance at life. The leader of the genie world, a dude named Kaf, saved me that day. Now, I'm the leader, and I'm here to save you. I can also give you a home." I tipped my glasses down and peered at him. "Groovy, hey?"

"Yeah, groovy."

He rolled his eyes, still skeptical. Or maybe cautious was a better word. Understandable, considering the horrible life he'd obviously been living.

"This is the point where I tell you about the conditions. Ready?"

After a long pause he said, "Sure. I got nowhere I need to be and nothing to lose. Tell me about your conditions."

"You have to become a genie."

His expression didn't change for many seconds, and then he burst out laughing and held out his hand. "You're hilarious. Give me some of whatever you're on."

Flashback to life in the commune. How many times a day had I heard someone say those exact words?

I continued with the conditions. If I kept pushing, eventually he'd believe.

"I'm the Wish Mistress, the boss. You'll serve me for a minimum of five years." I never thought it was fair to sentence people to fifty years like Kaf used to. "That means you help those whose wishes have been granted. I'll explain the details later. You have to agree first."

He sat quietly, looking at his dirty hands. Most likely at the burger and onion ring grease still coating his fingers. He picked up the drink cup and took a long draw through the straw.

"You'll give me a place to live?"

I nodded. "We all live together in the mountains. The Guides live in Mystic Lodge. I live in a renovated school bus."

"I've lived in Denver my whole life and never been to the mountains," he said. "Except for once on a school trip in sixth grade."

"You'll be the only male Guide." I never understood why there weren't others. Probably because Kaf liked having a harem. "Just you and two hundred women."

Clay shrugged. "I grew up with three sisters, five aunts, two grandmothers, and my ma. I'm used to women."

"No dating or hooking up." I couldn't deal with that kind of drama on top of everything else going on around there.

"No problem. I'm gay."

Well, at least dating wouldn't be an issue. "Are you ready to go see your new home?"

He started laughing again. "This has been fun. Don't know how you did that thing with the burger, but thanks for the meal. See you around."

He turned and started to walk away again. Damn. I hoped it wouldn't come to this. I touched my fingers together, and Clay dropped to the ground, pain etched across his face.

"Sorry," I said. "I'm so sorry, but this is the only way I can save you. If you don't agree to become a Guide and serve for a minimum of five years, the only way I can help you is to call for an ambulance."

Kaf would have added one more condition to this scenario.

Not only would he have sentenced Clay to fifty years, he would have said that if he did not complete his servitude, Clay would return to the condition he was found in. That meant curled on the ground in agony, bleeding to death like he was right now.

I wasn't Kaf, though. New leadership, new rules.

"Do you agree?"

"Nothing to lose." He was dangerously close to losing consciousness.

"You need to say the words. Say, 'I wish to live. I agree with the conditions.'"

"I wish . . . to live." He spoke so slowly and weakly, I wasn't sure he'd get all the words out. "I agree . . . conditions."

He passed out then but had said the words. I closed my eyes and concentrated fully on giving him powers. When I touched my fingers together, Clay started to glow with a warm, golden light.

He opened his eyes and stood. This time, not only had the blood stopped flowing, his wounds were gone. He was alive and whole. Thank the cosmos, I'd done it right.

The alley filled with strobing red and blue lights.

"Stop right there," a firm female voice cautioned us. "Put your hands in the air."

We both did as told, and I looked over at Clay. "Ready?"

"Don't move," the officer commanded. "Stay where you are."

"Ready," Clay said.

I envisioned Mystic Lodge, leaned toward him, and touched my fingers to his.

Chapter 3

Ainsley

We couldn't go. I'd had the best day of firsts anyone could have and tomorrow there would be more.

"Ainsley, get moving." Mum had one hand on the top of her head, holding her growing-out bangs out of her eyes, the other pointing toward my bedroom. "We pushed our luck staying here this long. We should have left at the end of the last school year."

She was absolutely frantic. I'd seen her anxious to get on the road but never like this. I had to calm her down. If I didn't, well, I had a lot to lose this time. Gabrielle and now Bryce. And all the other friends I'd made. My heart was breaking. I couldn't do this again.

As I set the box with my ghost fiddle safely in the corner, I willed myself to get control. All the other times I'd done this were practice for this moment. I took Mum's hands and wrapped mine around them. I stood there, silently staring at her, until she looked into my face. Before long, she mirrored the deep breath I inhaled and then exhaled slowly. When I nodded, questioning if she was better, she nodded back.

"Okay, what's going on?" I used the most soothing voice I could.

"They used your picture." Her voice was high-pitched. She started to panic again and tried to pull free from my grip. I held on tighter.

"What are you talking about?"

Her head dropped forward, and she blew out a long, slow breath. Good, she was calming down.

"I was writing down my schedule for next week." She nodded at the calendar laying on the coffee table. "I remembered that the talent show was coming up, and I wanted to make sure I had off for it. But I couldn't remember the date, so I looked on the school website."

"It's on Halloween, Mum. Remember?" Sometimes her memory wasn't so good, especially when she got stressed. She'd been working double shifts at the diner for the last month. That was a big stressor.

She yanked her hands out of mine. "They used your picture."

"What picture?" I'd never had school pictures taken. I either wasn't there for the day they were being taken or I wouldn't be around to get them once they were developed. "I don't understand what you're so upset about."

"Look!"

She pulled me over to the couch and wiggled the mouse attached to our ancient laptop, opening up the school website. After a few clicks, and a ridiculously long wait, a page advertising tryouts for the talent show appeared. I didn't know they'd dedicated an entire page to it. Seemed kind of over-the-top since there were flyers taped every four feet on every wall in the school. Gabrielle, the student chair, was super passionate about the show. Heck, Gabrielle was passionate about everything she did. Said nothing was worth doing if you weren't going to do it well and to the best of your ability. That girl had one solid work ethic.

Anyway, I saw immediately what Mum was upset about, but I didn't understand why. Dead center at the top of the page it read:

Tryouts for the Talent Show - Friday, October 17th.
Performance - Halloween Night.

Below that was a picture of a girl singing, the caption below it read: *Roxy Riddell rocks out!* Another picture showed a boy juggling rubber ducks—*Trying to get them to fly, Ernie Goodall?* The final image was of me. *Ainsley Blue astounds with her ghost fiddle.*

"Oh, I remember that now. Gabrielle came over one night while I was practicing—"

"I don't care when it was taken." Mum waved her hands, getting agitated again. "I don't care who took it or why. I care that they used it. I signed a paper when I enrolled you stating they did not have my permission to use your picture or your name anywhere. Not on the website, not on any printed materials."

"What's the big deal? Everyone knows everyone here."

"We have to go."

She went to the kitchen and searched the cupboards for anything that might be ours. The place came furnished, which was always a necessity because we had no furniture. Really, everything we owned would fit in the Volvo. Mum said the station wagon was too easy to break into, though, so it all went into the little four-foot-square trailer we pulled behind it.

She snatched the box with my glasses from the corner and headed for the back door. "Go pack your stuff."

"No! You're seriously telling me that you're freaking out because they put my picture on the school website? I'm not doing this again. I like it here, Mum. I have actual friends here. They want to do stuff with me. They invite me to their homes and ask me to go to football games with them." I took off my glasses to wipe away angry tears. "Until now, the only thing I've ever done with friends was to eat lunch with them at school. Gabrielle told me I get to be the closing act in the talent show."

Mum stared at me, her eyes wide and wild. "You should

have thought of that before you let her take your picture. Now, go pack your stuff or I will."

My clothes, my ghost fiddle, some books, and a small box filled with newspaper clippings and postcards from all the places we'd lived was the sum total of everything I owned. Exactly eighteen, sixteen-by-eighteen-inch boxes fit into the trailer. I had seven of them under my bed for my stuff. I'd packed so many times, I could do it half-asleep if necessary. One box was for my pillows and blanket. One was for my sheets and comforter. Three for clothes including socks, underwear, pajamas, and shoes. One for my ghost fiddle. One for those books, newspaper clippings, and a couple of stuffed animals. A big hound dog who sat in the corner and kept watch over me at night. And a little cow I'd had since I was a baby. Moo Cow still slept with me every night.

Mum also had seven boxes for her personal things. That left four for bathroom and kitchen stuff and whatever miscellaneous household items Mum felt we should hang on to. If it didn't fit into one of those eighteen boxes, it didn't fit in our life.

"No sense being tied down to possessions," Mum always said when I was little. I was about ten when I realized we basically had no possessions.

She was still standing there, hands on hips, waiting for me to follow her orders and start the process again.

I shook my head. "Not this time, Mum. Not unless you can give me a good reason, and using my picture on a website doesn't work."

She said nothing, which only made me angrier.

"I deserve to know why you're moving me. Again!" I yelled. "Who is *he*?"

"What are you talking about?" Mum spun and started tossing all of our toiletries and bath towels into the bathroom box.

"You said, 'They used your picture. He's coming.' Who is he?"

"Not now, Ainsley."

My body started to shake, my hands clenching and unclenching with anger.

"Yes, now. Bryce Dalton asked me out today. We sat on the bench around the corner and talked for two hours. He asked if he could kiss me, and then he asked if I want to go with him to watch the meteors tomorrow night. I can't tell you how much I want to do that, so if you're going to make me miss my first date ever, I deserve to know who *he* is."

She stood in the bathroom door with her arms hanging at her sides, our hair dryer in one hand and a stick of deodorant in the other. She dropped the items into the box and came over and wrapped her arms around me.

"I'm sorry."

"Sorry enough that we'll stay?" I wiped my eyes and nose on her shoulder.

"No." Before I could protest she added, "But I swear, I will explain everything to you. For now, we have to go."

I couldn't believe this was happening again. I was so sure we'd finally found a place where we could stay. Maybe not forever, but for a long time.

"Just tell me who he is," I bargained, my throat tightening. "Give me something, and I'll... I'll go pack my stuff."

A little piece of my heart hardened and broke off.

She released her arms from around me and turned away. In a voice so quiet I barely heard her, she said, "Your father."

☾

We loaded the trailer in silence, which was unusual. Mum and I never had a hard time talking to each other. Not even when we were mad. Another first for my journal.

How was I supposed to react to this kind of news? Other than complete shock. She said my father was coming for me. My *father* was coming for me? That kind of told me that he'd been looking for me. Was this a recent thing or had he been searching for years?

Every time I'd asked about him over the years, and there were many times, she always gave the same flippant, "you don't need to worry about him" answer. I just wanted was to know something, anything about him. Kids would ask me about my dad, and I never knew what to say. There wasn't one thing I could tell them about him, not even his name. Eventually, I started telling them he was dead. For all I knew, he was. If I ever pushed Mum too hard for an answer, she'd start freaking out like she'd done over the website picture. It was too much to deal with, so I stopped asking.

As she did every time, Mum left the apartment keys and a letter that we wouldn't be returning on the kitchen table. We never got a damage deposit back because we never gave proper notice. She said that it was only fair to the landlord who would have to find a new tenant.

We were almost three hundred miles east of Holly Lake, Colorado before either one of us made a noise. I sneezed. Mum said, "Bless you."

I stared at my phone in my hands and debated for half an hour about calling Bryce. There weren't many minutes left on the pre-paid phone, and I didn't want to use them all explaining why we were leaving out of the blue this way. I'd be able to buy more minutes, but who knew when we'd stop at a mobile store. Maybe calling Gabrielle would be a better idea since she was my best friend. She could explain things to Bryce.

"Go ahead," Mum said.

The sound of her voice in the silent car startled me. "Go ahead what?"

"Say goodbye to your friend and your boy."

Say goodbye. Another bittersweet first. I'd never gotten to say goodbye to anyone. Honestly, until today, I wasn't sure that was something people did. I mean, I said goodbye to Mum when I left for school in the morning. I said goodbye to

Gabrielle when I left for home at the end of the school day. I said goodbye before hanging up the phone. Those were more *see-you-later* comments. This would be a permanent *never-see-you-again*. I didn't want to say that to Bryce, because I definitely wanted to see him again. I certainly didn't want to say that to Gabrielle. She held a little piece of my heart. How could I possibly say *never see you again* to someone who held my heart?

We always left unexpectedly. We could go from snuggled in for the night to heading down the highway in an hour if Mum decided it was time. I always missed the kids I'd gotten to know, but my loneliness never lasted long. Making new friends had never been a problem for me. I'm sure the same would be true this time.

"Maybe later," I said. "All my bars just disappeared."

We were in the middle of absolutely nothing. Well, technically we were in the middle of Kansas, but there was nothing but prairie grass from one horizon to the next. I wouldn't hang out here if I was a cellular signal either.

"You may as well use up whatever's left," she said. "We're getting new phones wherever we stop next."

That meant new numbers. Gabrielle and Bryce wouldn't be able to call me. As far as they'd know, I dropped off the earth.

"Why?" I asked. "What's wrong with these phones?"

Mum shook her head. "Too many people have our numbers now. If he asks around enough, someone will likely give them to him. We have to start with a totally clean slate this time."

He. My father. He really was looking for me.

Shock set in again, so silence did, too. All of the moving, had that been Mum keeping us off the grid? We used burner phones with area codes from three states ago. New Mexico. She had no credit cards. Paid for things with cash only. Until Holly Lake, she only got jobs that paid her in cash.

Once, she told me that having no attachments, "Gave us a little more time." The comment seemed strange to me, but she'd worked a double shift that day, so I dismissed it as her being tired. But now I wondered, time for what?

"We've been hiding from him, haven't we?" A shiver of fear shot through me. We spent a lot of effort hiding from this man. Did that mean he was dangerous?

She wouldn't respond.

"That's the real reason we keep moving, isn't it?" I pushed. "Not because it's a big country and we should see it all. But because you didn't want my father to find us." The fear was turning into panic. If he was dangerous, what would happen if he did?

"Are you hungry?"

"Are you going to answer my questions?"

"I have to stop for gas. Do you want to eat now or wait until we have to stop again? That will be in three hundred miles. Maybe less."

My stomach grumbled. I'd been so nervous about the talent show tryouts after school, I skipped lunch.

"Fine. Let's stop for dinner."

While Mum filled the Volvo with gas, I went into the truck stop's diner, which wasn't big but was welcoming. Booths with cushy green vinyl benches lined the outside window wall. A row of small square tables, ready for customers with placemats and two chairs each, ran down the center of the dining room. The focal point was the classic diner counter with stools bolted to the floor along the kitchen wall. The place was a little better than half full. Fortunately, a booth was available. As much as I loved sitting at the counters, Mum and I needed to talk, which would require a little privacy. As I slid into the booth, I had to admit I was feeling a little nostalgic. We ate almost exclusively at truck stop diners when we traveled. The food was always good. Truckers were picky about their meals and didn't hesitate to let the cook know if something was below their standards.

"Anything look good?" Mum tapped the menu on the table in front of me as she sat.

"Chicken-fried steak, I think."

"Oh, yum. We haven't had that in a long time."

"More than a year." I couldn't even look at her.

The server, a lady in jeans and a truck stop T-shirt with carroty-red hair piled on top of her head came to the booth with two huge glasses of water. "Are you ladies ready to order?"

"Chicken-fried steak for both of us," Mum said. "With mashed potatoes and green beans."

"Do you have sweet potato fries?" I asked.

"We do. They're real good, too. Love your bangs, hon. That's a great look."

I touched my white fringe. "Thanks, they're real."

"Nice." The lady nodded her approval and pointed her pen at her head. "I have to dye mine. So, fries instead of mashed then?"

"Yes, please. And a sweet tea."

"Sweet tea for you, too?" she asked Mum.

Mum nodded. After the lady walked away she asked, "Sweet potato fries? You never eat those."

"I've been eating them for months. I never eat mashed anymore."

Gabrielle had introduced me to them. All the kids hung out at the pizza place at the far end of town on Friday nights. Their sweet potato fries were amazing, crispy on the outside, tender on the inside, and super salty.

Mum shook her head. "I always knew what you ate before. We've lost touch with each other. I knew we'd stayed in one place too long."

"Do you have any idea how crazy that sounds?"

"What?"

The server set two glasses of sweet tea and two straws on the table between us.

"I agree, we're not as up-to-date as we could be," I said after she walked away, "but do you seriously think that not knowing which type of potatoes I like means we should have moved sooner? Dinner together every now and then would've taken care of that."

Mum had just wrapped her lips around the straw and pulled back. "I've been working like a crazy person lately. That doesn't help."

She'd been working six days a week for over a month, and most of those were double shifts.

"Oh my god. You've been stashing away money. How could I be so blind?"

"I don't know what you're talking about." But her tone said she absolutely did.

Double shifts had always been the warning sign. We'd stayed in Holly Lake for so long, though, I missed it. I thought maybe she wanted a nicer place to live or a new car. We'd had the Volvo for nearly three years. Our cars were always old, usually close to falling apart when we got them, but that's all we could afford. The Volvo had been a trooper.

"You were getting comfortable there," I said. "You liked Holly Lake as much as I did. Once the new school year started, you realized how long we'd been there. That's when you started the double shifts. You were saving money so we could take off again."

"Lower your voice," she ordered. "People will think we're fugitives or something."

"Aren't we?"

"Of course not," she hissed as she ripped the paper wrapper off of my straw and jabbed it into my tea. "We haven't done anything wrong."

I pushed my glasses up on my nose. "Fugitive doesn't only mean running from the law. It can also mean something short-term or temporary. Something that can change or disappear. That's totally us."

"They were teaching you way too much at that school," Mum said flippantly.

"This isn't funny." I was actually mad at my mother. Yet

another first. "I don't want to move anymore. I liked staying in one place and having a best friend and a possible boyfriend. Don't you want a job, and a life, you can be proud of?"

"I have nothing to be ashamed of." But she wouldn't look at me.

"It's not too late, Mum. We can turn around and go back to Holly Lake. It'll be late, and I'll be tired in school tomorrow, but I can handle it."

And I'd be able to go out with Bryce and be in the talent show.

She shook her head.

I sat back and crossed my arms. "Tell me about him."

She shook her head again.

"I have the right to know about my own father." My voice was rising again, but I didn't care.

She looked around, trying to tell if anyone had heard me. "Not here."

"I won't get back in the car if you don't."

"Don't act like a child."

I leaned across the table and matched her scolding tone. "Don't make me act like one."

We were in the middle of a pretty intense stare-down when our food arrived.

"Everything okay?" the server asked, directing the question at me.

It was one of those looks adults give kids when they think they might be in need of help. I'd seen it a few times during our travels. Usually it was directed at kids who were getting chewed out by the adults they were with. A few times it was when men were getting rude with women.

"Everything's fine." Mum stared at the plate in front of her. "This looks great. Thank you."

The orange-haired lady waited for me to smile and nod before she walked away.

"I mean it," I told Mum in a tone low enough that no one else would hear. "Tell me about my father, or I won't get back in the car. You've been dragging me around the country for as long as I can remember. I'm fifteen years old. I have a right to have a say in my life."

"I don't want to talk about him."

"That's what you say every time I ask about him. You freak out and say you don't want to talk about it and then you go on and on. 'Why do you keep bringing him up, Ainsley? You know I don't like to talk about him, Ainsley.' Then you lecture me about how I should be grateful for my life and all you do for me until I give up and let it go."

She glared at me then. I'd pushed too far, but I was too mad to care.

I plucked three sweet potato fries off of my plate and shoved them in my mouth. Oh, my goodness. Despite my anger, I couldn't help but notice that these were even better than the ones at the pizza place in Holly Lake. I closed my eyes for a moment to enjoy the flavor. The next bite wouldn't be like this. Nothing was ever as special as it was the first time.

When I opened my eyes, Mum was jabbing at her steak with her fork.

"Your father isn't a good man." She scraped off some of the gravy and licked her fork. "He's a creep and a cheat. I've kept you away from him for all these years, because I don't want him to drag you into his life."

"If he was so horrible, why did you get involved with him?"

"Give me a little credit." She cut off a small piece of steak and speared it. "I would never get involved with someone like him." She chewed that bite like it was still alive and she needed to kill it before swallowing.

"But you did get *involved* with him. At least once." I held my hands up to my face.

She shoved a forkful of mashed potatoes into her mouth along with the steak in reply.

"Were you ever married?" I couldn't believe I didn't even know that.

"No."

"So that's it? We've had to live six months at a time for fifteen years because you hooked up with a bad boy? That's the big thing you didn't want to talk about?"

"Don't be crude," Mum said. "I didn't know any other way. I've always believed that keeping you away from them was the right thing to do."

"Them?"

"What?"

"You said 'keeping me away from them'."

A flash of something I couldn't decipher crossed her face. She was right. We *were* out of touch. I'd always been able to tell what my mum was thinking.

"Did I?" She shrugged. "Misspoke, I guess." She laid her hand on top of mine on the table. "I've never cared about anything but your wellbeing and keeping you safe. Tell you what, we won't stop this time until we find the perfect place. We'll be super choosey, and then we'll never leave again."

"Why don't we go back to Holly Lake? We both like it there. Why can't that be the place we never leave?"

"Because they used your picture."

I ate my fries, barely even tasting them, and replayed everything she'd said. Why didn't I believe her? I mean, I believed that *she* believed what she said, but why did it feel like there was something more she wasn't telling me? If my father was that bad of a person, why didn't she call the police on him? If we were in so much danger that we had to live in hiding, why didn't she have them put us in witness protection or something? Was he a mobster of some kind? A drug lord? A hardened criminal who had people looking for us?

It was like when you read down the middle of the page to get the general concept of your social studies homework, then you find out on the quiz the next day that you'd missed some key items doing it that way. I'd find out the truth eventually. I didn't know when, but now I had something to work off of. Sometimes, when she got overtired or was concentrating hard on something else, I could ask questions, and she wouldn't even know she'd answered me.

I finished my fries and steak. The server lady had brought us each a piece of cake in to-go containers for dessert. I grabbed my container and plastic fork and got up from the booth.

"What are you doing?" Mum asked.

"I'm going to go outside. I want to get some fresh air before we get back in the car."

"Okay," Mum said. "I'm going to freshen up in the bathroom. I haven't had a shower yet today."

That meant we weren't going to stop for a long time. We'd keep driving until she was too tired to go any farther. Then we'd get a motel for a few hours so she could sleep, and once she was rested enough, we'd continue on.

"It's dark already. Are you sure you don't want to stay here for the night?"

I didn't like it when she pushed herself like that. Not only would she be in danger of falling asleep, she'd turn the radio way up and sing so loud I wouldn't be able to sleep, either.

"I'm sure," she said in the tone I knew not to bother questioning.

Across the two-lane highway from the truck stop was a little park. It was nowhere near as tiny as the one where Bryce and I sat earlier today but still small. I went to the bench there, and even though there were plenty of lights from the truck stop, I could see bazillions of stars.

The night was a little cool, and I wished I'd grabbed my fleece from the car. As I stared up at the sky, eating my carrot cake frosting first, I saw a streak of light almost directly overhead. The meteors!

A few seconds later, another meteor shot across the darkness. Did they ever collide with the stars? How long until they burned out? Was a meteor the same thing as a shooting star? Would wishing on one be the same thing as wishing on a star? Couldn't hurt to try.

I stared without blinking until the stars started to blur. Finally, when another meteor shot past, I closed my eyes and clasped my hands together over my heart.

"I wish—" My voice caught. "I wish I could know the whole truth about my parents. And I wish I could have a home. A *real* one that I never have to leave until I'm ready to. Please. Amen. Thank you."

I'd never gone to church. Mum had never taught me any kind of religion, so it felt a little disingenuous adding the *Amen*, but I figured whoever or whatever might be listening to me would know that I wasn't being disrespectful. I meant those words with my whole heart.

Chapter 4

Desiree

Clay stared out the windows at Mystic Lodge on the far side of the lake. I had transported us to Gypsy V, my renovated school bus home, when we left the alley. I knew Olanna would be smoking-mad, waiting for an explanation for why I'd left so suddenly. But, not only did Clay need time to deal with the events of the last hour of his life, I needed time to figure out how to introduce him to the Guides.

Clay walked through the bus, investigated my little kitchen, and stopped at the entrance to my bedroom. "Nice place. Where are we exactly?"

"In the mountains, still in Colorado, in a valley that's nearly impossible to get to. If someone did wander by, they wouldn't see anything. I've enchanted it. Planes flying over can't see us either. Not the Lodge, not the little cabin perched next to it that I use as an office, not Gypsy V."

"Kind of like Hogwarts." He gave a tired smile.

"Exactly." I loved it when others came up with ideas I could borrow. I went to his side and pointed at the massive log-cabin-style lodge. "That's your new home, by the way. No rush to get over there."

He was breathing hard. Mostly from the high altitude, I assumed, but also because he was still weak from . . . whatever had happened to him. I had healed his wounds, but I couldn't bring him to full health. Only time could do that.

Now that we were away from the shadowy alley, I saw how thin and broken down he was. I sent a little plea to the cosmos to provide more of his story so I didn't have to ask him. I knew the look though. He'd been using a drug of some kind. I'd seen that same vacant, skittish look on half the people in the commune I'd lived in back in 1970. He was strung-out and would need help getting clean.

What were the drugs covering up? What had he lived through?

"You look like you could use a shower." Clay wasn't simply dirty. Only someone who'd been literally rolling in mud could have been dirtier. His fingernails were caked beneath and around with gunk. His face was greasy with grime and lined with streaks of dried blood that must have transferred from his hands. He'd respectfully taken off his beanie when we came inside Gypsy V. His hair was so dirty it was starting to look like Rasta's cords.

"Yeah, I stink." He was so exhausted, speaking was hard work. "Haven't had a shower since . . . Can't remember."

"Maybe a haircut, too? And a shave?"

He smiled. "You're gonna make me want to stay, lady." He held up a hand to stop the words I was about to say. "I know, I know. I'm here for five years."

Glad he understood that.

"You gave me these magical powers," he said. "Can't I magic myself clean?"

"You can. But would you deny yourself the luxury of a hot shower?"

He closed his eyes and sighed. "Not gonna argue with that."

I touched my fingers together. "Your shower is waiting."

Outside, tucked among the pine trees near the lake, I manifested a shower hut made of large mountain stones. It was fully enclosed except for a roof. Taking a shower beneath the stars sounded like a bit of nirvana on earth to me. I couldn't believe I'd never thought of it before.

"Take all the time you need," I said. "You can manifest yourself some new clothes."

"How do I do that?"

"Remember the cheeseburger?"

Clay nodded. "Just think of what I want?"

"That's it."

As he cleaned up, I climbed onto Gypsy V's roof. When I was a Guide, I moved my bus all around the world. Kaf could find me no matter where I went, so I set up in the most remote mountain valleys or on secluded islands in the middle of the ocean. I even spent a few weeks in the middle of an African plain with wildlife all around me. I'd start every morning this way, sitting on top of my bus, first meditating and then drinking a big mug of tea while watching the animals. One day, I saw a baby zebra being born. It was one of the most perfect moments in my life.

My charges' needs always came first, but I had the freedom to go anywhere I wanted. I missed that. As the Wish Mistress, the boss, I had to take these moments when I could get them. Like now, sitting on my roof to stargaze. And listening to Clay singing in the shower. In Spanish.

Helping him tonight gave me that bitchin' little thrill I used to get whenever I helped a charge get his or her wish. I didn't get to experience that part of things with this job. I assigned wishes, but had no interaction with the charges. In order to be a happy boss, I was going to have to tweak a few things.

"That was amazing," Clay said, walking toward the bus in dark straight—but thankfully not skinny—jeans, a striped T-shirt, navy blazer, new beanie, and a pair of the coolest wingtip shoes I'd seen in a long time. "Checkin' out the threads, aren't you?"

"I am. I can see the real Clay now. Feeling better?"

"Much."

"I've got an idea for that shave and haircut."

He hesitated before asking, "What?"

I summoned Indira. Moments later, the woman with crazy-curly hair and cocoa-brown skin arrived. I gave her the quick version of how Clay had come to be a part of Team Genie, and told her he could use a little of her TLC. A few minutes later, her *vardo*, her gypsy wagon turned mini-spa, was sitting next to my bus.

"Come inside." Indira held a hand out to the wagon.

Silks in gorgeous jewel tones adorned the *vardo* walls. Candles in dozens of beautiful Moroccan-style lamps hung from the ceiling and cast flickering shadows all around. A comfortable salon-style chair sat at one end next to an ornately carved cabinet that served as a hair washing station. Indira touched the back of the chair and told Clay to sit.

Clay remained by the door, hands clasped in front of him, eyes cast down.

"You can trust Indira completely," I reassured him. "She's not a genie. The only power she has is to transport herself and her wagon to where she's needed. Her gift, to transform people into more beautiful versions of themselves, comes naturally."

Sheepishly, he looked up. "What're you gonna do to me?"

"Let's start with a simple haircut," Indira suggested. "You can let me know afterwards if you want me to shave you."

"Okay. A cut is good." Slowly, he sat and slid his hands along the sides of his head. His voice shook slightly as he explained, "Shorter here, longer on top."

Little beads of sweat appeared on his forehead as Indira put a cape around him. When she ran her fingers through his thick, shoulder-length black hair to get a feel for it, he jumped out of the chair and headed back for the door.

"What's wrong?" I asked.

"Touching." His breath came in ragged gasps. "I don't like being touched."

Again, I wondered what had happened to him?

"She's not going to hurt you," I promised. "I'll stay right at your side. She's got to touch your hair if you want her to cut it, right?"

He considered this for a few seconds then nodded.

"Tell me if I'm doing something you don't like." Indira was a true pro, not at all upset by Clay's reaction. She'd helped hundreds of people over the years who had been as broken as Clay was now. "You say stop, I'll stop."

As she ran a comb through his hair, her bracelets jangled and Indira started humming. The tune was an Asian, Middle Eastern, Native American blend and unbelievably soothing. It worked like magic on Clay. When she was done, he was happy with the cut.

"What about that shave?" Indira asked.

He shook his head. "Don't think I can handle anyone coming near me with a blade for a while."

I explained he'd been stabbed and tapped my fingers together. Instantly, he was clean-shaven and looking like a new person. Or, more accurately, he looked like the person he was supposed to be.

"Sorry." He watched the ground as we walked back to my bus.

"For what?"

"You know what."

"You don't have to apologize." I echoed Indira's soothing tone. "I get it. Something bad happened to you. If you want to tell me about it, you can. If you don't, that's groovy, too. If you need someone else to talk to, I'll find someone for you."

"Thanks. There is one thing I need."

"Sleep?" I guessed.

"How'd you know?"

"Because even though you're clean and smell good, you still look like hell. You take my bed for tonight. Tomorrow you'll meet the Guides and can move into your room in Mystic Lodge."

"Where are you gonna sleep?"

"On top of the bus." A little thrill rushed through me. "I haven't slept up there in a long time."

"I've been sleeping on the street for over a year. Always on alert for someone coming up on me. I'd give anything for a good night's sleep. So, if you're sure—"

"Done." I enclosed the bus in a bubble so quiet he had to speak to ensure I hadn't struck him deaf.

As he settled into Gypsy V, I went to Olanna. She'd been at the little cabin I used for an office for hours and had summoned me twice.

"You need to work on your communication skills," Olanna attacked the moment I appeared.

I was prepared for her to be angry. What I hadn't prepared for was to find Kaf there with her. They'd been sitting next to each other in the overstuffed leather chairs I provided for the Guides.

Everyone knew that Olanna was in love with Kaf. She had been for a long time. So my immediate reaction was to assume that they were *together*. Logic told me that if I'd caught them doing something scandalous, one of them would have jumped to their feet and started explaining that nothing was going on. Instead, when Olanna saw me, she inched a little closer to Kaf, letting her knee graze his.

"Sorry I had to leave so quickly." I went to my chair across from them.

"You can't disappear that way," she reprimanded. "I had to summon Kaf to assist me."

"Don't know as much about my job as you'd thought?" Childish, yes, but I couldn't help poking her every now and then.

A blush broke out along her high cheekbones, and she pouted her full lips.

"I went to help a boy who'd made a wish."

"That is a job for a Guide." Kaf rose from the chair and positioned himself between Olanna and I.

"He was dying," I said. "His wish was to live."

Kaf understood immediately. "A dying wish. What did you do for him?"

There were two ways to handle a dying wish. If death was due to a fatal disease, cancer for example, I could cure the disease. If death was due to an injury, as it had been in Clay's case—and mine and Olanna's and many of the other Guides—I would heal the injuries. Either way, a dying wish meant that death was coming within minutes.

"He's our newest Guide, of course," I explained as though that should have been obvious.

"There are no male Guides," Kaf objected.

Olanna jumped to her feet and went to Kaf's side, joining forces. "It isn't done."

I had been one hundred percent on the side of girl power for as long as I could remember. I believed that women were equal to men. Logically, that meant men were also equal to women. Therefore, there was no reason Clay couldn't be a Guide.

"There never have been," I said. "That doesn't mean there can't be."

"Actually," Kaf admitted, "there were male Guides when I became Wish Master two hundred years ago."

It was a tie between Olanna and me for who was more shocked by this revelation.

"What happened to them?" I asked, sure my harem theory was finally about to be proven.

"I sent them away," he said. "For the wellbeing of my sister."

"For Adellika?" I asked. "Why?"

"I brought Adellika to the magical world not long after I got here." Kaf completely softened as he talked about his sister. His voice, his expression, even his rock-solid muscles relaxed. "For reasons that are not mine to explain, she couldn't be around men. I released the male Guides and have allowed only females since."

Kaf's caring side. I didn't get to see it often, and I didn't always understand it when I did, but it always melted my heart.

The last time was when Crissy's boyfriend, Brad, was attacking her. I wanted to rush in and save her. I wanted to pull Brad off of her, manifest the most poisonous snake imaginable, and drop it down his pants. It made me physically sick to know what was happening to her, and I was furious when Kaf held me back. He literally grabbed me by the elbow—the first time he had ever touched me—and told me I had to stay away. The pain on Kaf's face had been as real as what I'd felt. He was right, though, and I knew it. If I'd stormed in and saved her, Crissy wouldn't have found the courage to stand up to Brad. The truth was, Kaf cared about our charges every bit as much as I did.

"Protecting your sister. How honorable of you." I locked eyes with him, my heart stuttering when I did, and he bowed his head in thanks. "You'll see. Clay will be a great Guide."

"That's what you said about Dara." Olanna's bratty voice yanked me out of the moment.

I cringed. Dara never should have become a Guide. Yes, she had made a dying wish and agreed to the conditions, but an exception should have been made. She should have been healed and allowed to return to her real life. That mistake led to Robin, her first and only charge, nearly dying.

"I have a plan for Clay," I said.

To my horror, Kaf smirked. "What is your *plan*, Desiree?"

That smirk was like a punch to the gut. It took my breath, but I had to stand strong. I couldn't let either of them see me doubting my decisions.

"I'm implementing an apprentice policy for all new Guides." I felt stronger with each word. "They will have to observe a number of wishes from beginning to end before being allowed to take on their own charges. Following more than one Guide would be even better since each Guide has their own process. They can see a few different styles that way."

"That's actually a good idea," Olanna said.

Olanna agreed with me on something? I pinched my arm to make sure I really was in my cabin and not still on top of my bus in a meditative trance.

"There are a handful of Guides I'd suggest they follow," Olanna continued. "New Guides deserve to learn from the best."

"Glad you feel that way," I said. "Clay will start by following me."

"You?" Kaf nearly choked on the question. "You are the Wish Mistress. You no longer guide charges."

It was more of an order than a point of fact.

"Correct me if I'm wrong," I said, "but part of the reason you chose me as your replacement is that I was the best Guide here."

Kaf didn't respond. But that lack of response confirmed my suspicion and boosted my confidence.

"If we want our world to be successful, we need to have quality Guides. To be the best, you must learn from the best."

"Take care," Olanna cautioned, "that your head doesn't inflate so much that you float off into the pines."

"This isn't me being arrogant," I countered. "If I'm confident about one thing, it's that I was a good Guide. I have made mistakes—all of which you have pointed out to me, Olanna—and I don't want to make any more."

"This is wrong," Kaf said. "Your job is ruler of the Guides. Not teacher."

I settled into full lotus pose in my meditation chair.

"Kaf," I said, "for my first three wishes you followed me so closely we practically shared a shadow. Basically, you did with me what I want to do with Clay."

By the way Olanna's head snapped toward him, Kaf hadn't trailed her the same way. Curiouser and curiouser.

"Who will be in charge while you are off guiding?" Kaf challenged.

"Indira is the second-in-command," I said.

"What if she's working with a charge?" Olanna asked. Trying to win back a few points from Kaf? "You do have a tendency to disappear."

"You're right again." I tapped my fingers thoughtfully. "Our chain-of-command doesn't have enough links." Another flaw in Kaf's system. A sudden, impulsive thought occurred to me. There's a saying: keep your friends close and your enemies closer. "Olanna will be our third."

I'd known Olanna for years and had never seen her look so surprised.

Just then, a new wish came in, its aurora bouncing around my feet like a playful kitten. This aurora was coppery-red with patches of white. It reminded me of a peppermint candy, the kind with the pinwheel design.

I scooped up the wish and was about to toss it at the window when Olanna said, "I'll leave."

"No, you can stay. As third-in-command," I said as though knighting her, "it is your responsibility to perform the duties of Wish Mistress if for any reason Indira and I are not able to."

"Isn't that the oath of the runner up in beauty pageants?" Olanna asked.

"Yeah." I made a face. "I'm not a fan of that whole display, but the oath is good."

Sorting and assigning wishes was a job that only the Wish Mistress or Master could perform. Out of respect for the wisher, I normally did the job in private and kept the details private. The only people to know them were me and the Guide assigned to the wish. Just this once, as a display of trust, I tapped my fingers together and gave Olanna the ability to see everything about this wish.

I tossed the candy-cane-like aurora at the big window. A pretty girl with coppery-red and white hair and oversized black-plastic glasses appeared. Information started populating the screen along with her picture. Ainsley Blue was fifteen, had lived with only her mother since she was born, and had lived . . . wow, in more places than I thought possible in only fifteen years. The list of all those places was quite long. Her list of friends, short. Of course, if those friends were as good to her as Mandy and Crissy were to me, she was all set.

Ainsley's voice, a little on the raspy side, filled the tiny cabin next. "I wish I could know the whole truth about my parents. I wish I could have a home. A *real* one that I never have to leave until I'm ready to. Please. Amen. Thank you."

"Sweet girl," Olanna said.

I nodded my agreement. "On the outside, she's bubbly and bright. The kind of person anyone would want to be around. Something's wrong, though. Do you sense it?"

Olanna turned to me, her head tilted in question. "No. What do you see?"

"It's in her eyes." I pointed at Ainsley's picture. "There's an emptiness in those beautiful baby-blues. Her eyebrows are scrunched together a bit. She's sad."

The words *connection, family, friends,* and *home* popped up on the window.

"This is how the universe gives us a little help," I explained. "We get an image and information about her life that helps us figure out what her soul truly wants. And that, as you know, is the crux of every wish."

Two of those words, *connection* and *home,* tugged at my heart and formed an immediate bond to this girl for me. People who care that you're alive, a place where you felt safe and like you belonged. What more did a person need?

"Far out. I needed a wish, and the universe gave me one." A ripple of excitement rushed through me. "Clay will apprentice with me for Ainsley's wish."

Kaf pushed his shoulders back. "This is not a good idea."

"Can't imagine what you could possibly have to complain

about." I narrowed my eyes at him. "Is it that I'm changing things or that I'm allowing another male into our world?"

"Bringing a rooster into the henhouse is not a good idea." Kaf crossed his arms as though punctuating his point—the signal that he had made his decision—and the conversation was finished.

I stared at him then turned to Olanna, hoping she was as offended by this as I was. The purse of her lips told me she was.

"First," I said, "we're not hens. Second, if you're insinuating that we won't be able to stop ourselves from being swayed by his masculine charms, you're an ass. Third, you're an ass. Fourth, trust me, allowing this *rooster* in won't be a problem for anyone."

Olanna took a step closer to me, one arm held tightly across her belly, the other hand fluttered near her throat.

"I agree with you, Desiree." Her voice had lost its signature confident edge, and she seemed to be almost pleading with me. "The majority of the Guides will be fine, but some of us are not comfortable in the presence of a male."

Immediately, I understood what she meant. Olanna had been near death from injuries she received during a gang rape when Kaf saved her. Another Guide, Amber, had been drugged and abused by a man. She was huddled in a cardboard box in an alley when Kaf went to her. Kaf's sister, Adellika, must have gone through something similar.

"I'm sorry." I placed my hands in Namaste and bowed to Olanna. "I never intended to make you feel unsafe. You'll see when you meet Clay, he's got a gentle soul."

She didn't argue with me but looked a little gray.

"When will we get to meet him?" Olanna asked.

"He's sleeping in my bus right now," I said. "He's had a rough time and needs to rejuvenate. Once he's rested and ready, I'll introduce him to you all and we'll get started on Ainsley's wish."

I couldn't say what I was more pleased about, that things had gone as well as they had with Olanna and Kaf or that I was going to get to guide a wish again.

Once Kaf and Olanna had left, I opened Ainsley's file on my tablet and read more about her. The list of places she'd lived left me shaking my head: Maine, Vermont, Pennsylvania, Kentucky, North Carolina, Florida, Alabama, Mississippi, Missouri, Kansas, Oklahoma, Texas, New Mexico, Arizona, Utah, Colorado. Sixteen states in fifteen years, currently on their way to number seventeen, and multiple cities within most of those states. Her mother called it traveling, seeing the country.

I'd done a lot of traveling when I first became a Guide. Until the road trip to Woodstock and then the move to the commune in San Francisco with my boyfriend and best friend, I'd never left Texas. I loved the idea of seeing the world, so I would move Gypsy V to a new place every couple of months. When not tending to a charge's wish, I'd wander through the streets of quaint villages in France. I'd have dinner at outdoor cafés in Bavaria while watching people pass by on the cobblestone streets. Once, I even transported myself to the top of Mt. Everest so I could watch the sunrise from the top of the world.

Traveling was exciting. It was easy for me, too. All I had to do was concentrate on a new destination, and suddenly I was there. It came with a price, though. I'd established a reputation as a recluse, the strange hippie girl who thought she was too good to hang out with the other Guides. That wasn't it at all. But after a reputation took root, it was ridiculously hard to change it. So, I kept to myself for forty more years.

I looked down to find Rasta sitting in front of me.

What's the matter? he thought at me.

"What makes you think something's the matter?"

Because you are sweating.

"I am?" I put my hand to my forehead, and it came away damp. My tunic had started to stick to me. "Is it hot in here? I can't breathe."

I touched my fingers together, and the door opened.

It isn't hot, Desiree. What's upsetting you?

I shook my head and reread the keywords and details of Ainsley's life. "They live like nomads. They barely have any possessions, and they've moved every four months or so."

Possessions are important?

"To some people. Why is it so hot?" I flicked the windows open, too. "Ainsley has never even known that she has family other than her mother."

I had to get up from my chair and push my shoulders back to get any decent amount of air into my lungs.

Is it the girl or the wish that's upsetting you?

"I don't know. I feel bad for her. What her mom is doing isn't right. All Ainsley wants is a home. Someplace she doesn't have to leave."

Isn't that what her wish will give her?

"You're right." I reached down and scratched his ears. "You're absolutely right. It's stupid for me to sit here and get upset about something that will be resolved soon. Let's go home."

When we got to the bus, I climbed the ladder hanging off the back and attempted to relax with a little yoga on the roof before going to sleep. My body was tense and tight from all the drama going on in the magical world. At first the stretches hurt, but in less than a minute, my muscles loosened and responded the way I wanted them to. Unfortunately, my brain was so distracted with thoughts of Ainsley and Clay and the Guides and Kaf, I nearly fell off the bus.

I sat with my legs in full lotus and tried to meditate instead. I calmed my mind with a number of long, deep breaths and focused on the partial moon that hovered over the mountain peaks. The crisp air was refreshing, but my brain wandered to thoughts of the hippies I had lived with in the commune, many of whom lived much like Ainsley and her mum. No possessions. No home. Few true connections.

I still lived like a hippie. Everything I owned fit inside Gypsy

V. The only family I had left was my sister Carol. We were trying to repair the wounds of the past, but it was slow going.

"Ainsley's wish will give her the stability and happy home she wants." I repeated this over and over like a mantra. It didn't settle my mind though.

Finally, I had to give up on meditation, too, when a single thought hijacked my mind. *The hippie life isn't for you anymore.*

Chapter 5

Ainsley

It took six days before Mum decided we'd found our new town. The one we were supposedly going to stay in forever. We'd gone clear through Kansas, to the midpoint of Missouri, and north through Iowa before we finally stopped about fifty or sixty miles over the Minnesota border in Lake Bellwood.

"At least they have a lake here," Mum said as if that was a selling point.

The lake was nice, I had to admit. Holly Lake not only didn't have a lake, unless you counted the reservoir as a lake, it had no holly, either. Must've been named after someone named Holly.

Mum had three checklist items that determined if we'd stay in a place. First, it had to be off the beaten path. We passed many beaten paths, aka dirt roads, on the way to Lake Bellwood.

Second item, the town had to have a population of between five- and seven-thousand. Mum claimed it was easier to find a place willing to pay cash in a small town. Too small, though, and everyone knew everyone. Mum preferred a little anonymity.

Third, there had to be a diner with a *Help Wanted* sign in the window. She claimed if there was a sign in the window it was almost a guarantee she'd get the job, because in a small town they'd put the word out if they needed help, and a sign meant they were having a hard time finding someone.

I had no idea if she was right about any of that, but Lake Bellwood ticked all of Mum's boxes. The city sign read *Pop. 6203* beneath the name, and across the street from where we stopped for gas was the Bellwood Diner.

"Do you see what I see?" Mum pointed at the old brick building.

"Yep. See it." I assumed she meant the sign in the window.

Not talking wasn't an option with Mum. She let me have my quiet for the first night, and then insisted I speak because, "It's excruciating to sit in a car with someone for this long and neither of us says a word." I had to agree with her on that one. Although, I was still so mad at her, I couldn't manage more than three words at a time. Luckily, that counted.

She handed me some money. "You gas up the car. I'm going to go see if they're still looking."

I went in to pay for the gas and bought myself a piece of something called *lefse*. I had no idea what it was, but it looked like a thin pancake smeared with butter, sprinkled with cinnamon and sugar, and rolled into a tube. Since I'll eat almost anything with cinnamon and sugar, I figured, what the heck.

It was chewier than a pancake but not as chewy as a tortilla. The salty butter and sweet cinnamon sprinkle danced happily across my tongue.

"This is amazing," I murmured to the clerk with my eyes closed.

"Thanks. Make them myself." Mina, according to the name embroidered on the pocket of her denim uniform shirt, was probably in her mid-twenties. Her face was scrubbed clean of makeup, and she was pretty, in a natural rather than supermodel way.

"You make these here? In the gas station?"

"Small town," she said like that explained everything. "We have to multi-task. The town lawyer also cuts hair. I've got a dedicated spot, so it's not like I make it among the cans of oil. Want to see how it's done?"

"Of course." This was one of the cool things about traveling. What were the chances I would have ever gotten to watch lefse being made in a gas station otherwise? I made a mental note to add *ate and learned how to make lefse* to my journal.

Mina led me to the far corner where a mini kitchen was set up behind a glass partition. She pulled her long blonde hair into a ponytail and then took a little blob of dough from a refrigerator beneath the counter. She said the dough was made from potatoes, flour, sugar, salt, and cream. With a rolling pin covered in little nubs, she rolled the blob until the dough was about twelve inches round and paper thin. She placed the rolled dough on a big round griddle, and after thirty seconds or so, she flipped it and let it go another thirty seconds. Then she smeared it, sprinkled it, rolled it, and handed it to me.

"That's it?" I asked.

"Well, I've been making lefse for over ten years," Mina said. "Rolling and frying are important, but the dough is what makes it good."

The little bell over the door rang out, and Mum walked in.

"Here you are." She held up a light blue uniform dress and a white apron. "Got the job. Now, we need a place to stay."

"I've got a place," Mina offered.

Mum looked at me and then Mina. "You do?"

"Sure." Mina pronounced it *shur*. "I got a loft over my barn I can rent to ya'." She pointed at me. "What's your name?"

Barn? I'd never lived on a farm before. "Ainsley. Ainsley Blue."

"Great name," Mina said with an approving nod. "If Miss Ainsley Blue is willing to learn how to roll and fry lefse in time for the Lefse Festival, I'll only charge you three hundred a month for rent. And I'll pay you ten bucks an hour, too. I'm desperate for help."

"Is it furnished?" Mum asked.

"Nothing fancy," Mina said. "There's one bedroom and a futon in the living room. Little bathroom. Kitchenette."

"Sounds good. We'll take it, and she'll learn. What's lefse?"

Mina handed Mum a little rolled-up piece of heaven. Mum took a bite and her eyes fluttered shut. "She'll definitely learn. This is delicious."

As usual, Mum didn't check with me before deciding on a place. I already liked Mina, though, and lefse was my new favorite thing. So, what the heck. Besides, having my own money would be pretty awesome.

"Did you say *Lefse Festival*?" I asked. "You seriously have a festival to celebrate lefse?"

"Every year, second weekend in November," Mina said. "It started back in the late 1800s. There was this Norwegian couple, the Wilhelmsens. Their land was about half a mile from where my place is. They grew potatoes and pumpkins. One day, Mr. Wilhelmsen suffered a massive stroke while plowing his fields and died. They'd never had any children, and while the townspeople did what they could to help, it was up to Mrs. Wilhelmsen to earn the money."

"Let me guess," I said, "she could make lefse."

"Could she!" Mina slapped her hand on the counter. "She figured out that she could make more money selling lefse and pumpkin pies than she could selling the crops outright. After a couple of years of her doing so well, the other women in town decided to try, and before long, Lefse Fest!"

"Cool story," I said.

"It's a lot of fun," Mina replied, "and an excuse for everyone to get together. The farm families are too busy with their crops in the summer, so we wait until things have settled down. It's nice to see everyone before we all hole up in our houses for the winter. So, you've got two weeks to learn the fine art of lefse-making. You up for it?"

"Of course. Can we start tomorrow though?"

"Sure. I want you fresh and alert. Looks like you've been on the road for a while."

The bell over the door tinkled again, and a man in a green and white John Deere hat poked his head in.

"Not to rush you, but you're blocking the air pump. I've got a flat."

"Oh, sorry," Mum said. "I'll get out of your way."

As I watched Mum go through the door, I noticed a flyer with orange letter announcing Trunk-or-Treat would be held at the Syversen farm this year.

"What's Trunk-or-Treat?" I asked.

"It's Trick-or-Treat, but instead of going house-to-house kids go car-to-car. Houses are spread pretty far around here, so we hold it in a field instead. We have a potluck and games and Mrs. Syversen said something about karaoke this year." She shrugged a shoulder." Gives us another reason to gather. You and your mom should come. You can meet the town."

Two things. First, I just fell in love with Lake Bellwood. Not only did it have that quaint, old-town feel, the people actually liked to get together.

Second, I realized that tomorrow was Halloween. I was going to miss the talent show. Like I missed my date with Bryce.

The messages from him and Gabrielle were still trapped in my phone. Since I didn't have enough minutes to check all of them, I didn't check any of them. Didn't seem fair to those that would get left behind.

"Is there a cellular store in town?"

"Keep going two more blocks," Mina said. "Store's on the other side of the street. They also sell hunting licenses if you're interested. I hear small game is pretty hot this year. They sell fishing licenses and bait, too, if you prefer fishing. The walleye are biting."

I could surmise that a walleye was a fish but, "What's small game?"

"Rabbits, raccoons, fox, 'possums, badgers. You know, little furry things."

That would be another first for my list. I might try fishing at some point, but I couldn't imagine killing a little furry thing.

Mum had given me way more money than I needed for the gas and lefse. Enough to buy more minutes. Hopefully the cellular/license/bait store could help me with that. I had to know what those trapped messages said, and, even though Mum wouldn't be happy about it, I had to call Bryce and Gabrielle and let them know what happened. It wasn't right to disappear on people. Especially people who had become friends.

"We'll need directions to a few places," Mum said as she reentered the gas station. "Where is your place? Where's a grocery store?"

"Pretty much everything in town is on this road and the one over." Mina pointed across the street. "Grocery store is on the one over. To get to my place, go half a mile down and take a right at the white fence. Go another mile and there you'll be. White house with a bright blue door, red barn. The loft is open so go ahead and move on in. Not much need to lock things up around here, but I'll give you a key if you want one."

"Can't tell you what a relief it is to come across you like this," Mum said. "It's almost like magic is on our side. Do you have internet at your place? Mina does high school online, so we'll need access. Otherwise, do you know of a place she can go? A library maybe?"

Online? That's news to me. Guess that's one way to prevent my school from using my picture. And my father from finding me.

Mina nodded. "My connection is a little glitchy, but I've got it. Otherwise the best reception is in the county library about ten miles north of here."

"Ainsley can't drive yet, and I'll be working," Mum said

thoughtfully. "I'll gladly pay for half of your service if we can use it."

Mina gave us all the Wi-Fi info, Mum thanked her again, and we headed for our next new home.

Just like Mina said, half a mile up the road we came to a field surrounded by a white fence. Then, we came to a farm.

"That must be it," Mum said.

The house was one of those old farmhouse kinds, a two-story box with a wide covered porch that wrapped around three sides. Both the house and the porch looked like they hadn't seen fresh paint in decades. Two white metal chairs sat on either side of the Superman-blue front door. Mina wasn't kidding about that blue being bright. The plants, in what surely had once been an amazing flower bed across the front of the house, had given up their struggle for life long ago.

A split-rail fence, half of its rails broken or missing, formed a line between the backyard and what I assumed was a cornfield. I didn't know anything about when corn got harvested, but the field looked like it hadn't seen a plow, or whatever, in years.

Thirty yards to the right of the house stood a big red barn. The barn, ironically, was in great shape and looked like it had recently been painted.

Like with every new place we moved to, Mum clapped her hands once, rubbed them together, and said, "Let's check it out before we move stuff in."

How bad would a place have to be for her to decide we wouldn't stay? It hadn't happened yet, and some of the places were pretty bad.

We slid aside one of the two wide barn doors and found what looked like a farm equipment museum. I could identify two tractors and an old wagon that horses probably used to pull, but everything else was just equipment to me. The barn was stuffed full and immaculate. Not that everything was shiny and new, but it was clean and orderly.

Mum motioned for me to follow her to a stairway along the

left side of the barn that led up to a door. Beyond the door was the loft. White paint covered everything—the walls, floors, and ceiling. Across from the door was the kitchenette made up of three white cupboards with a white sink set into a soft-gray Formica counter. On one end stood a small white refrigerator and on the other, an ancient-looking white stove.

Immediately to the right of the door was a wobbly little dining table made from the same soft-gray Formica as the counter and two metal chairs with padded seats. Past that, a living room with a metal futon topped with a black mattress, two mismatched wooden chairs, a rickety coffee table, and a stand that held an old television. The all-white bathroom was so small it would be a struggle for Mum and me to stand in there together. In the far corner was what had to be the bedroom.

"Well," Mum said with a deep inhale. I knew what was coming. "It's not the Ritz, but it's fine for us."

Every single time, she said those two sentences in exactly the same way. *Let's check it out before we move stuff in.* Followed moments later by *It's not the Ritz, but it's fine for us.*

Mum didn't need a lot to be content. I didn't either, but this time, I felt a strange little tug at my insides. The loft was fine, and the town was great, but something felt off. Usually, a new place meant a new adventure with new people and places to be discovered. This time I felt empty, like something was missing, and I didn't like it. Maybe it was because I was tired from all the driving. More likely, it was that I'd left actual friends behind.

I helped Mum unload the trailer and brought my boxes to the bedroom. Mum said I could have it, and she'd use the futon. "You'll need privacy to do your homework."

"Online schooling?"

"Don't know why I never thought of it before," Mum answered. "It's the perfect solution."

Although it wasn't the most fun thing I could imagine, I didn't mind the first day at a school and being the new kid. For the first week or so, I had kids fighting over who was going to play with me at recess and where I should sit for lunch.

My first day at Holly Lake High had started the same as at any other school I'd been to. *Welcome our new student, Ainsley Blue, everyone.* By midday, Gabrielle and I realized we'd had every morning class together. She showed me how lunch worked—every school was different that way—and ate with me. We had two afternoon classes together and were besties by the end of the day. I'd never latched on to someone so quickly before.

I blinked away some stinging, threatening tears as I stood in the middle of the loft's bedroom. It was only about eight feet wide and maybe twelve feet long. It had a door which meant privacy, so I could deal with it being small. There was a twin-sized bed covered with a thick patchwork quilt of every color imaginable. It was beautiful and stood out like a neon sign in this otherwise monochromatic space. There was a narrow four-drawer dresser, a tiny table just wide enough for a laptop and notebook, and a wooden chair with a rattan seat. Everything looked like it had been handmade and was covered in a thick layer of white paint that only emphasized gouges and gashes. I laid my hand on the table and instantly felt connected, like the spirit of whoever had made the table was giving me a hug to welcome me to my new bedroom.

I snatched my hand back and swept away the spirit. First Mina, then the town, now the bedroom. I didn't want to feel welcome here. There was no sense in that, since we'd probably leave in a month.

"I'm going to go for a walk," I told Mum. "Get some fresh air. I'll help unpack the boxes when I get back."

The boxes that we never got rid of so we could make a speedy getaway when the need arose. They were pre-labeled and covered in packing tape. Some spots had become so paper-thin from having tape pulled off so often, I wasn't sure how they held together anymore.

"Okay," Mum held her hand out to me. "Can I have the change from the gas money, please? I'll run to the grocery store."

My heart sank as I took the money from my pocket. Mina had promised to pay me for making lefse. How long until I earned enough to buy more minutes?

We tucked the trailer around the far side of the barn, and I waved as she drove away. What would I do if she never came back? I'd always assumed I didn't have any other family, but apparently I had a dad. What would happen to me? Would I end up in foster care? Would they be able to find my father?

Behind the house, I spun in a slow circle and took it all in. The backyard was more weeds than grass. I imagined kids playing on the rusty swing set or in the weeded-over sandbox off to the left side, and a mom hanging clothes on the clotheslines over to the right. Drying clothes there hadn't happened in a while. Four of the six lines were broken and hung uselessly from the poles. Beyond the fence at the edge of the backyard sat a fallow cornfield. The dad would have plowed that field using one of the tractors in the barn. An old-fashioned, traditional family. What would it be like to be part of one of those?

Was this the house Mina grew up in? Did her mom hang clothes on those lines? Was her dad the farmer who had planted the last crop of corn?

A breeze blew through the yard, making me shiver. Minnesota was colder and damper than Colorado. I untied my fleece from around my waist and pulled it over my head. Then I hopped over one of the broken fence rails to walk among the ghost-rows of corn. Stalks so old they were practically dust and corncobs picked clean of kernels littered the ground. How long ago had this crop been harvested?

At the far side of the field, I came to a line of tall pine trees. One of the trees had fallen, so I sat on the trunk and scanned my surroundings. The sun was getting low, maybe an hour of daylight left. I'd have to head back before long, or I'd be stumbling through a cornfield graveyard in the dark. I could still see the house and barn. They were far enough away, though, that if I held my arm straight out in front of me, I could cover both with my thumb. I could cover the entire town with my other thumb. Blotted out, like they didn't exist at all.

"Wouldn't it be nice if we could get rid of all things we don't like that easily?"

I screamed, jumped up, and spun to find a couple standing ten feet away. My immediate reaction was to be scared, to reach for my phone and call Mum for help. But as quickly as my heart rate spiked, it dropped again. They weren't scary. In fact, they kept their distance, didn't even move, as I studied them, my hand still cautiously on my phone. They were together but not *together*. He looked trendy in dark jeans, a T-shirt, blazer, and a beanie. She was head-to-toe boho with jeans that were wider than any boot cut I'd seen, a filmy tunic with daisies embroidered along the bottom, a flowing lacey sweater that hung to her knees, and no shoes.

"Of course, in this case, the opposite is true," the boho girl said. "It's not that you don't like the farm and the town, it's that you like them too much."

A tingly feeling, like a million ants crawling all over me, skittered across my skin. That's almost exactly what I was thinking. How could she know that?

I stared into her blue eyes and saw a bit of the same emptiness there that had been slowly taking over my heart every time we left a place. What caused the emptiness for her?

"Close," I responded, pushing my glasses up with my thumb. "I was thinking that I liked them too quickly."

The only other time I could remember feeling such an immediate connection was with Gabrielle, but that took an entire school day. I'd only been in Lake Bellwood for a little over an hour and already had a strong feeling that I was meant to be here.

So, who were these two? And how did they sneak up on me

so fast? They could have been hiding in the trees. I was so deep in thought I wouldn't have noticed them there.

I pointed at her feet. "Doesn't it hurt to walk through a cornfield without shoes?"

"We didn't walk here," she said.

I frowned and was about to say, *that's crazy, how else could you get here?*

"Did you see us as you were walking?" The girl spread her arms wide to take in the vast, flat field. "You would have."

I shrugged and offered her the excuse I told myself. "I was deep in thought."

"You were. About life and family and what it all means for you. And about why you're feeling such a bond to this place."

She was in my head. I didn't know how or why, but she was in there and wanted me to know it.

"You're right," I said, "I would have seen you, so you couldn't have walked. You could have parachuted or hang glided, but considering how you're dressed, that doesn't seem likely, either. And I would have noticed a parachute. You're not covered in dirt, so you didn't tunnel. The only other option is that you magically appeared."

She froze, just for a second, then smiled. "What if I said you're right?"

"Then I *should* say that's not possible. I should wonder if you're crazy, and if I was in some kind of danger."

She held up a peace sign. "I'm Desiree. This is Clay. You're not in danger. Not from us, anyway."

I didn't feel like I was in danger. I felt curious. Maybe there was a logical way they could have appeared in the middle of a cornfield without me seeing. If I tried hard enough for long enough, I probably would have come up with something. Honestly, though, there was only one thing I wanted to believe.

"I made a wish. For a home that I didn't have to leave until I was ready. You're here because of that, aren't you?"

Desiree's face paled and went slack. She held my stare,

confused, studying me for a good ten seconds, and then shook back her long, straight dark-blonde hair. "What makes you think that?"

I shrugged. "You want me to believe you appeared here out of nowhere. That sounds like magic to me. And not the kind that corny magicians do at parties. I've never wished for something life-changing before. Kinda feels like the two are related."

She squinted, like she was trying to figure me out. "You're doing my job for me."

"Is that a bad thing? Most people like having things done for them."

Desiree shook her head, flustered. "Yes, we're here to grant your wish. We're genies. Clay is my apprentice, and yours is his first wish. He's here to learn how to do this properly."

"Oh. I understand. Sorry. Didn't mean to mess with your process. Let's back up, and you can do this the way you're supposed to." I rewound the last few minutes in my head to the point where Desiree read my mind. "You knew that I was thinking about life and family and how I already feel connected to this place. How'd you know all that?"

Her shoulders visibly relaxed. "I know because I need to know. You made a wish, the universe decided that wish was worthy and sent it to me. In order for me to grant it and be sure you get what you want in the end, I need to know you and what you're thinking."

"So? What do I want? What did I wish for?" I played along for Clay's sake, but also because I didn't want to risk missing out on anything. I mean, how many people got their wish granted?

"You want a real home," Desiree answered. "One that you don't have to leave until you're ready to. You also want to know the truth about your parents."

I gasped. "I forgot about that last part. Can you do that? Let me know the truth about them, I mean?"

Desiree looked skyward, as though conferring with the universe on that point.

"By the time your wish has reached its conclusion," she reported, "you will know the truth about your parents."

My knees were about to give out, so I sat back down on the fallen tree. This meant everything was going to change.

"So how does this work?" I asked. "Is it like a truth serum? Do I ask Mum about my father again, and now she'll tell me?"

Desiree turned to Clay. "Lots of questions and a bit of panic. This is closer to how these things usually go."

"I figured accepting so quickly wasn't normal," Clay replied. "Took a cheeseburger, fries, and pain like my guts were being ripped out for me to believe you."

"Your reaction was pretty typical. Except for the pain. We don't usually do that." She turned to look at both of us at the same time. "This part is super important. You both need to pay close attention." She pointed at Clay. "You need to know what to say when you guide your own charges." She pointed at me. "You need to decide if you want to accept this wish."

"If?" I asked. "Why wouldn't I want to accept it?"

"You've heard the saying be careful what you wish for, right?"

"Of course," I said. Who hadn't?

"Finding out the truth about your parents could be pretty heavy. You might learn some things you don't like."

I sat up straight and shook my hair back. "I know my mum pretty well. And anything I don't know, I can handle."

Desiree looked me dead in the eye for a little too long. If she was trying to unnerve me, she succeeded.

"You think you can handle it," she said. "I hope you can. But here's the thing, once the wish starts, there's no way for me to stop it if you can't."

"Thanks for the warning," I said, a little chillier than was probably necessary. "My mum taught me to accept people for who they are. I've always known my life wasn't like other kids'. I wondered why, asked a few times, but never pushed the question too hard. Maybe I shouldn't accept things quite so easily, but I do. So, I'll be able to deal with anything I learn about my parents."

Desiree placed her hands together like she was praying and gave me a little bow. "I didn't mean to upset you, but you're asking to learn something your mom has kept secret from you for fifteen years. I wanted to make sure you understood how monumental that could be."

When she opened her hands, a flat, oval, green stone was between them. She either really was magic or she was a pro at sleight of hand. She handed me the stone which had a peace sign carved into it. Well, almost. The circle part of the sign wasn't complete, it had a little opening in it.

"A peace sign made from a Zen circle," I said. "How cool."

Desiree hesitated before saying, "You're the first one to ever recognize that as a Zen circle. I'm impressed."

Clay held out his hand. "Can I see it?"

He studied it closely, turning it over and over.

"A Zen circle represents different things to different people," Desiree said. "To me it represents an ongoing journey or an incomplete life path. I added the peace sign because they're bitchin'."

"Of course." I got it immediately. "Life isn't done until we die. If even then."

Desiree nodded. "You'd be good at my job."

"No thanks. I'm happy being a human," I said. "Besides, I've got truths to learn and a forever-home to find."

Clay handed the stone back to me.

"If you place a finger on the circle your wish will begin," Desiree said. "If you need me or Clay for any reason, place your finger there to summon us."

"Why would I need you?" The feeling of being unnerved got stronger.

"I told you, you may not like some of the truths you learn." Desiree was dead-serious. "Once started, I cannot stop your wish for any reason. No matter how unpleasant things may become, you must complete your journey."

I swallowed. "I will know the truth in the end, though, right? And I'll have a home?"

Desiree bowed her head in agreement. "You will."

"Then, I accept. Thank you for honoring me with this opportunity." I gave her a little bow in return and placed my thumb over the peace sign.

Chapter 6

Desiree

When Clay and I got back to my cabin after leaving Ainsley, he was excited and had a million questions about wishes and Zen stones. I, on the other hand, felt numb. In all my years of guiding, I'd never come across a charge like Ainsley. She knew everything before I could say it and didn't doubt for a second that her wish was being granted.

"This summoning thing. What do I do if that happens?" Clay sat across from me, eager to learn everything right then and there. I knew he'd be a good Guide.

"You'll find out at some point during Ainsley's wish. They always summon, and they always want to back out, because things get rough."

"But they can't. No way, no how."

"Right." As much as I wanted to, I was too flustered by Ainsley to give in-depth instruction right then. So, like a parent with a hyper toddler, I gave him something that would distract him. "You haven't seen your room in the Lodge, yet. Go check it out. It's all yours, do whatever you want to do to it. Give me an hour and then come down to the commons area and you can meet the other Guides."

"Where's the commons?"

"It's pretty much the whole first floor of the Lodge. You can't miss it."

I touched my fingers together, and Clay vanished.

"Rasta," I called to my dog, who was laying in the corner like a giant pile of yarn. "Let's go for a walk."

We'd gone from my little cabin near Mystic Lodge clear around the lake to my bus in complete silence. We turned around to make the return trip when Rasta, usually an extremely chatty dog, sent me a Jamaican-accented thought.

What is wrong?

"This new charge," I told him as we strolled along the shore. "She wants to learn the truth about her parents, but unfortunately, it's not something she could possibly expect."

You explained that things don't always go well?

"Of course." Did animals make wishes? If they did, Rasta would be a far-out animal Guide. "She says she can handle whatever the truth is. That she won't judge and just wants to know."

Then you should believe her. We walked a few more yards. *That's not all though.*

"It's not. There's something different about her."

Different how?

"She knew why I was there."

She knew her wish had been granted? Why does this upset you?

"It's not only because she knew about her wish."

Never once during the forty-five years that I served as a Guide had a charge known why I was there before I told them. I suppose it was inevitable that one would be different from the others at some point. Mandy and Crissy were different. They became my best friends. That wasn't until after their wishes had completed, though. As much as Mandy's, Crissy's, and Robin's wishes had rocked my world, I knew Ainsley's was going to, too. It's like she was here for me as much as I was for her.

How could I possibly explain all that to a dog? I stopped

walking and looked down at him. What was I thinking? This dog practically had a mainline to my brain. I sat and scratched his head through his thick cords.

"You know how you instinctively seem to know things about me? Like now, you knew something was wrong."

Of course. You are my mistress. We are connected.

"Exactly. That's kind of how it was with Ainsley."

You feel connected to her?

"Yeah. It's like she was looking into my soul." Then, more to myself than Rasta, I mumbled, "What did she see?"

Abandonment.

"What? Why would you say that?"

Kaf left you. Dara left. You rarely see your friends. You live alone in your bus.

"You sound like Dara, poking me about how I choose to live. The majority of the Guides have private rooms, you know. My private room happens to be a bus instead of space in the Lodge."

Gypsy V was a part of me. I hadn't realized how much until I almost lost her to that loser hitchhiker a few months ago. Since then, I couldn't imagine ever living anywhere else.

"Dara didn't leave. I sent her away because she never should have been here to begin with. I live in my bus because I need somewhere off-limits to the Guides where I can be alone. And, for the record, Kaf came back. So none of that counts as abandonment."

I crossed my arms and the lights of the Lodge glistened off the lake, taunting me.

For those who did not leave you, Rasta continued like I hadn't spoken, *you feel guilty that you left them. Your sister. Your parents. Your best friend Marsha. Your boyfriend Glenn. Mandy and Crissy. For Ainsley, she keeps leaving her home and friends. And now, there is a father she has been kept from. It is a different definition, but abandonment goes both ways, does it not? Whether the pain is due to being left or due to doing the leaving, it's still pain.*

"It's not the same thing." I manifested my granny glasses.

Why are you hiding?

"I'm not."

It's nighttime.

I sent the shades back to Gypsy V.

This is the life of a Guide. People come into your life. You know almost everything about them, but they know very little about you. You must leave them when their wish is complete, and you don't see them again. It is hard to leave people you have come to care about.

I was about to tell him to stay out of my head, but he was right. Like Ainsley, I was missing a permanent connection to people I really cared about. Yes, I had Mandy and Crissy, but I didn't get to see them as often as I'd like. Same with my sister, Carol. None of them truly understood my world. Not the way a Guide, for example, would.

"Let's go." I rose to my feet.

You are mad?

"No, not mad. I feel bruised."

I bruised you? There was a panicky tone to his thoughts.

"Not on purpose." I reassured him with an ear scratch. "You're right. People shouldn't go for so long without connecting to other people. I've done that for nearly fifty years, and it's damaged me. Can you imagine how—" I stopped dead in my tracks.

What is it?

"I'm damaged after almost fifty years. Can you imagine how lonely and broken Kaf must feel after two hundred? Could that be why he is the way he is?"

Maybe you should talk to him.

"I will." I dropped to my knees and wrapped my arms around Rasta. He licked me all over my face. "Once again, Rasta Dog saves the day."

Twenty minutes later, I was in the commons area of the Lodge, waiting for the Guides to gather. The room was massive with one wall of windows that looked out at the lake, a huge circular stone fireplace at the center, and a kitchen that ran the length of one side. The kitchen's counter, a four-inch thick marble slab lined with stools, was my preferred perch when I had to address the Guides. It was like a stage, and all of them could see me there.

A general grumbling created a buzz in the room while we waited. The Guides didn't like these gatherings, but over the last couple of weeks they'd become more tolerant of them. Guess I was finally making progress.

"I think everyone's here," I said, amplifying my voice so they could all hear me. "Those not here are with their charges, so let's get to it. I think, by now, you all know about our new Guide."

A new buzz filled the room. Some were simply acknowledging. Some seemed excited. Some were obviously angry.

"His name is Clay," I began, "and I think you're all going to love him."

"There's never been male Guides," someone called out.

"There has, actually," I stated. "Kaf and those who have been here a long time can verify that. It's time to welcome all into our world again. Clay is apprenticing with me, and I think he'll be great at this."

"Men just cause problems," someone else shouted above the crowd.

"I won't disagree with you about that," I said, and many of them laughed. "Can we give him a chance, though? If anyone has issues, please come to me."

"If I have issues with them, can I come to you, too?" Clay appeared at the back of the room.

I waved him up to the front and motioned for him to join me on the bar. "Of course you can, but we've all learned to live together pretty well. Mostly, we're trying to adjust to new leadership."

Clay climbed up onto the bar with me, and color rose on his face as he looked out at the sea of Guides.

"Everyone," I said, "this is Clay."

A chorus of hi's and hey's and how ya' doin's rang out. Many scowled and weren't at all happy to have him among us. Others seemed friendly enough. A few gave him head-to-toe scans that said they were happy in more than a *let's be friends* way to see him.

Tentatively, Clay raised a hand in greeting.

The Guides' frustration wasn't only about Clay. Bringing in a male Guide was simply the latest in a series of changes I'd made. I was about to talk about that when Kaf walked in at the back of the crowd.

When the Guides realized he was there, they moved to the side to make way for him. Some darted like the spectators avoiding the charging beasts at a Running of the Bulls celebration in Pamplona. Others moved but held their hands outstretched, like crazed fans as their favorite celebrity walked past.

"How many changes are you planning to make?" he asked. Many in the crowd murmured their agreement with the question.

"You say that like change is a bad thing," I replied. "You gave me the Wish Mistress position. There are some tweaks I feel we can make that will benefit our world." I turned to Clay, linked my arm through his, and gave him an encouraging smile. "I think Clay will be a huge benefit."

Kaf glared at Clay. I'd never seen that expression on him before. Was he . . . no, it couldn't be. Was Kaf jealous? Well, well, well. Guess he should have considered keeping male Guides on staff. Or he should have stuck around as the boss if he didn't like me making changes. Either way, as my adorable little grandma would have said, *You burnt your butt, mister. Now, sit on the blister.*

"Like you would a new female Guide," I told the group, "you need to give him a chance and get to know him. So, is anyone willing to show Clay around the Lodge? It's a big place that's easy to get lost in."

The Guide, who Kaf had found drugged and dying in the cardboard box in an alley, stepped to the front.

"I will." She smiled up at Clay who was still on the bar with me. "Hi, I'm Amber."

Clay jumped down to stand by Amber's side.

"I can help him with other things, too," Amber offered. "You know, with learning how to be a Guide."

It was happening again. Like that little pull between me and Ainsley, the same connection was forming between Clay and Amber. A little spot in my chest flared with jealousy, but I tamped it down right away. It wasn't like Clay and I could be friends; I was his boss. Besides, this wasn't about me. This was about Clay being accepted.

"That's great," I told Amber. "Knowledge is power. You teach him your ways, and I'll teach him mine. He'll be an awesome Guide." To Clay I said, "Remember, Ainsley is your first priority. You'll be notified when she summons us. Find me immediately when that happens, and we'll go to her."

The other Guides had already scattered, so Rasta and I went to the cabin. Kaf was there, waiting for us.

Just like every time I saw him, my breath caught. When he first returned to the genie world, I insisted that if he was going to stay, he had to start wearing a shirt. I manifested one for him that fit snuggly across the chest but was roomy through the body. He acted like I'd put him in a straightjacket. He squirmed and tugged at the collar and stretched the sleeves.

"If you gave me some powers," he'd said, "I could manifest my own clothing."

"Why would I do that?" I'd asked. "You gave your powers and control over the genie world to me. If you wanted to still do magic and be the boss, why did you give it away?"

He'd flinched at the word genie. He didn't like it, never had. Said it made what we did seem like a carnival act.

Eternally loyal, his sister Adellika manifested a shirt that fit him like a second skin. Impossibly, the black T-shirt made him look even hotter than when he was bare-chested. How was I supposed to maintain control with him being that distracting?

Of the Guides. How was I supposed to maintain control of the Guides?

"What are you doing?" he asked me as I approached the little cabin.

"I was going to check on status updates for the Guides and their charges."

"That is not what I meant. Why are you making all of these changes? Do you not see how much that is upsetting everyone?"

How many times during the years I was a Guide had Kaf shown up at Gypsy V unannounced? He'd always claim he was there because of some issue with one of my charges. Now, he was showing up at the cabin claiming it had something to do with the Guides. Had he ever hovered around the other Guides this way? There were two hundred of us. After doing his job for nearly three months, I knew there was no way to go to each and every Guide as often as he had come to me.

So maybe . . . Could he be coming around for a different reason? My heart fluttered with the possibility of what that meant. Now, as he stepped closer to me, his aggravatingly familiar sweet-and-spicy, bitter-and-sour aroma surrounded me. Like a hug. What I wouldn't give to be wrapped in his arms. And what did the little smirk on his face mean? Was he purposely trying to aggravate me? Or did he know that he made my heart flutter and was purposely trying to fluster me?

"I'm busy, Kaf." I turned and opened my tablet. I was still mad at him for leaving me alone to figure out the Wish Mistress job. "It's getting late. I want to finish what I need to do and go home."

"You are changing things that do not need to be changed," he insisted. "Soon there will be nothing left of the world I created."

"Is that the problem? You're mad because I'm changing *your* world?" I stabbed at my tablet, opening random emails without even looking at them. "Are you regretting your choice to make me the leader?"

When I finally glanced up, I saw a look of longing on his face that stopped me cold. What was he missing? The world? His magical powers? Me?

He looked away and shook his head. Almost too softly for me to hear, he said, "I do not want this anymore."

What did *this* mean? That he didn't want me to be the Wish Mistress, or that he didn't want me? Why did he keep coming around then?

"Nothing is keeping you here, Kaf."

"You asked for my help."

"No." I slammed my tablet shut. "I needed your help on my first day here. After a couple of weeks, I accepted that you were gone and that I'd never see you again. I figured your life path had simply led you away from me. I admit, it hurt that you didn't at least say goodbye. Your *sister* is the one who decided I needed help running things. I had moved on. *She* brought you back, not me."

He took two more slow, cautious steps closer to me and, I could feel the warmth radiating off of him. It was comforting. It was agonizing.

"Perhaps I was wrong." He looked straight into my eyes. "Perhaps my plan was not the best. It would have been better if I'd stayed."

"Bitchin' apology. Really heartfelt." I turned back to my tablet.

"Desiree, I am sorry for leaving you the way I did. It was not the right decision. I was . . ."

I held my breath, waiting, willing him to say something about us. That he had left because he needed time to figure out what to do about us—we had been boss and employee, after all. Or, that he had been trying to accept that he had feelings for me. But he didn't complete his thought.

"I am here now," he said instead. None of the familiar

swagger in his voice. Only sincerity. "I will offer my guidance if you want it. Anything you want or need, let me know."

He placed his hands together in Namaste, bowed, and left the cabin.

What *I* wanted? If only I could find the courage to tell him.

Chapter 7

Ainsley

Mina was a stickler for perfection when it came to her lefse. Beneath the counter in the gas station kitchen were two little refrigerators. One held ingredients, the other was stuffed full with cartons of premade dough.

"Have everything ready to go before you even take the dough out of the refrigerator," Mina said, to begin my lesson. "The reason my lefse is so good, is because I have fine-tuned my process over the years. After making the dough, the next step is rolling out the rounds."

While the griddle got good and hot, she slid a pastry cover over the two-foot square board—like putting a pillowcase on a pillow—and pastry sock around the two-foot long rolling pin. Then she grabbed a sifter filled with flour. The sifter looked like an oversized soup can with a handle. When she squeezed the handle, flour came out, like tiny snowflakes, and covered the board and pin. With all her tools prepped, Mina took a container of dough out of the fridge, dumped the dough onto the table, and divided it into twelve little balls.

I never would have guessed there were so many steps. I expected it to be simple. Lefse was basically a little rolled-up pancake, after all. Guess that was true of a lot of things, though.

School. Friends. Life. It seemed like those should be simple things, but really, they took a lot of work.

"Watch now," Mina said. "This is what you will be doing." She set one of the little balls at the center of the floured board. "You're watching?"

"I'm not even blinking." Seriously, I thought my eyeballs were going to dehydrate.

"Apply even pressure as you roll," Mina continued. "Start rolling from a different spot each time. That keeps the dough perfectly round. And try not to squish down the edges."

Once the circle of dough measured about sixteen inches across, she declared it ready.

"Run your hand over that." She gestured at the round.

The surface was smooth and the tiniest bit gritty from the flour.

"Feel how it's even all the way across?"

I nodded.

"That's what you're aiming for. Smooth and level. Now, we transfer to the griddle. Ready?"

"You bet'cha," I said, mimicking Mina's funny Minnesota accent.

She took a long stick and slid in under the dough right at the center.

"Lift carefully, line it up with the edge of the griddle, and unroll it."

The motion was part rolling, part spreading. Then she hit the button on a timer. I could tell by watching her sure, confident movements, that Mina truly was a lefse-making pro.

When the timer went off, she flipped the dough and hit the timer again.

"Once the timer goes off again, transfer it to this cloth." A large cloth, twice the length of the lefse, sat to the right of the griddle. "Brush off any leftover flour, cover it with the end of the cloth, and you're done. Eventually you'll know by looking when it's time to flip and remove and you won't need the timer. Ready to try?"

I spent the next two hours rolling, transferring, flipping, and covering. I ruined a few at first, and I wasn't fast, but by the time I rolled and cooked up all the little dough balls Mina had prepared, I'd found a rhythm.

The repetitive job was exactly what I needed right then. My head was full of thoughts: Gabrielle and Bryce and their messages held captive in my phone. My mum and why she'd been hiding me from my father, and any other family members I didn't know I had, for the last fifteen years. This new home we'd found and why I was so drawn to the place. And the people. Well, I'd only met Mina so far, but I liked her a lot.

Mostly, I thought about my wish. I was going to find out the truth and fill in all those blanks in my life. I could hardly wait. Was I supposed to do something or hang out and wait for stuff to happen? Desiree said this was a journey, a path I needed to follow. One thing I knew for sure about journeys and pathways, they could be very long.

"Want to check my work?" I called to Mina.

She came over from the cash register and closely inspected every piece. She pulled out about half and set them aside.

"I'm going to give you some criticism," she said. "It's not meant to upset or offend you. I need your help, but I also need quality work. Okay?"

I threw my shoulders back and stood tall. "As long as you don't yell, I can take it."

"I won't yell," Mina promised.

She showed me where some of the pieces had torn. Others hadn't been rolled quite level so were a little doughy in those spots. A few had gotten overcooked.

"The spots on the second side should be like golden brown freckles. Not dark brown. Okay?"

"Yes, ma'am."

"Now for the praise." Mina winked at me. "You did lots

better than I expected. When I first learned, my mom threw away every batch I made for three entire days. That's how I learned to do this so well."

My chest swelled a little with happiness.

"I'm about ready to close for the day. Would you like a ride home or are you going to wait for your mom?"

"She's going to be there for a couple more hours," I said, glancing across the street at the diner. "I've got some schoolwork to do, so I'll take a ride."

There was a ton of stuff I had to review and information to fill out for my new online high school. I was actually anxious to get to work. I could go at my own pace, which meant I might be able to graduate earlier than I had expected.

Plus, a ride meant I could learn more about Mina.

"Does anyone else live with you?" I asked, climbing into her old light-blue pickup.

"No. It's just me."

"That's an awful lot of house for one person, isn't it?"

She got quiet for a minute. Clearly, I was asking about a sensitive topic.

"Sorry. Didn't mean to stick my nose where it shouldn't be."

"No, that's not it." She waited a few seconds and took a deep breath. "I grew up in that house. It used to be full of my family. My mom and dad, two brothers, one sister, my mom's mom . . ." She smiled, but her gray-blue eyes were misty. "Three cats, two dogs, and more chickens than I could count."

I wanted to know more, but I'd already pried open something that probably should've stayed sealed up tight, so I didn't dare ask. I guess my silence was the same as asking, though, because after a bit, she told more of her story.

"I was out with my boyfriend one night." She paused at a stop sign before turning right onto the road that led home. "It started out as the best night ever. It was the last night of Lefse Fest, and a bunch of us made a bonfire out in the middle of a field. Everyone came with the backs of their pickups loaded.

Wood, cornstalks, broken furniture." She laughed. "You could see that fire a good mile away."

"Sounds like fun. I've never seen a bonfire."

"There's always one on the first night of Lefse Fest, so you'll see one in a couple of weeks. Anyway, we wanted one that night, too." She got quiet again and then blinked a bunch of times. "I stayed out late that night. It was close to two in the morning when I got home. As soon as I walked in the house, I knew something was wrong."

The hair on my arms stood up and prickly gooseflesh crawled all over me.

"The house was quiet, like it should be in the middle of the night, but it was an unnatural kind of quiet." She glanced at me then back to the road. "A dead quiet."

"Oh no," I whispered.

She nodded and slowed to turn into her driveway. "Carbon monoxide poisoning. It was the first really cold night, so my parents turned on the furnace." She blinked and cleared her throat. "The house filled with the gas. My whole family, except for my oldest brother, died that night." She took a deep breath and shook her head. "Hans had moved into the barn loft about a month earlier. He was twenty-two and said he'd stay and work the farm with dad as long as he could have his own place."

I waited, but she didn't say anymore. "I'm so sorry."

She nodded. "Since I was only sixteen at the time, Hans was made my guardian. He stayed with me until I turned eighteen, and then he enlisted in the Air Force." She laughed and simultaneously choked on a sob. "He wanted to learn how to fly helicopters. He did, and then he was sent overseas. He got shot down during one of his first combat flights."

"Oh, Mina." My chest clenched with pain. I could only imagine what she must be feeling. "I'm sorry. You don't have to tell me anymore."

"It's good to talk about it." She tapped her forehead. "The

thoughts get trapped in there otherwise and mess with my mind."

We sat in her truck in the driveway. The night air was stuck somewhere between warm and cool. Fireflies blinked in the used-to-be landscaping around her house. I could see why she stayed, but I couldn't understand why she didn't leave.

"Why did you ask me about my house?" she asked.

"I don't know." I lifted my shoulders. "Just a feeling."

Mina perked up. "A feeling? What do you mean?"

"You know how sometimes you go to a place and you immediately feel like it's a good place and you want to stay? Or, it's a bad one and you want to leave right away? It's like that."

"You're very in tune with your surroundings."

"Yeah, I guess I am."

Mina turned to face me. "Why do you think that is?"

This was the conversation I sort of started with Bryce on the bench that day. I was glad to be able to continue it.

"I think it's because Mum and I don't stay in one place for long. Guess I've trained myself to take in as much of a place as I can before I have to leave again." I gave her the quick version of our travels. "Maybe when I take things in so quickly, I take everything in. Now and then, a place will sort of speak to me. Your loft does."

"Is it a good place or bad?"

I smiled. "I was in the bedroom for the first time and got the overwhelming feeling of being welcomed, like the room was hugging me."

She glowed with happiness over this. So I didn't tell her that her house felt like it was pushing me away.

"Your family was close, wasn't it?"

"We were." A sad smile darkened her face. "It's been eight years, and I still miss them so much sometimes."

"Why do you stay here?"

She shrugged. "This is where I've always lived."

"Do you have any other family?"

She shook her head.

"There's nothing tying you here. You could go anywhere. Absolutely anywhere. Mum says it's a big world and you should experience as much of it as you can."

The look on her face told me she didn't agree.

"Why would I leave? There's no reason for me to, Ainsley. I don't have family, but I have friends here who are almost like family." She studied me for a bit. "Wouldn't you like to stay someplace where there were people who love and care about you?"

The question hit a little close. "I thought that's what Colorado was going to be. I made some good friends there."

"That's what Lake Bellwood is for me." Mina placed her rough hand on mine. "You can stay with me for as long as you want."

I nodded, my throat too tight for speech.

"I agree that it's a big world, and it would be great to see more of it," she said. "I'd like to travel someday. Tell me something. You've trained yourself to absorb as much of a place as you can while passing through, but how much do you *really* experience?"

I couldn't answer that. I'd been to many places, but the only one I got to know well was Holly Lake because we stayed there for over a year. And it wasn't the place that was special, it was the people.

I leaned over and gave Mina a quick hug. "I'd better get busy on my schoolwork."

When I entered the barn this time, I looked at the tractors and farm equipment with different eyes. All of this had belonged to Mina's family. The extreme cleanliness of it all told me this was more of a shrine to them than a storage facility. I assumed none of it had been used since her brother left. I imagined her in here after receiving news of his death methodically cleaning and specifically placing every piece. Was she keeping it ready to be used again or simply honoring memories?

I climbed the stairs to the loft, grabbed a glass of milk, and went to the bedroom. I set the milk on the little table and changed into my favorite baggy sweatpants with the *Ski Vermont* logo on the left thigh. They were Mum's before I stole them from her. When had she gotten them? Must've been a long time ago because there were holes forming in the butt and right knee. I pulled on a tank top we picked up at Stone Mountain in Georgia. It was chilly in the bedroom, so I slipped on the fleece I got two years ago from Zion National Park in Utah.

The little room felt too small for anything but sleeping, so I moved out to the wobbly kitchen table. I opened the laptop and tapped in the password to my new school. As I waited for the website to open, I drank my milk and imagined Mina's dad and brother building the loft. That feeling of being welcomed with a hug came over me again.

Next thing I knew, I was transferring Mum's stuff from the corner next to the futon to the bedroom and putting mine in the corner of the living room. Maybe she'd let me pick up a set of plastic shelves or drawers from the hardware/alternative medicine store for my stuff.

By the time I'd moved everything, not only did I feel less claustrophobic, the school website was ready for me. I was reading the last class syllabus when Mum walked in.

"What a long day." She kicked her shoes off by the door and dropped her purse next to them. "Good tips, though."

"Great," I said, waiting for her to notice. It took approximately three seconds.

"Why is all your stuff out here?"

"I switched us."

"Why?" She slumped into one of the wooden chairs next to the futon and rubbed her achy feet.

"You should have the bedroom," I said simply. "There's more room for me to spread out on the table here. I'll probably be up all hours studying, too, so . . ." I waved my hand at the bedroom.

"You're a sweet girl, Ainsley Blue." She sat up straight. "I forgot dinner in the car."

"I'll get it. Go change your clothes."

There were two bags on the passenger seat of the Volvo. One from the grocery store filled with breakfast food. The other from the diner filled with what was now dinner and tomorrow would be leftovers for my lunch. As I turned away from the car, I realized that all of the lights were on in Mina's house. Every window on both floors were lit up.

I couldn't stop myself. I went to the house, quietly climbed the porch steps, and peeked inside. The first room was a living room. A fireplace took up most of the far wall. Toys lay strewn across the floor. A pile of knitting, with needles in place as though waiting for the knitter to return any moment, sat on one of two sofas. Everything was covered in a thick layer of dust. Eight years' worth, I'd guess. On the floor at the doorway just inside the room was a single footprint. I imagined Mina carefully stepping in that same spot every time as she reached in to flip the light switch near the doorway.

In the next room, the dining room, a crispy bouquet of ghost flowers sat on the table. Mina's mom, or maybe Mina and her sister, had probably picked them from the beds outside around the house eight years earlier. One chair, a bigger version of the one in the loft's bedroom, was pulled away from the table. A book lay open on the table. Again, as if waiting for the reader to come back, maybe from the kitchen where he or she had gone to get a snack.

The only other room I could see from the porch was the kitchen. It more closely resembled the barn in that it was spotless. A coffee maker and a dish drainer were the only two things on the counters. There wasn't a crumb to be seen, not a speck of dirt on the floor. Mina's tall boots sat in a tray by the backdoor, her wallet-on-a-string hung on a peg next to it.

Through the windows of the backdoor, I saw a staircase that led to the second floor. That had to be where the bedrooms and bathrooms were. I expected that one of the bedrooms and bathrooms were pristine, the others dusty tombs like the living and dining rooms.

Had she changed the sheets on the beds after the paramedics took the bodies of her family members away? Or had she left everything like the rooms downstairs, frozen in the last moments that her family was alive?

Mina hadn't been honest with me. I didn't think she lied on purpose; she probably didn't know she'd done it. And she hadn't lied to just me, she was lying to herself, too. She didn't stay because she had close family-like friends here. Friends wouldn't let her keep living like this after eight years. She stayed because she couldn't leave her family.

Chapter 8

Desiree

Clay and I spent days discussing the fine art of being a Guide. Okay, maybe it wasn't a fine art. It was more a hit-and-miss instinctual thing.

"Once a wish is underway," I explained, "every step and decision leads the charge to where they want to be."

"And how much of that is our doing?"

"I've learned the hard way that it's best to say and do as little as possible and let the wish take its own course. That said, sometimes I'll provide people or things that I believe will help."

"So were you responsible for Ainsley crossing paths with Mina?"

"Guilty as charged." Inserting people—like Lexi for Mandy and Lance for Crissy—had been standard practice for me. "You need to know your charge well for something like that to work. If you don't, they might pass each other by and your efforts will be wasted."

Clay opened Ainsley's file and read it again. He was anxious for her wish to move forward. "Shouldn't she have summoned us by now?"

"Most charges would have by this point," I agreed. "Ainsley is different."

"That bothers you."

"Why do you say that?" I asked.

"It's all over your face. What's up?"

Very intuitive, this boy.

"Sometimes a wish will be something you want for yourself, or it will bring up a memory of something you'd rather forget about." I thought of Mandy and how bitterly envious I was that she got the chance to right some wrongs that had been eating her up. And how not being able to help Crissy reminded me of how I couldn't help my best friend Marsha. "You have to do your best to separate yourself from it and think only of your charge. Dig?"

"Is that happening for you with Ainsley?"

Amber appeared at the door before I could answer. Good, because I didn't understand yet why Ainsley's wish was getting to me.

"One of my charges summoned me," Amber told Clay and gave him a sassy smile. "Wanna watch?"

"You make it sound naughty." Clay bumped shoulders with her.

"Only via video screen," I reminded them. Guides and their charges formed a tight bond. Clay coming in mid-wish could damage that bond. I wasn't going to risk another disastrous wish like Robin's had been. We'd enchanted a computer monitor so Clay could observe Amber without being right there.

"We know," they said in unison, like I was their mom and had told them to remember to shut the door when they went out to play.

As I sat in my meditation chair and stared out the windows at the mountains, I thought about Robin. It was a daily struggle for him, but he was doing well now. He met with Dr. Bell, his psychiatrist, once a week to discuss his suicide attempt and the other things going on in his life. He had a good friend now, Jeremiah. He did something with his parents at least twice a week, even if it was simply eating dinner together, which made them happier, too. He would be okay.

I, on the other hand, still suffered the aftershocks from his wish. At one point, he and I had talked about the world requiring balance, a constant yin-yang effect.

"Where there are floods in one area," I had told him, "there are droughts in another. Where there is wealth and overabundance for some, there is dire poverty for others."

Robin claimed this meant some people were destined for unhappy lives while others had blessed ones. That made me wonder, when one person had their wish granted, was someone else losing something important to them? This thought would not leave me alone. It nagged and picked and made me question everything the Guides and I were doing.

How could we be doing good if the world would simply restore balance again? Were we actually making a difference in peoples' lives by granting wishes, or had the universe already decided everyone's paths? And if our paths were predetermined, was there anything any of us could do to change our destinies?

Rasta nudged my hand, rescuing me from my spiraling black thoughts.

I would like to walk.

The sun was sparkling warmly off of the snow and the lake. The air was crisp.

"Good idea, let's go." My head needed clearing.

This was a rare silent walk, for which I was grateful. That dog knew me so well. We went to the far side of the lake, and when we got back, I didn't want to go to the cabin. There was nothing for me to do there today. Only twenty-seven wishes had come in. It hadn't taken me any time at all to assign them to Guides. And now, Clay was with Amber, so I didn't even have my apprentice. I fully understood if Kaf had been bored at times.

I decided to go see what the Guides were up to and went to the commons area in Mystic Lodge. I expected to find it buzzing with activity and conversations. It was empty except for Indira.

"Where is everyone?" I asked. It was eerie; the commons area was never empty. Even in the middle of the night there were usually a few Guides here laughing, whispering, or crying about something. Thankfully, I had Indira. She was like my Guide liaison.

"Most of them are in their rooms," Indira answered. "The rest, I believe, are attending to their charges."

"This isn't because of Clay, is it?"

"Not directly," she said. "Change can be exciting or terrifying. Sometimes both. Clay is a big change, and there are differing opinions about him."

"Are they hiding from each other?"

"I think it's more that they're tired of fighting with each other. A lot has happened since—"

"Since Kaf put me in charge." I knew what I had to do. "Guess it's time for me to talk to Kaf and get him on my side. He decided I should be the boss, now he has to back me up. If he supports my changes, things should settle down."

Of course, getting him on my side wouldn't be easy. He wasn't any happier about my changes than some of the Guides were.

"Can I make one suggestion?" Indira asked.

"Of course." I'd take any help I could get.

"Negotiate."

"What? With Kaf?" I laughed. "I thought it was standard policy to never negotiate with terrorists."

Indira put her hands palm-up in the air and rocked them up and down like a balance scale. "Not all of those who disagree with you are doing so because of Kaf. They simply don't agree. A good leader tries to serve all by finding the balance point."

Indira vanished, off to help with a wish.

I went to the far side of the huge circular fireplace at the center of the room, chose a chair I could sink into, and touched my fingers together to start a fire. The crackling flames comforted me, and the heat soothed my tight, tense muscles. I held out my hand to manifest a mug of tea and thought of ways to fix things around here. Rasta jumped up onto the hearth and immediately fell asleep.

Just then, I heard voices. I peeked through the center of the fireplace and saw Clay and Amber at the far end of the room. They were in the middle of a serious conversation. My curiosity got the better of me, and I enchanted the room so I could hear them.

"He seriously kicked you out?" Amber asked. "As in, out onto the streets?"

"He gave me fifteen minutes," Clay said, "to pack whatever I wanted to take and get out of his house. He gave me no money. Told me to never come around again. I lived on the streets of Denver for over a year. When it got cold, I'd try to get a spot in the shelters. They filled up fast, though. If I didn't get there soon enough, I wouldn't get a bed that night."

"My father was a drunk, "Amber said. "He beat my mom, every day sometimes. I begged her to leave, but she was too afraid. I stayed to try and protect her, but the day he took a swing at me, I left. I was nineteen, so it was time for me to go anyway. Leaving her was the hardest thing I ever did."

"Where'd you go?" Clay asked.

"To a friend's. I got a couple of jobs. One at a convenience store and another waitressing at this disgusting corner diner. I got the night shift at the diner so had to clean up lots of puke and got my ass grabbed by plenty of drunks. I could pay my own way, though." Amber got quiet for a second. "Me and my friend went out one night to celebrate my twenty-first birthday and the fact that I got a new job as head server at this swanky restaurant. They said I could be an assistant manager in six months. Anyway, I let this guy buy me a drink."

"Let me guess," Clay said. "Roofies?"

"Yep. He *helped* me outside, so I could get some air." Her voice got thick like she was fighting back emotion. "He was big, like he lifted and worked out a lot. He wanted to have a little fun right there in the alley. When I tried to fight him off, he snapped.

Not even my dad got angry that fast. The guy beat me up and tossed me into a cardboard box by a dumpster. I wished to not die in that box and for my life to change. That's when Kaf found me and saved me."

I could hear the smile in her voice. Amber idolized Kaf. There was nothing he could do that she didn't approve of. Funny that she approved of Clay, a Guide Kaf never would have brought here.

"Desiree found me in an alley, too," Clay said. "I couldn't get a job because I had no ID or address, but there were plenty of men looking for a little companionship from boys. They cruised the streets on cold nights. Sleeping in the beds of men who didn't ask anything more about me than my name meant I wouldn't freeze to death those nights."

"Oh, Clay."

"I'm not proud of it. I did what I had to do to stay alive," Clay snapped, like she had accused him of something rather than empathized with him. "They all wanted something different from me. I'll spare you the gory details, but that's when I changed my name from Diego to Clay. Mold me. Form me into whatever you want. Just give me a warm place to sleep and some food to eat."

I turned off the enchantment. My heart ached for him, but at the same time, I felt happy that I was able to rescue him from such a horrible existence.

While Clay had sort of become the poster boy for change in the genie world, he also represented courage and survival. He was exactly the motivation I needed. My worries over the yin-yang, world rebalancing itself problem was gone. Because restoring balance, no matter how many times the scales got knocked out of whack, was what I did best.

Chapter 9

Ainsley

By the time Lefse Fest got underway on a cool, crisp Thursday afternoon, I could roll and bake lefse with the best of them.

"We've got about a hundred pounds of dough in the refrigerator in the back room and there are probably four-thousand pieces in the refrigerator ready to sell," I told Mina as we set up a table for lefse and hot cocoa outside the gas station/bakery. "What are you going to do with all that lefse?"

The streets of downtown Lake Bellwood weren't much busier than they normally were. I would have spent days making all that lefse for nothing if more people didn't come.

"Don't worry, we'll sell it all," Mina promised. "The fest doesn't officially start until tomorrow. Today is for the town. Everyone will close up shop in about an hour. Then we'll wander around and sample the food and see the handmade crafts and gadgets people will sell this year. There will be a bonfire tonight over by the fire station."

"Awesome!" I couldn't wait for the bonfire experience.

As Mina stirred the big electric kettle of cocoa, I wondered how to ask about a paycheck. I still hadn't been able to put more minutes on my phone, and I was dying to listen to those messages. Of course, by now, Gabrielle and Bryce had probably given up on me.

"So, um, Mina?"

"Yeah." She dug under the table for Styrofoam cups to set next to the cocoa kettle.

"You had said something about a paycheck?"

She stood straight up like she'd been zapped by electricity. "Oh my god. I haven't paid you yet?"

I shook my head but was relieved she had at least remembered that she was going to.

"I'll get your money right now."

I was about to say *no, that's okay it can wait,* but I wanted that money. She came back a few minutes later with a space heater to put under the table by our feet and five hundred fifty dollars in cash.

"I'm sort of a scatterbrain," Mina said. "Don't be afraid to ask me for your pay. This will cover you working the table with me this weekend, too. Is that okay?"

"Sure." I'd never had this much money all at once in my life.

"I included a little bonus in there because you caught on so quickly."

"Thanks, Mina." I looked down the street, worried that the cell store would close and I'd have to wait even longer. "Can I ask a favor? Is it okay if I take a few minutes to go to Fred's?"

Mina laughed. "Going fishing?"

"No, I need to put more minutes on my phone."

"Oh, sure. Take what time you need." She stood back to look at our table. There was a big covered tray of lefse, a bowl of sugar, a shaker of cinnamon, a few different jars of preserves, chunky applesauce—all of which could be eaten on the lefse—and the hot cocoa. "This will cover us for tonight. We should probably make up another batch of applesauce for this weekend, so I could use some help peeling apples in the morning." She smacked a palm against her forehead. "Marshmallows! How could I forget? Go, do your thing. I'll catch up with you later."

I took off before she could change her mind. "See you later."

Across the street, I could see Mum wiping down tables in the diner. I walked a little faster, so she wouldn't see me and ask what I was up to. She'd told me, again, when she handed me my new phone with the new number that this was the best idea.

"A fresh start," she said. "The only way we could be any fresher would be if we changed our names."

The way she paused after the statement, as though waiting for my reaction, told me she was at least a little serious about the idea. That was the craziest thing I'd ever heard her say, and I'd heard a lot of crazy from her. No way was I changing my name.

I got to the cellular shop and found a big guy in denim overalls behind the counter, his arm in a fish tank up to the elbow.

"One sec," he said. "Got some floaters I gotta get outta here. Makes the others feel badly to see their compatriots belly-up." He chuckled to himself, pulled out a net with a few dead minnows in it, and dumped their little carcasses in a trashcan. "What can I do you for?"

I jerked a thumb over my shoulder at the cell phone counter. "Is there someone that can help me with my phone?"

"Surely." *Shurly.* He wiped his wet arm off with a towel. "I can. Just gotta switch hats."

He literally took off the cap that said *Fred's Bait 'n' Tackle* and put on one that said *Phones Galore.* He held a big, beefy hand out to me.

"I'm Fred. What do you need?"

I shook his hand. "Can you help me put more minutes on this phone?"

I handed him my bare bones, no-frills flip phone.

"I can, this phone is pretty old, though. Must be hard to text on it. Are you sure you don't want to upgrade? You pay for the month and get unlimited talk and text."

I couldn't text on this old phone. Well, I could, but it only had an old-school number pad. It was such a pain, I rarely texted anyone. I pulled out the new prepaid smart phone Mum had given me. Never had a smart phone before. She said it wasn't super fancy but did have a map feature on it, so we wouldn't get lost in the wilds of Minnesota. And, I could text.

"You got another prepaid one like this?" I asked, handing him the phone. If I got the same one, Mum would never know the difference, and I could text with Gabrielle and Bryce.

What was I doing? Hiding things from my mum? What was the matter with me?

Fred didn't ask why I wanted a second identical phone, just reached into the cabinet and pulled one out. I imagine he got people coming in all the time with questionable requirements. He was like a good hair stylist or bar tender. What was said in the chair, stayed in the chair.

"Question. Can I keep my number?"

Fred gave me a nod. "It's called porting. I'll set it all up for ya'."

Thirty minutes later, I had two phones in my bag. Fred put a tiny peace sign sticker on the phone he'd set up for me. That way I could tell the two apart.

I walked until I got to the end of town then took a left toward the firehouse. I couldn't believe the size of the towering cone of wood they'd stacked up for tonight's bonfire. It was as tall as a single-story house and probably twenty feet around. No wonder they set it up by the fire station.

I went another hundred yards or so to where I was sure no one would see me, sat on the ground, and leaned up against a tree.

My hands shook a bit as I dialed into my voicemail box. What if there weren't a ton of messages from Gabrielle and Bryce? What if all this time I'd been stressing over calling them and it turned out they each tried once, shrugged, and said, *oh well, guess she's gone*? What if I had felt connected to them this whole time but they hadn't felt anything for me?

Once I managed to dial my number and enter my PIN, I

heard, "Your mailbox is full. You have twenty-two messages." My entire body started to shake.

The messages started the night we left. The first one was from Gabrielle. "You and Bryce? I had no clue. Well, I had a little clue. Call me and share the joy!"

The next two were from Bryce. His voice was a little husky and soft, like he was talking quietly into the phone so anyone around him wouldn't hear. "I can still taste your lip gloss. Mango, right? *Mmm.* I'll never again look at a mango without thinking of you. Talk to you later."

My heart raced and a shock of electricity rushed through me. I put my fingertips to my lips, closed my eyes, and pulled up the memory of kissing him. Soft and tender and ever-so-slightly moist. And he was right. Mango.

He left the second message a couple of hours later. "Doing my homework and I keep smelling mangoes. It's a little confusing to be thinking about mangoes and kissing while doing biology. Well, I guess kissing and biology sort of go together, but you know what I mean."

Another from Gabrielle was next. "A real friend would have called back by now and shared these sort of luscious tidbits with another friend." She paused. "Kidding. Sort of. I'm going to bed in an hour. Call me if you can. See you tomorrow if you can't."

Then Bryce once more. "I forgot to ask you to call back. I wanted to say goodnight. I'll say it now in case you can't call for some reason. Goodnight, Ainsley Blue."

My chest clenched and then a violent sob burst free. It wasn't fair. I was supposed to go on my first date with Bryce Dalton. I was supposed to watch my first meteor shower with him and get my fourth, fifth, and hopefully many other kisses. Then I would've called Gabrielle, or more likely she would have called me and demanded details. We'd talk for an hour, giggling in the darkness.

I sat there next to the tree with my arms on my knees, my forehead resting on my arms, and tears dripping onto the dirt.

"It's not fair," I whispered. "Why couldn't Mum have waited two more days?"

"To hear the next message, press four."

My phone was prompting me. I still had seventeen more messages to listen to. I ran my sweatshirt sleeve across my eyes and pressed four.

The next five messages—two from Bryce, three from Gabrielle—were from Friday morning. They all basically wanted to know where I was, was I sick, did I think I'd make it to the talent show the next day?

"Crap. Forgot all about the show. Wonder who won."

I made a mental note to check the school website when I got back to my computer.

The next came at the end of the school day from Bryce. "Hey, Ainsley, it's Bryce. I'm standing outside your apartment. Gabrielle gave me your address. Hope that's okay. Um, so where are you?" He gave a nervous-sounding laugh. "We're supposed to go look at meteors tonight. Remember?" I could hear what sounded like him knocking on the door. "I'm right outside. That's me knocking. Guess you're not home. I'll try again later."

Next came three from Gabrielle. "The rehearsal is starting. Where are you?" Then, "Rehearsal is like a third done. You're last in the lineup, so you still have time, but seriously, you should be here." Finally, "I'm getting worried. Where are you?"

Then another one from Bryce. "I asked around. No one's seen you today. Is everything all right? Call me. Okay?"

With each message I listened to, my body shivered harder. It was cold and damp outside, but I was shivering because of guilt. I should have called. Even if I only had enough minutes to call one of them, I should have called. Or I should have used Mum's phone or borrowed Mina's. What kind of friend was I?

Two more calls came in on Friday night. The first from Bryce.

"I hope this isn't totally creepy, but I'm looking in your windows. You left again, didn't you? Is this how this goes?" There was an angry edge to his voice. "You're here one day and then gone the next without letting anyone know? I'd at least like to know if you're okay. Call me, please."

"Ainsley, this is your supposed best friend Gabrielle Fernandez. What the hell is going on? Bryce called and said your apartment is empty. You moved? You're supposed to be in the show tomorrow night. You're practically guaranteed to win. Not that that's the important thing." Her voice caught. "Where'd you go, Blue?"

The next was from Gabrielle, and she was not happy. "The talent show is starting. You're supposed to be here." A sniff. "Regardless of the show, you're supposed to be here. Bryce told me that you and your mom leave without saying goodbye. Is that what happened?" Her voice shook. "How could you leave and not let me know?"

I was scum. I was worse than scum. Was this how all of my friends felt when I left? No, not all of them. I'd never gotten this close to any other friends. Had any of them felt this way, though?

For the first time, I truly understood what abandonment felt like. Bryce and Gabrielle were hurt, worried, and scared. An aching hollowness, like a heavy fog, was slowly taking me over inside. It wasn't my fault, Mum gave me no choice, but I should have found a way to call sooner.

Next came three from Gabrielle's number. I heard her muffled voice say what sounded like *not answering* in the first, a frustrated sigh in the second, and "Whatever" in the last one, like she'd finally given up on me. I hated that she thought I'd abandoned her. I hated that she was mad at me. I had to let her know I was okay. I hung up the phone and tapped the messaging icon.

Gab, it's me. Ainsley. I'll call you as soon as I can and explain. I'm okay. It's a long story, but I'll tell you everything. If you want to hear it.

I read the message a dozen times, deleted a few words, then put them back. Finally, I added *Yes, I can text like a normal person now*, hit send, and said a little prayer that she wasn't so mad she wouldn't want to speak to me again. I felt a little better that at least she'd know nothing horrible had happened to me.

I looked at my phone. A little light was blinking at the top, alerting me to a voicemail. I dialed back in.

"You have twenty-one saved messages. You have one new message."

I pressed four and waited for the message to play.

"Hi, Ainsley. It's Bryce."

My heart did that fluttering thing again as soon as I heard his voice.

"I hope you're okay. I don't know if you'll get this message, and it's okay if you can't call me back. I understand your life is complicated. I wanted to let you know about a weird thing that happened. I went to the talent show tonight, hoping you'd show up there. Anyway, there was this guy asking everyone about you. He said he was your dad. He said he saw your picture on the school website and was trying to find you. He told me your mom—"

"Your mailbox is full."

Chapter 10

Ainsley

I stood up. I sat down. I stood up again and thought about running to tell Mum. I sat back down and decided I needed more details. What time was it in Colorado? An hour earlier than Minnesota, which meant it was a little after three and school was out.

I pressed the button for his number and waited while it rang. What should I say?

"Ainsley?" He sighed like the world had just centered on its axis again. The next moment, his relief turned to panic, and he rapid-fired questions at me. "Are you okay? Do you need help? What can I do? Where are you?"

"Minnesota," I blurted without thinking. Maybe he didn't hear.

"Minnesota?"

Too late.

"Yeah. I'm so sorry." Maybe if I started talking as fast as he had, he'd forget. "You were right. Mum freaked and insisted we leave again. I got home that afternoon, you know, after we, um . . ."

"Mangoed?"

I could hear his smile. My heart fluttered again. My face flushed hotly.

"Yeah." I smiled back and remembered the kissing again. "Anyway, when I got home, Mum had most of our stuff packed. She saw my picture on the school website and said we had to leave. I had forgotten all about that picture."

"So, this guy, is he really your dad?"

"I don't know. I've never met him. Never seen a picture of him. I didn't even know he was looking for me until that night."

"You're serious? Your mom never told you about him?"

The phone buzzed with an incoming text. I held the phone away and along the top a message that could only have been from Gabrielle scrolled past: *Do you know how worried I've been?!?! I'm sobbing so hard I can barely type. Are you okay? Where are you?*

I heard Bryce calling my name.

"Sorry. Gabrielle is texting me. What did you say?"

"I asked if your mom really never told you about your dad."

"Right. No, she told me he was a creep and a cheat." The phone buzzed again. Was there a way to talk and text at the same time? No, I'd call her as soon as I was done talking to Bryce. "Does he look like a creep and a cheat?"

For the first time, something in my gut told me that maybe I shouldn't believe everything Mum said about him.

"Not sure what a creep or a cheat would look like," Bryce said.

Buzz.

"Well, what *does* he look like?" I ran my fingers over my red braids and then reached up to my white bangs. The bit of research I'd done on piebaldism said that usually one of the parents would have the disorder. "What color is his hair?"

"Bald. I wasn't paying attention to stuff like that. I think his eyebrows might have been brown. He looks like a normal dude. He had on khaki pants and a short-sleeved shirt."

"The button-up kind or a polo?" I closed my eyes to get an

image of my dad in my head. I had khaki-covered legs and a bald head.

"Button-up," Bryce said.

"What color?"

"Geeze. I didn't know there'd be a quiz. I would've taken notes."

"Close your eyes and try to remember."

He exhaled. "Green, I think. Yeah. Tan pants, light green shirt with pockets on the front."

"Keep going," I whispered. "Show me my dad."

"His eyes were blue."

"You're sure?"

"Yeah." The smile was in his voice again. "They're just like yours with that dark blue ring around the outside. His face is soft and oval-shaped, like yours."

I placed my fingers on my face. It was pudgy and I'd always hated it. It never seemed to fit with the rest of my body which was a bit scrawny. I had my dad's eyes and face? Suddenly, I wanted to squeeze my own cheeks the way old ladies would. *Look how cute she is with her daddy's pudgy cheeks.*

The phone buzzed with another text from Gabrielle. If I didn't respond, she'd keep sending one after another.

Hang on. I'll call you in a few.

"How tall is he?" I asked.

"Average, five-nine or -ten, I guess. A bit on the heavy side." He paused and then, matching my whisper, asked, "Am I doing okay?"

"You're doing great." My throat tightened, and I could barely ask the next question. "Did he seem like a nice guy?"

"He did," Bryce said immediately. "He shook my hand—"

"Firm or weak?"

"Firm, but not hard. He introduced himself as Eddie Freeman."

My eyes shot open and a shiver ran over me. My dad's name was Eddie Freeman. Mum's last name was Blue. Until Mum told me that night in the diner that they'd never been married, I always assumed they had the same last name.

"What does his voice sound like?" I asked Bryce.

"His voice? I don't know. Not real deep, but toward the deep spectrum. Smooth, not gravelly. Kind of raspy, like yours."

I smiled. I liked it when he added the little bits about me. Familiar, like we'd just seen each other at school a few minutes ago.

"He said he was looking for a fifteen-year-old girl with red hair and white bangs," Bryce said. "I asked why and he said, 'I'm her dad. I've been looking for her for a long time.' Then he told me he saw your picture on the website."

"Did he say my name?" There was a tug in my chest. What I wouldn't give to hear my dad say my name.

"He showed me a black-and-white printout of a screenshot off the school website. He held it out and said, 'This girl. The school webpage said her name is Ainsley Blue.' It was like your name wasn't familiar."

"Why? What do you mean?"

"Because he said it slow like a question, or like he wanted to make sure he was pronouncing it correctly." He paused and then cautiously asked, "Ainsley? Why doesn't your dad know your name?"

I shot to my feet, like his words had shocked me. "Is that what you think? That he didn't know it?"

"That's kind of how it sounded."

Maybe it was the truth. It would explain why, if he'd been looking for me for fifteen years, he couldn't find me. After all, there couldn't be many Ainsley Blue's in the world. That name would be easy to track down. I leaned one hand against the tree's trunk to steady myself because the world had gone all swimmy.

"Do you think *Ainsley Blue* isn't my real name?"

"I'm not sure what to think. It kind of makes sense, though, doesn't it? The sudden picking up and moving? That's not adventurous. That's panic."

"You're right." I felt heavy, like I was trying to walk through thick goo. "When I got home that day, Mum was definitely panicking. All she would say was 'Pack your stuff. They used your picture. He's coming.' She wouldn't tell me who *he* was until I refused to get in the car."

"That doesn't sound like someone who just wants to start a new adventure."

I shook my head. "No. It doesn't."

"Ainsley?" He sounded sort of apologetic. "Did your mom kidnap you?"

That must have been what the rest of that cut off voicemail said. *He told me your mom . . .*

I started pacing then. "Why would you think that? What a horrible thing to say."

"Think about it," Bryce said, persistent but not accusing. "If this guy is your dad, why hasn't he been able to find you? Maybe your mom changed your name and took off with you to keep you hidden."

I heard a ringing noise. It took a second for me to figure out that it was my other phone. I picked it up to see Mum's blonde hair, brown eyes, and angular face staring at me.

"What should I do, Bryce?" I didn't like the fear I heard in my voice.

"He *really* wants to find you. I told him I knew you pretty well."

"You did?"

"Well, everyone knows you."

Everyone knows my girlfriend. That's what I wanted the comment to mean. That was a little presumptuous, though.

"He gave me his phone number and asked, no, he begged me to call him if I heard from you." Bryce waited a few seconds before asking, "What do you want me to do?"

My other phone rang again. Mum. She didn't leave a

message the first time. That meant she was waiting for me to call her right back and I hadn't.

"I'm not sure," I said. "Give me a little while to think about this."

"Okay," he said. "Ainsley? Are you okay? Honestly?"

Good question. "I'm not in any physical danger if that's what you mean. She wouldn't hurt me." I played with my white bangs. "I can't believe any of this." The phone rang again. "I've gotta go. I'll call you back."

"I'll call you if I don't hear from you soon."

"Don't worry. I'm fine. Finer than fine."

I hung up with Bryce and sent a quick text to Gabrielle.

Hang on. Mum's calling non-stop.

Gabrielle would know exactly what that meant. She'd been with me a few times, football games or whatever, and Mum started calling like this.

I answered the again-ringing phone. "Geeze, Mum, give me a minute."

She exhaled a big sigh of relief. Like she did every time I didn't answer the phone on the second ring. What was she so afraid of? That someone had taken me?

"I gave you six minutes," she said. "Where are you?"

"I'm over by the fire station. I wanted to check out the bonfire set up."

"Well, the diner is closed, and I wanted to wander around town with you. Come back to the diner. I'll wait for you."

I took my time walking back through town, so I could talk to Gabrielle.

"I'm fine, I promise," I said. "Listen, I've only got a few minutes so ask Bryce what's going on."

"You can tell him but not me?" She was half-joking, half-hurt.

"Of course not. His last voicemail to me was all panicky. He had information for me."

"About that guy who was looking for you at the talent show?"

"Yeah. If I say anything you're going to want the whole story, and it's a super-long one. Ask Bryce. He'll tell you everything."

Two blocks down, Mum was standing outside the diner, waiting for me. If she saw me on the phone, she'd want to know who I was talking to. She might check the history on the new phone she gave me and see that there were no calls made and the only ones received were from her. Then she'd figure out I was talking to Gabrielle or Bryce. She might dig through my stuff and find the second phone. If she found it, she'd probably take it away from me. I'd lose Gabrielle's and Bryce's numbers. They wouldn't be able to find me. I made a mental note to memorize their numbers.

"I've got to go," I said. "Love you, Gab."

"Love you, too. Ainsley? Be safe. Please?"

"Promise. I'll call you soon as I can."

I hated lying to and hiding things from Mum. But this feeling that she wasn't being honest with me wouldn't go away.

☮

Pretty much the whole town showed up for the pre-Lefse Fest celebration, which meant close to five thousand people were walking up and down Main Street. Literally. They put up barricades at the furthest ends and directed any vehicle traffic through the residential streets.

Mum and I walked with Mina while she introduced us to townspeople and explained what some of the unusual food was. There was something called lutefisk that I guess was fish, but it looked like gelatinous glop and smelled like something that had been dead for about two months. A lot of other places had lefse for sale. That was the reason for the fest, after all, but everyone said Mina's was the best.

"Believe it or not," Mina said, "every single piece of lefse will be gone by Sunday afternoon. People will come from every little community around to party with us."

Mum came up to us, munching on some of that awful lutefisk stuff. She saw me looking at it and held out a spoonful. "Want some?"

I backed away. "I'll try almost anything, but I'm going to pass on that."

She shook her head and swallowed a mouthful as though tasting a bit of heaven. "I don't know how we're related."

I stopped dead in my tracks but didn't respond to the statement.

We ate until we were stuffed and met family after family. They all welcomed us to Lake Bellwood and said they hoped we liked it there. Later, after the sun had fully set and everyone was waddling due to full bellies, we all gathered at the firehouse for the bonfire.

Someone started a countdown and when we got to *one*, a woman shot a flaming arrow smack into the middle of the stack. The flames started slowly, and in minutes, they soared twenty feet above our heads. For safety, they'd cordoned off the stack so no one but the volunteer firefighters could get closer than ten feet. The heat was so intense I couldn't get any closer than that anyway.

Mina came up to me with two folding lawn chairs and two hot cocoas. Between the fire and the cocoa, I was contently warm despite the near-freezing temperature.

"Hope it's not this cold tomorrow," I said. "People won't like to be out in this."

"We're Minnesotans." Mina knocked a closed fist against her chest. "We're a hardy lot. A little cold won't keep people away."

We sat in friendly silence while the town buzzed around us. Mum stood about ten yards away, talking with a few of the other diner employees. As I watched them, my vision tunneled until I saw only her. She had a big smile on her face and appeared to be happy, but her body language told a different story. She held a beer in both hands, centered over her heart. A protective stance? I'd seen her do that hundreds of times, but it never occurred to me that she might be keeping a barrier between herself and whoever she was talking to.

That smile. Big, opened-mouthed, usually accompanied by a laugh. A laugh, I realized, that rarely reached her brown eyes. Eddie Freeman and I had blue eyes.

Mum's chin and cheekbones were so sharply defined, I used to tease her that they were going to cut right through her skin. Eddie Freeman had a pudgy egg-shaped face. Like me.

She was flat-chested. I had no problem filling out a bra.

She was tall, five-eight. I had to stand straight to make five-three.

We didn't share a single physical characteristic.

I don't know how we're related.

I wish I could know the whole truth about my parents.

"I'm going to use the portable," I blurted to Mina and pointed at the line of Port-a-Johns set up near the firehouse. "Be right back."

"I'll be here." Mina leaned her head back against the chair and closed her eyes, like she was laying on a beach, taking in the warm rays of the sun.

I shot to my feet and got so dizzy I had to hold onto my chair for a few seconds to keep from tipping over. When things finally stopped spinning and I could walk a semi-straight line, I went behind the firehouse where no one would see me. With shaking hands, I took out my phone. I had to blink repeatedly in order to see clearly enough to dial Bryce's number.

"Hi. I'm in Lake Bellwood, Minnesota. Would you let Eddie Freeman know that?"

Chapter 11

Desiree

I didn't always understand why a person's life path led them to what it did. Why, for example, did Mandy's path involve losing her sister and Crissy's mean enduring Brad? Why did Robin's swing past a suicide attempt? Why did mine take me away from the magical world only to return me there again? Whether I understood it or not, I always trusted that I was where I was supposed to be, when I was supposed to be there. At this point on my path, I was supposed to be the leader of the magical world. Most days it felt like I was destined to fail at this job, but if I had any say in it, I wanted to do it well. That meant I needed to fix the problems in my world, and to do that, I needed help. So, I invited Kaf to my cabin to negotiate.

"You made the right decision by calling me." He strode through the door and around my cabin like it was his. The way he glanced down at me in my chair said he thought I was finally seeing the wisdom of his ways.

"I didn't call you here to cry uncle." I could tell by the furrow of his brow, he had no idea what that saying meant. "I'm not giving up on what I believe is right for the world, Kaf. I hoped you would help me find common ground."

He considered that and then said, "I learned much during my

two hundred years as Wish Master about how to rule this world. I created the rules I did for a reason."

"I understand that."

As I got up from my chair, I thought of what had worked and what hadn't in the commune. Other than day-to-day life being a lot harder than many of us expected it would be, there was one thing that divided us. We let one person make all the big decisions for us. Giving away our voice did us in.

"Your way is like a monarchy." I stood behind my chair. My little cabin suddenly seemed way too small for the two of us. If I was going to remain level-headed, it was best to keep some distance between us. "While your rules may not be wrong for some, there are more sides that need to be considered. There's no reason Clay shouldn't be here. There's no reason every Guide has to agree to fifty years of service unless they want to. There's no reason the Guides have to stay away from their family and friends. Your reasoning, that humans will reveal our world, isn't good enough. Not when we have magical ways to keep our world safe."

It was heartbreaking and infuriating to think of all that I had missed out on with my family and friends by being subjected to his one-size-fits-all rules.

His expression revealed nothing. Was he considering my points or ignoring them?

"You know this latest blow up isn't really about Clay," I reminded him.

"Correct. It is about the many changes you have made." He stepped closer to me. "Perhaps you should rethink what you are proposing."

I moved further away. "Why do you refuse to accept that only half of the Guides want to go back to your ways? Is it impossible for you to admit that maybe it's time to consider some different options?"

He looked down. "No, it is not impossible. It does appear that you have swayed many of my Guides to your side."

"I didn't *sway*." Why did everything feel so double-edged with him? Couldn't he give me credit without taking it back right away? "I did what I felt was right, and many of them agree with me. And they're not *your* Guides anymore."

Kaf closed his eyes and shook his head. Softly, he said, "You have a habit of misinterpreting my words. I am not as against you as you would like to believe."

"So you see how chaotic things are right now? These disagreements are pulling us apart, and our world will implode if the problems aren't fixed."

"I would have to be blind to not see the chaos," he agreed sadly.

"Two hundred years ago, your ways were fine," I continued. "But our charges are different now. Their world is different, and we need to change with them if we are going to be able to give them what their hearts truly want. Charges who need a Guide like Clay deserve to have a Guide like Clay."

He crossed his arms then went to the window and stared out at the lake. "Not even my home was good enough for you."

"What are you talking about?"

"You moved everyone here." He motioned out the window at the mountains, forest, and lake.

"That's because I don't like the desert. Besides, there were too many memories for the Guides there." And for me. Everywhere I looked, I saw Kaf. It was agony. "It would have been even harder for me to rule with all those old memories in the way. I thought a fresh start was important."

He turned to face me. "I could not find you." The tops of his cheekbones reddened. "The magical world, that is."

My breath caught. He corrected his words, but I'd heard what he said. "You looked for me?"

"For two hundred years, I was available to the Guides day and night." He sounded and looked exhausted. "I thought all would be well for a few days. You simply needed to ensure that wishes were guided smoothly. Indira was there to help you assign the new ones. I did not anticipate that leaving you for a few days would cause such turmoil."

He seemed to be talking as much to himself as to me.

"You're telling me that you went back to our desert home?" I asked. "That you planned to return and help me all along?"

He hadn't meant to leave forever? Why didn't he tell me? None of this would have happened if he had. Or not all of it, at least.

"Of course I was going to come back." He stared at me for a little too long then blinked and turned away. "Do you think I would trust all of this to you without providing proper direction? I had always intended to come back to instruct you."

"Maybe you should have shared that fact with me, hey?"

"I went on—what do you always call it—a walkabout? When I returned, everyone and everything was gone." His breathing got faster, his tone frantic, like he was in the middle of the search. "I did not know where to look and had to wait for Adellika to come to me. I had instructed her to give me time, but I neglected to state how much."

"Wait. Adellika knew? Of course, she knew. She retrieved you when she decided I needed help." I paced the cabin, my chest heaving, hands on my hips. "The whole time I'd been struggling with how to do things around here, your sister knew you'd be back and she never told me?"

Because of the struggles and mistakes I made, the Guides who didn't like me before pretty much hated me now. My friendship with Dara had almost been destroyed. Robin nearly died. And Adellika never said a thing.

"You know what? I don't *need* your help." I couldn't remember ever feeling this furious.

"Desiree—"

"No. If you would like to work with me to find neutral ground, you may stay. If not, then get out of my world. I can't take any more of this from you. I *can* run this world on my own."

Finally, he seemed concerned because he knew that was true. "What are you planning to do, Desiree?"

All I'd ever wanted was to help people have good and happy lives. That's exactly what I'd done as a Guide, via my sometimes unconventional ways. No reason to follow the *rules* now.

"Those unwilling to accept the changes I decide are best for our world and our charges, will be released from their contracts. They can return to the human world and move on with their lives. The rest of us will go on and recreate the magical world without them. One way or another, we will have peace around here."

Chapter 12

Ainsley

Bryce contacted Eddie Freeman immediately and then left me a voicemail to report how it had gone.

"Wish you could have heard that call," Bryce said. "He gasped and thanked me over and over. He repeated 'Lake Bellwood, Minnesota' about ten times and thanked me again. I don't know what the story is, but this guy is desperate to find you."

A mixture of excitement and guilt filled me immediately. I absolutely wanted to meet my father, but what if Mum's fears were legitimate? What if I'd made a horrible mistake by letting Bryce contact him?

I barely saw Mum during Lefse Fest. She was at the diner from fifteen minutes before it opened until the floors had been scrubbed and everything was prepped for the next day. She walked in the door of the loft around ten-thirty on Saturday night. She kicked off her shoes, shuffled into the bathroom, and then went to her bedroom.

I casually typed *Mum home, gotta go* onto a sign-off text to Gabrielle and shoved the phone in my back pocket. In the bedroom, I found Mum on top of the bed in only a T-shirt and panties, her uniform and apron in a crumpled heap on the floor.

"Would you like me to wash your uniforms?" I picked up the grease-splattered clothes from today and tossed them on top of the second set in the basket under the little table.

"You've been working as much as I have," she mumbled into the mattress. "I'll do it."

"Yeah, but I get to sit on a stool. You're on your feet all day, carrying heavy trays of food."

"You're the best. Will you take the tip money out of my purse and put it in the box?"

I pulled a wad of cash, rubber banded into a roll, out of her purse sitting on the floor by her uniform.

"Holy crap. How much is here?"

"Couple hundred," she mumbled. "Fest-goers are generous tippers."

I flipped through the bills and counted two hundred eighty-three dollars. "We should put this in a bank, you know."

"Thank God tomorrow is the last day."

She ignored my bank comment. Opening a bank account would create a trail. Eddie Freeman probably would have found us a long time ago if we'd left a trail.

Mum fell asleep approximately two seconds later, so I pulled a blanket over her and went down through the barn/museum to the little utility room in the back. Mina had said it had originally been a bathroom her father had built so he wouldn't need to go into the house in his dirty clothes.

"My mom kept every surface in this house clean enough to eat off of," Mina had said while showing me where the laundry supplies were one day. "That was pretty remarkable considering all the people living here."

The smile on her face as she talked about her mom nearly broke my heart. How horrible to lose one person you loved so much, let alone your entire family.

"Hans turned the bathroom into a laundry room when he built the loft. The machines are old but they still work. You're welcome to use them."

After I started Mum's uniforms washing, I climbed into one of the tractors and took out my phone. Gabrielle, Bryce, and I texted throughout the day. Sometimes two of us back and forth, other times we did group texts.

As I sat in the tractor, waiting for the wash cycle to finish so I could move everything to the dryer before tucking into my futon for the night, I scrolled through the texts we'd sent each other over the last few days. Gabrielle told me some guy whose talent was balancing things had won the talent show.

He was pretty good, her text said. *Balancing a golf club on top of a golf ball was pretty impressive, but you would have won easily.*

Wish I could have seen that, I'd responded.

I was happy for the guy, but I wished I had gotten to compete and win that first place trophy. Or ribbon. I wasn't sure what they gave the winner.

"And I wish I'd gone on that date with Bryce," I whimpered to myself. "I wish we'd gone to the reservoir and sat under a blanket together to watch the meteor show."

I started crying. I missed them so much.

As I sat there, wondering for the thousandth time if I'd done the right thing by letting Bryce contact my father, images of Mum wiggled their way into my mind. They were quick flashes, but as soon as I saw the image, I remembered where we'd been.

Mum with pixie cut white-blonde hair. North Carolina.

Mum with shoulder length, light brown hair. Missouri.

Shoulder length, dark brown hair and bangs. Kansas.

Short reddish-brown hair, bangs grown out. New Mexico.

Now her medium-blonde hair was past her shoulders, bangs growing out, usually pulled into a ponytail, but sometimes she let it hang free in lots of big, loose curls. She'd changed her hair so many times, I honestly wasn't sure what her natural color was.

The screen on my phone timed out, and I didn't turn it on again. I sat straight up on the tractor seat as more images came to me.

Me with short, sticking-out pigtails. Kentucky.

Me with shoulder length hair and bangs cut straight across and thick so the red blended with the white. Mississippi.

Long, wildly-curly permed hair, parted down the center, my bangs long enough to tuck behind each ear. The small stripes of white were barely noticeable in the curls. Texas.

"Oh, Mum," I whispered, numb with the realization. "You were disguising us."

She got me new glasses every time we moved, claiming it was good to keep the prescription up-to-date. We only had a few outfits each but always got new ones wherever we went.

"To blend in with the locals," she said. "No one likes to stick out like a weed in a flower garden."

When I was little, she wanted us to wear hats all the time.

"We have to keep the sun off of our fair skin."

Except, her skin was anything but fair. Sometimes it was paler than at other times, but it didn't take long for her to get a tan. One weekend in the sun and she'd be so dark, I'd barely recognize her.

The buzzer on the washer went off, startling me. I climbed down from the tractor and transferred her uniforms to the dryer. I sneaked upstairs, quiet as I could be, and grabbed my jacket and tote bag draped over a chair by the door. I crept back down the stairs, across the driveway, and through Mina's backyard. Once I'd made my way, by moonlight, over the fence and far enough into the corn graveyard, I dug the stone Desiree had given me out of my bag and placed my thumb on the peace sign.

Less than thirty seconds later, Desiree and Clay appeared.

"I was wondering if you'd ever summon us," Clay said. "What's going on?"

"I'm remembering things." I was numb but wasn't sure if it was exhaustion or shock. "At least, I think I'm remembering things."

"Memories can be slippery," Desiree cautioned.

"What did you remember?" Clay asked.

"All the times my mum changed our appearance. It was practically every time we moved."

"And why is this poking at you?" Desiree asked.

"Did she kidnap me? Do you know? That's possible, right? For a mother to kidnap her own child. She did, didn't she?"

What did this mean? Was Eddie Freeman a liar and a cheat like she said? Or was Mum the liar and a fugitive, like both Bryce and Gabrielle seemed to think, and we were on the run because of something she had done? Maybe both of my parents were criminals, which meant I'd end up . . . where?

Clay looked at Desiree who shook her head. What did *that* mean?

"This is the truth my wish is supposed to reveal, isn't it? My mother kidnapped me from my father, and he's been looking for me for fifteen years. This is what my wish has been leading me to, hasn't it?"

Wishes didn't come true every day. I expected mine would be something a little more dramatic. Not that this wasn't. I mean, finding out that your mother had kidnapped you was pretty darn dramatic. But I felt unfulfilled. Wishes were supposed to have happy endings. Weren't they?

"Everything that happens to you is part of your life's path. Your journey," Desiree said. "Every day brings either more of the same or something new and different."

I waited, leaning in closer, so I'd hear what else she had to say. But that was it.

"Did you answer my question?" I asked.

"You wished to know the truth and to have a home that you didn't have to leave until you were ready," Desiree stated.

Again, I waited. Again, nothing more. So, I waited a little longer.

"Do you have either of those things?" Desiree finally asked.

I looked to Clay for help.

"Why are you asking these questions?" He pointed at the barn. "Is this place a home you'll never want to leave? If your mom tells you that you're leaving here tomorrow, how will you feel?"

They had slightly different approaches, Desiree spoke in riddles while Clay answered questions by asking questions, but the result was basically the same. Non-answers.

"All granted wishes result in satisfying conclusions," Desiree added. "Are you satisfied?"

"No. I'd want my money back if this was all I was going to get."

Desiree smiled. "Good thing we don't charge."

"Is this part of it?" I hoped they'd tell me something. Anything. "Now that I remember how Mum constantly changed our appearance, it's pretty obvious that we've been hiding. That's a piece of my truth isn't it?"

"I can't tell you what things mean," Desiree said. "But I can tell you that your wish isn't over yet."

"So there's more to come." Good to know that, at least.

"Are you ready for it?"

I shivered but not from the crisp night air. Desiree's words were a challenge.

"You're trying to scare me, aren't you?"

She raised her eyebrows in an expression that said, *if I am, what are you going to do about it?*

I stood tall and lifted my chin. "I reject your scare tactics and choose to look at my wish as a gift. Some gifts are exactly what you always wanted, and you love them immediately. Some you hate and re-gift in the next classroom gift exchange. Other gifts are things that you need, like socks and underwear. It's okay if you don't like this kind of gift right away, you'll appreciate it later. My wish seems to be that last kind of gift, one that the universe feels I need."

Desiree glanced at Clay and then back at me. "I like the way you think, Miss Ainsley. Since you're handling this so well, I'll give you a little hint."

She touched the thumb and pointer finger of her right hand together, and I got a flash of four wrapped boxes.

"What's inside them?" I asked, knowing she wouldn't tell me.

"Part of the fun in receiving a gift," Desiree said, "is the anticipation of having to wait to open it."

"You're mean," Clay said.

"I prefer the term mischievous. You should go to bed, Miss Ainsley. You've got a big day tomorrow."

Shivers again. "Why?"

Even in the darkness I saw a little glint in her eye. "It's the last day of the fest. You've got many pieces of lefse to sell."

"I love lefse," Clay said. "I had this Norwegian friend. His mom made it all the time."

"We should get some then." Desiree nodded like the decision was made. Then they disappeared.

☾

By mid-day on the last day of the fest, I'd stopped believing Desiree's prediction that this was going to be a big day. Maybe I'd interpreted it wrong. I thought she meant that something big was going to happen. The crowds had been good in the morning but not *big* in comparison to the others. After lunch, when the streets were getting less and less populated, a lady with wild hair, a long flowing skirt, and a heavy shawl came up to our table.

I had a mug of hot cocoa clutched in my cold hands and the space heater beneath the table cranked to high. The sun had been shining bright and warm all day, but I couldn't warm up.

"You're not from around here," I said and took a sip of the cocoa.

"What makes you say that?" the lady asked.

"Your clothes. No one wears skirts around here. At least not when it's this cold out. I haven't been here when it's warm, so maybe they do then."

"I heard that you and Mina make the best lefse in all of southern Minnesota." She flipped her hair over her shoulder, the dozens of bracelets circling her wrists jangling as she did. "This is a beautiful place."

Lake Bellwood was smack in the middle of farm country. There were a few hills here and there, but basically it was as flat as the lefse on the table in front of me. Lines of trees were strategically planted as windbreaks to keep the topsoil from blowing away when the winds picked up. I'd learned quite a bit about farming by listening to people talk over the last three days.

"It is beautiful," I agreed. "Would you like some lefse?"

"That's what I was sent here for. Do you have two hundred pieces?"

"Two hundred? Are you feeding an army?" Then I figured it out. "Desiree sent you, didn't she?"

"Clay did. I guess he really loves lefse." She held her hand out. "I'm Indira."

I looked left then right to make sure no one would hear me. "Are you a genie, too?"

She shrugged. "Of sorts."

I bagged up the two hundred pieces, and Indira handed me two hundred dollars.

"Mina will be happy." I tucked the money into the lock box on the little table behind me. "She was worried we made too much. I warned her . . ."

I turned back around to find Indira studying me with her head cocked to the side and her eyes narrowed.

"There's something I'd like to do, if you don't mind," she proposed.

"What's that?"

"Come around to this side of the table."

When I did, she removed the cap I'd been wearing.

"Oh, no," I objected. "I went to bed late last night and didn't have time to shampoo it this morning."

"Trust me."

She ran her fingers through my hair, humming softly as she did so, and fluffed it up. That itchy, can't wait to take a shower feeling went away. After she'd fluffed it, she positioned my bangs around my face.

"There," she said, "much better."

"Thanks. But why the urgent need to do my hair?"

"Have a beautiful day, Ainsley." She gave me a little wink and turned away. Then I swear, she vanished into the crowd. *Poof*, gone.

I had no idea why she was so worried about my hair, but I did feel better now that my head didn't itch.

"We're down to the last two hours," Mina said. "I'm going to start packing up the plates and napkins from under the table." She looked at me, surprised. "What did you do to your hair?"

I was about to explain that this genie who looked like a gypsy fixed it for me, but that would require more explanation than I wanted to give.

"Oh, you know." I wiggled my fingers near my head. "Just fluffed it up."

She was staring at my bangs. I'd already explained the whole piebaldism thing to her so she knew why they were white.

"Sorry." She shook her head and returned to the excess inventory under the table. "Your bangs look even whiter all of a sudden."

When she left, her arms full of paper goods, I leaned down to add two hundred to the sold count for the lefse Indira bought.

"Ainsley Blue?"

The man's voice stopped me cold. When I stood up, eyes identical to mine in an egg-shaped face were staring at me.

"It is you." His voice quivered with emotion. "I saw those white bangs from a block away."

My mouth had suddenly gone dry, but I was able to croak, "Eddie Freeman?"

Chapter 13

Ainsley

Even without Bryce's description, I would have known this man was my father. Or at least a close relative. It was like staring into a mirror. Well, a fun house mirror maybe, since he was a man and I wasn't.

"You know me?" he asked cautiously.

"You know me?" I echoed.

"I'd know you anywhere."

He reached for my bangs. I probably should have flinched or backed away or something. But this was my father. I'd never, as far as I could remember, felt his touch. First, a little flick of my bangs. Then, maybe a hug.

"Fewer than two hundred thousand people in the U.S. have this condition. Factor in a teenage girl with red hair, and that number becomes quite low." He blinked twice quickly and then once more. His voice shook as he said, "I've been looking for you for fifteen years."

"You have?"

"I know this has to be a real shock for you. As much as I wish you would have been at the school when I got there that night, it's good that Bryce was able to talk to you first and prepare you. He's a nice young man, by the way."

My dad likes my boyfriend, skittered happily across my brain.

"It would have been too much for you if I'd shown up out of the blue," he continued.

"How did you finally find me?" I wanted him to keep talking. I liked the sound of his voice. Deep, but not too deep. Comforting. Warm. I felt sorry for all the bedtime stories he never got to tell me.

"Your mom never told me that she was pregnant," Eddie said. "She didn't even tell me you'd been born until you were almost six months old. I contacted the police to try and find you. When that didn't work, I hired a private detective and told him he was permanently on this case until the day we found you. Your mom told me about your hair. I told the P.I. that would be a good way to narrow our search field."

"You've been paying a detective for fifteen years? That had to cost a fortune."

He waved a hand, dismissing the issue of money as if it were as insignificant as the dirt on the bottom of his brown-leather loafers.

"It's a long story," he said. "Anyway, I don't know how he does what he does, but he called me one day to report he had a lead. He came across this during an internet search." He pulled out the screenshot from the school website. "I couldn't get to Colorado fast enough."

"Mum was right. She knew that picture would do it."

"Mum?"

"That's what I've always called her." I'd already waved a dismissive hand before I realized I'd done it. Was it possible to inherit a gesture?

His jaw clenched, and the muscles in his neck tensed for a moment. Then he relaxed again.

"I'd love to talk with you some more. We've got fifteen years of catching up to do." He pointed across the street to the diner. "I thought I'd pop in there, grab some coffee and a bite. Will you join me when you're done here?"

I almost said *yes, of course.* "Mum works there. It might be best to talk with her first."

Eddie stiffened and shoved his hands into his jeans pockets. "She's not keeping us apart any longer. I'll go talk to her."

That guilty feeling, over letting him know where I was, poked at me again. "She won't take this very well. Just so you know."

"No, I'm sure she won't," he said with a cool, calm defiance that both chilled me and made me feel protected. "No more than I've liked being kept away from my daughter for fifteen years."

His daughter. The label made my heart skip.

"I'll see you in a little while." He gestured for me to come out from behind the table.

Then it happened. He placed his fingertips under my chin and turned my face up to his. His eyes misted with tears, and he placed a gentle kiss on my forehead. Then he wrapped me in a hug that conveyed love, strength, and security. I'd never in my whole life felt as safe as I did at that moment.

"Who is that?" Mina asked as he crossed the street.

"My father," I said.

"Your father? I thought you didn't know him."

"I do now."

He paused on the other side and looked back at me. Mina stiffened when he did and looked from me to him and back a few times. She must have seen the resemblance.

"Long story," I said. "I don't know all of it yet, but I'll tell you when I do."

⚸

"They're out back." Hank, the diner owner, indicated with a flick of a finger that I should go through the kitchen. "Might want to approach slowly."

My excitement over the fact that I was about to be in the presence of both of my parents at the same time, for the first time in my life, quickly vanished. To say Mum wasn't reacting well was probably the biggest understatement in the history of ever. She paced with her arms wrapped so tightly at her middle, I wasn't sure how she could breathe. Eddie sat on a column of stacked pickle buckets, his long legs stretched out, crossed at the ankles.

"You have no right," Mum accused.

"You keep saying that," Eddie said, his voice as calm as Mum's was frantic. "I have every right. *You* have no right."

"Don't you say that." Mum charged him with fists raised like she was going to hit him.

"Mum, stop!" I positioned myself closer to my father. "What are you doing?"

The color drained from her face when she saw me there, next to him—a breach of loyalty I felt instantly guilty for. She was panicking, like the day we left Holly Lake. This time, I could at least understand why. I knew she wouldn't take Eddie's arrival well. I didn't expect she'd take a swing at him, though. What had I done?

I took her hands, wrapped mine around them, and tried to calm her down the way I always did when she got like this. I silently stared into her eyes and inhaled deeply. She mirrored my deep breath with one of her own and then ripped her hands out of mine.

"Ainsley, I want you to go home."

I knew that tone. Normally, the next words out of her mouth would be, *start packing*. She stopped herself this time, though. There was no reason to go anywhere. We couldn't run from him anymore.

"What are you two talking about?" I asked. "What rights?"

Eddie chuckled, a deep, ironic sound. "You never told her anything, did you, Virginia?"

"Who's Virginia?" I asked. "Mum's name is Judy."

Red spots grew in the center of Mum's pale cheeks, hands

still fisted. Dad sat there, waiting for her to speak. When a minute passed and she hadn't said anything, he did.

"When I first learned about your . . . mum, her name was Virginia Rosen. Your birth name was Kira."

Kira? My heart sank as I realized Bryce was right. I turned to Mum. "You changed our names?"

She wouldn't look at me. That single, small thing made my knees go weak, and I dropped to sit on the ground. Eddie was at my side in an instant.

"I'm okay," I said. "I think."

"You never told her anything." Eddie's deep voice held an edge of anger. He reached into an inside pocket of his jacket and pulled out a piece of paper.

"What's that?" Mum's eyes went wide.

"A picture of Noelle." It was a challenge. What was she going to do about it?

What she did was lunge for the photo. Then she spun, ran to the dumpster, and threw up next to it.

I went to her and placed a hand on her shoulder. "Mum? Are you okay? Who's Noelle?"

She shook her head and put her hand to her mouth. Her whole body shook, and she'd gone so pale, I worried she'd pass out.

"Eddie, please. I've taken excellent care of Ainsley for fifteen years. She's fine. You know where we are. I won't take her away again. Please, leave the rest alone."

"We've been without our daughter for fifteen years—"

"That's not *my* fault," Mum snapped.

"We? We who?" But my voice was like a whisper in a windstorm. Neither of them responded.

"It's entirely your fault," Eddie said.

"She left her." Mum stepped between me and Eddie. A shield protecting me from him? Or a barrier, keeping me from whatever he was about to tell me?

I held out my hand for the picture. "I'd like to see it, please."

Mum spun and took hold of my arms. "No, Ainsley, you don't need—"

I jerked out of her grip and took the picture from Eddie. The woman in it had hair the color smack in between auburn and copper penny. Her bangs, and a little triangle of her forehead, were white. I saw it, but I didn't understand what I was seeing.

"Who is this woman?"

"Your mother," Eddie said.

My mother? What was he talking about? This person didn't look anything like Mum.

They were both at my side, bombarding me with words I couldn't hear. My brain was spinning, trying to put together the bits and pieces of what Mum had told me at that diner the night we left Holly Lake.

"Your father isn't a good man," she had said. *"He's a creep and a cheat. I've kept you away from him for all these years because I don't want him to drag you into his life."*

"I would never get involved with someone like him."

"I've always thought keeping you away from them was the right thing to do."

The pieces were trying to come together, but the windstorm that drowned out my voice swirled them wildly around me.

"You said keep me away from *them*," I told Mum, my brain ready to burst with wanting the whole story.

"What?" She spoke so softly, I barely heard her.

"That night at the diner when I said I wouldn't get in the car until you told me about my father." Eddie stood behind me and put a supportive hand on my shoulder. "You told me that we kept running because my father was a bad person and that you thought it was best for me to stay away from *them*." I held up the picture of the woman who had my hair. "Piebaldism is almost always passed directly on from a parent."

Mum opened her mouth to speak, but I held up my hand, silencing her. I turned my back on both of them and closed my eyes. In my mind, I saw the puzzle pieces spinning and twirling. *Slow down,* I silently commanded them. They did. *Now stop.*

When they did, I saw pieces that made Eddie's egg-shaped face and blue eyes.

Others created Noelle's red-and-white hair.

"Were you ever married?"

"Not even for a day."

"Oh my god." I turned, the picture still in my hands, and looked at Mum. "You're not my mother."

My father stood beside me, his arm around my shoulders to keep me from dropping to the ground again.

"I'll tell you everything," he said.

"*We* will." The color returned to Mum's face as she composed herself. "If she's going to hear the story, she's going to hear the truth."

I didn't mean to, but I laughed. "Are you sure you're capable of telling me the truth?"

It was mean and said with spite. That wasn't me. I wasn't a mean person. But, to find out my whole life—even my name— had been a lie?

"Are you prepared to tell her *everything*?" Eddie asked, and Mum paled again. "Because she deserves to know."

For a second, Mum looked like she was going to throw up again. Then she stood tall and nodded.

Fifteen minutes later, we were climbing the stairs to the loft. When Eddie walked in, he frowned.

Dishes were piled in the sink. My school work lay all over the table. The futon was pulled out, ready for me to climb into. Except for my clothes in neat stacks against the wall, the place was trashed.

He didn't approve. Suddenly, I was so embarrassed, my face burned with it.

"It doesn't always look like this," I explained lamely. "It's been a crazy few days."

"Would you like to start or should I?" Eddie asked Mum.

She nodded at him after a short pause. "Go ahead. I'll get us some glasses of water."

"Some things won't make sense to her." They locked eyes, communicating something I didn't understand. "Should I—"

"No!" Mum said. "I'll tell her my parts."

I pulled my bedding off of the futon and pushed it back into couch position. I sat at one end, Eddie at the other, leaving Mum with only the hard, wood chairs.

"I told you earlier," he began, "I didn't even know you were alive until you were nearly six months old. Your mother, Noelle, and I met at a medical conference."

"Medical?" I asked. "You're doctors?"

"No. Your mother was a physician's assistant at that time. I'm a hospital administrator."

That was cool. It was easy to see by looking at him that he was a professional. His clothes, shoes, and even his haircut suggested it.

"It was the end of a long day," Eddie said. "We had both gone down to the hotel bar for a drink. Noelle was sitting alone at the far end of the counter, and I couldn't help but notice her." He wiggled his fingers near his forehead indicating bangs and touched the spot of our triangle of white skin. "She looked upset, so I sat next to her, and we started talking."

His eyes darted to Mum. She had turned partially toward us, listening to every word, while washing three glasses to fill with water.

"I asked her what was wrong. Noelle said it was a personal matter that she didn't want to talk about." He shrugged. "So, we talked about the conference and our jobs instead. I bought her another drink, and we talked. She bought me a drink, and we talked."

His voice trailed off, but I could fill in what he wasn't saying.

"You ended up together, and made me." Not the most romantic story, but I wanted the truth, not rainbows and unicorns.

He glanced toward Mum and quickly away, as though ashamed, then nodded.

"We exchanged phone numbers and email addresses. I didn't see her again until after you were born." He frowned. "During all the times we talked, she'd never said anything to me about being pregnant. I had fallen in love with her by that point, and I'd begged her many times to get together. She could come to me. I'd come to her. We could meet somewhere else. She kept saying she was busy with work or the time wasn't good for some reason or another."

He was right. Things weren't making sense.

"So how did I end up with Mum?" I turned to her. "Did you adopt me?" If she had, why did we run?

"*She* left you with me," Mum blurted, handing us each a glass with hands shaking so hard the water nearly sloshed over the rims. Pure loathing had etched into every line on her face. "She left you with me and went to him."

There had to be a reason for that. Mother's didn't just leave their babies, did they?

"Virginia—"

"My name is Judy," she roared.

He nodded once. "Judy. I didn't know about Ainsley. Or you."

"Wait." I held up a hand. The pieces had started spinning again. "I'm missing something. Why did Noelle leave me with you?"

"We were friends," Mum said too quickly.

Eddie cleared his throat. "You said you'd tell her the truth. You do it, or I will."

Hatred flowed hotly from Mum to him.

Your wish is to know the truth. Desiree had said. *Are you ready for it?*

"Hang on." I shot up from the futon. Suddenly, this was too much. "Give me a minute."

I stepped out of the door onto the landing that looked down

at the barn museum. I inhaled deeply, trying to slow my racing heart, and stared at the bits and pieces below that were all Mina had left of her broken family. I had bits and pieces, too, but mine were about to come together. This is what I wanted. This is what I'd wished for.

There was one last spinning piece that hadn't connected with the others. A gaping hole in the story.

I'd been raised by a woman who was neither my birthmother nor my adoptive mother. My father had been searching for me since I was a baby because my birthmother hadn't told him about me. What shocking thing would this last piece reveal?

I turned to go back into the loft and spotted a message scratched into the wall just above the railing. *Always in my heart, Hans.* Mina told me that when their family died, her brother, Hans, added the bedroom to the loft so they could live there together and each have some privacy.

"Being in the house was too awful," Mina had said. "Neither of us could stand it for more than a few minutes."

When had Hans left this message? Did he leave it after their family had died as a memorial to them? Or was it meant for Mina, left before he enlisted?

I placed my fingers on the etching, and like when I placed my hand on the little table in the bedroom, a feeling of warmth spread through me. Then the words, *everything will be okay,* sounded in my ear as surely as if one of Mina's family members had whispered them to me. A man's voice. Was it Hans? Or maybe Mina's father, encouraging me to move forward.

"Thanks," I whispered and went back inside to find Mum and Eddie looking anywhere but at each other, the tension between them about at the breaking point. I took my seat on the futon again. "Okay, I'm ready. Tell me."

Mum stared at her hands in her lap as she spoke.

"Noelle and I were more than friends. We'd been living together for two years when things started going badly. She went to that conference for professional reasons, yes, but also because we needed a little space. A little time to think about where things were going and how to move forward."

"Wait." The piece twirled faster as new questions entered my head. "So you were roommates, and she was thinking about moving out?"

Even as I said the words, I knew how naïve they sounded.

Mum shook her head. "We weren't just roommates."

The silence in the room grew so intense it was nearly claustrophobic. I waited, but Mum wouldn't say anything more.

"Judy?" Eddie prompted.

"I'll tell her," Mum snapped. "Give me a minute."

I knew what was coming. I could have said the words for her, let her off the hook of having to come out to me. My whole life had been a lie, though. I was the one who had to calm her down when she had one of her many paranoia-induced attacks. I'd played the parent role long enough. It wasn't, or shouldn't be, my job to make this easier on her.

"Noelle was my girlfriend." Mum's voice was thick with emotion. "We met in college our sophomore year. For our junior year, we decided to be roommates. By the end of our senior year, I realized that I felt more than friendship for her. One night, I worked up the courage and kissed her. She didn't push me away, and we were together for the next three years."

The words were out, but she still wouldn't look at me.

"She told me that she'd found this conference and was going to go to it. I told her she couldn't afford it. She had so many student loans to pay off." A sound escaped Mum's throat that was half hysterical laughter, half sob. "She said she couldn't afford not to go. Not only was it important for her career, she needed some space to figure out what to do about us."

"She wanted to break up." I guessed the truth.

Mum finally lifted her head and looked at me then. She seemed surprised by . . . what? The lack of judgement in my voice?

"Mum, I couldn't care less that you're lesbian. I admit, it's a surprise but not a very big one." I always thought it was strange that she'd never had a boyfriend. It's not like she didn't have the opportunity. She never had any interest in the many men who had shown her attention over the years. When I got a little older, I figured it was her being a single mom and putting me first. "You raised me to accept people for who they are. This is not a big deal to me. What I care about, is the fact that you've lied to me my entire life. About everything."

"Noelle told me that she loved me and didn't regret our time together." Mum sat taller and looked straight at Eddie, her voice stronger now, her eyes shining with happiness. It's almost like she was reporting an achievement or a win he couldn't take away from her. "She said she wasn't sure if our lifestyle was right for her."

Eddie hadn't said a word since Mum started talking. He didn't make a sound. Hadn't even shifted positions on the uncomfortable futon.

"Did you know all of this?" I asked him. "Did my mother tell you about Mum?"

He cleared his throat. "When Noelle agreed to see me, after you were born, she flew to Oregon. That's where we live, near Portland. Anyway, that's when she told me about Judy. She had never given me any reason to believe there was someone else in her life. She said that after more than a year of soul-searching, she'd realized that being with me was what she wanted."

Mum flinched. The pieces were coming together for the two of them as well.

"She told me," Eddie said, "that she wanted to break things off with you, Judy, and move to Oregon. That trip was to verify her feelings and to see if that's what I wanted, too, before moving everything across the country."

Did that *everything* include me, or had she planned to leave me behind? How could a mother walk away from her child like that? I understood that she'd been going through a lot, but I was having a hard time extending my accept-everyone-for-who-they-are philosophy to my birthmother right then.

"Once we decided that we did want to be together," Eddie continued, "that's when she told me about you." His jaw tightened and his expression went a little cold. "I missed the pregnancy. I missed your birth. It took me a long time to forgive her for that."

"So you wanted me?" I asked.

I couldn't tell if he looked more confused or shocked.

"Of course I wanted you. I never for one second didn't. And your mother wanted you, too."

I believed him. Or at least I believed that's what *he* believed. I'd have to hear the words from her to know for sure.

"For the record," he said, "that decision, to not bring you with her right away, made her sick. Literally. She couldn't function. She stopped eating and sleeping." He shook his head at the memory. "I had to hospitalize her."

"Is she here?" I could understand if it was hard for her to see Mum again after all that had happened. But maybe she was waiting for me in a hotel somewhere close.

"No, she's back in Oregon."

"Why isn't she here?" Mum snapped, asking the question I was about to.

"She's not allowed to travel," Eddie said.

"Not allowed?" I asked. "Why not?"

"Because the baby is due in about a month. Flying, and all of this, would have been too stressful."

"The baby?" I asked.

Mum dropped her head to her knees. Eddie smiled at me.

"She'd like you to come to Oregon," he said. "Your little brother, Noah, would love to meet you. He's five. It would be pretty great if you were there to meet your sister when she's born." He gave me a minute to take in all of that. "I want to bring you home with me."

A little spot in my chest tightened. Or expanded. All I knew was I couldn't breathe.

"What an idyllic little tale you've told." Mum's whole body shook with rage as tears caught in the lines and dark circles which had formed beneath her eyes. "No. You can't take her."

"You don't want to try and stop me." There was a finality in his tone, an assurance that he would win this battle, so she should back down.

What was I supposed to do? For a couple of years, I'd felt an emptiness that I figured was due to not having friends. Holly Lake, specifically Gabrielle and Bryce, had quieted that feeling, but I still felt restless. Maybe it was because we'd been in one place for over a year, and I wasn't used to that. Maybe it was this thing I can do, the sensing thing. Maybe I'd been sensing my father looking for me. As happy as I was that he'd finally found me, how could I leave Mum?

"I won't let you," Mum said with less conviction this time.

"You can't stop me. I have two plane tickets to Portland for tomorrow morning."

Whoa.

"She's not going with you." Mum was on her feet now.

As much as I didn't appreciate finding out his plans this way, I didn't like Mum just making that decision for me, either.

"Okay, you know what?" I stood between them. "It's late, and we're all exhausted. Why don't we get some sleep and talk again in the morning?"

My father gave me a smile, half-pride, half-pain. "Peacekeeper, hey?"

I took him by the arm and walked him out to his rental car. "Where are you staying? There aren't any motels in Lake Bellwood."

"I'm not going to a motel." He tucked my hair behind my ear. "Honestly, I'm not sure you'll be here in the morning if I leave. I'll sleep in my car."

"It's freezing out here." I shivered and pulled my jacket tighter around me. "You can sleep on the futon."

I turned him back toward the barn. Mum was standing there like a bouncer with her arms at her sides and a murderous look on her face.

"Not a good idea," he said. "Judy might kill me in my sleep."

"Dad," I scolded, and we both froze.

He looked as surprised as I felt. I'd called him *Dad*, and it felt one-hundred-percent right. He pressed a hand against my face, and I closed my eyes to imprint the moment.

"She's not going to kill you in your sleep." I continued with what I was going to say. "Her world kind of turned upside down today. And what's the deal with that 'I've got two plane tickets' thing? Not cool. For either of us."

"Sorry. I shouldn't have said it that way," he admitted.

"Yeah. And I should have warned her that you were coming." I knew full well we'd be two states away by now if I had, though. "I have an idea."

I took Dad's hand and pulled him over to Mina's house.

"Ainsley!" Mum shouted. "What are you doing?"

"It's okay. Go back inside, Mum. I'll be right there."

I had to knock twice before Mina opened the door. Her wide eyes, like a scared rabbit's, bounced back-and-forth between us.

"Ainsley. Hi. What's up?"

"Mina, this is my dad."

She stood straighter and, after a pause, held her hand out to him. "Nice to meet you."

"And you. Thank you for giving my daughter a place to live."

My daughter. The words said in his soft baritone warmed me.

"He needs somewhere to sleep tonight," I said. "Can he stay with you?" I looked up at him. "I'm not going anywhere, but if you want, you can block in the Volvo with your car."

"Oh, Ainsley," Mina said, "I don't think so."

"He'll sleep in his car otherwise." I gestured toward the living room, only a small slice of which was visible. "I understand what I'm asking. I looked in your windows one night. I know there are rooms you haven't gone into since . . . that night."

She clenched the neck of her tattered bathrobe. "You looked in my windows?"

"Isn't it time to open your world back up?" I asked when she pushed the door closed a little. "What would you do if your dad suddenly appeared?"

She glared at me. "That's a low blow, Ainsley. You know that's not even close to the same thing."

"Please, Mina. It's late. The closest motel is half an hour away."

"It's okay," Dad said. "I'll sleep in my car. Do you have a blanket I could borrow?"

Mina started swaying side-to-side, her breathing so spastic I thought she was hyperventilating.

"Okay," she finally blurted. "The bedrooms are, well, you'll see. We'll figure something out."

"Thank you. I'll go grab my bag. And I am going to block the Volvo."

"You looked in my windows?" Mina asked again after Dad was in the driveway. "I don't know if that's more creepy or invasive."

"All the lights in the house were on one night." I explained, embarrassed now about having invaded her privacy. "I was worried something was wrong."

She shook her head. "No. You were being nosey."

Couldn't argue with that. "I'm sorry. Do you have a thing of some kind?"

"A thing?"

"Yeah, about letting people into your home. If it's a phobia or something—"

"No. It's just, no one ever comes out here I mean ever. No

one has been here since they died." She looked over her shoulder toward the living room and then back to me. "It was only going to be fore a little while. I figured I'd leave their stuff where it was until it wouldn't be so painful to deal with. Guess I got used to having their things around me." She gave a small, sad laugh. "Maybe it is a *thing*. Guess it's time I face it."

"No one ever comes?" I asked. "I thought you said these people were your friends."

She cocked her head, confused, like she'd never thought of it that way.

Dad returned with a small duffle bag. "Are you sure this is okay, Mina? I can figure something else out."

"It's fine." She answered him, but her eyes were solidly on mine. "It's time."

Chapter 14

Desiree

While Kaf and I were *negotiating*, Olanna stood outside my cabin and listened. I should have known. Immediately, she told the Guides what she heard. Only a few, she claimed, but those few spread the word, and the rift between the two sides grew even bigger. The half that were in favor of the changes I'd made cheered because I'd taken a stand. I wasn't sure what to do about the half that hated me. A couple of hours later, the biggest rumor was that I was going to sever their contracts and banish them, like some barbarian, if they didn't agree to my terms.

"How could you do that?" I asked Olanna as I paced my cabin. Just when I thought things couldn't get worse. "Now, they all think I'm going to send them to their deaths or back to situations they'd been desperate to get away from."

"They have the right to know what's going to happen to them." She stretched her neck like a cornered animal trying to make itself look bigger.

"Olanna, nothing has been decided yet."

"You are considering it as an option."

"Yes, but did you hear all of what I'd said?"

"You said you'd release them from their contracts."

"Right. I would release them and allow them to return to the human world." I stood before her, my hands clenched as though trying to keep hold of the last bits of my non-violent, love-not-war hippie ways. At the same time, thoughts of stringing her up by her swan neck skipped through my head. "I am not Kaf. I would never send anyone to their death or back to a horrible situation. Everyone who chose to leave would be taken care of and have a new chance at a normal human life."

"What about Sarah?" she challenged with wavering emotion.

Sweet Sarah. The elderly Guide who simply wanted to be done guiding. I knew I should have told them what I'd done with her.

"I didn't kill her," I said, but Olanna didn't seem to believe me. "Everyone knew how miserable and lonely Sarah was. The only reason she agreed to be a Guide in the first place was because Kaf allowed her to watch over her family. Her children had wonderful lives and her husband had died. If the universe permitted it, she has been reunited with him." My voice quivered as I talked about her. "I allowed her to die peacefully, like she wanted. I'm not some bloodthirsty beast. And you're going to tell the Guides that."

Olanna's regal shoulders slumped forward a bit. A sign that she understood the damage she'd done?

"What if they don't want to return to the human world?" she asked. "Many of the Guides are happy with their lives here."

I stopped myself from preaching about how life was constant change and how they needed to accept that. No one knew better than a Guide how life could change. I needed Olanna's help if this was going to work. But, I needed to stay in charge at the same time.

"My best friend, Marsha, always told me that being a hippie meant we bent with the wind that blew through our lives. If the Guides want to stay, they'll have to bend and accept the changes that will most certainly help our charges. Because all of this, the sole reason we exist, is for our charges."

For that, I received a nod from Olanna. It was so tiny I wasn't sure she'd really done it.

"You're not helping anyone by spreading untruths. I thought you cared about what was best for this world."

"I do." She wouldn't meet my eyes. A sign of repentance or rebellion?

"Then don't make me regret my decision to make you my third." As a final dig, I couldn't help but add, "I think you're a little blinded by Kaf. You'll agree with him no matter how little sense he makes."

"And you'll argue with him no matter how much sense he does make."

I dismissed her then, stinging a little from her words, and tasked her with diffusing as much of the damage she'd done as possible. She said she'd do her best, but emotions were running high.

Word of my intentions was out and spreading. I didn't want to say anything more to them until I had a definite plan. If I didn't respond soon, though, it would look like I was hiding or planning to run the world as a dictator.

They knew me better than that, didn't they?

Exhausted from all the Kaf and Olanna drama, I climbed to the top of Gypsy V and encircled her in a protective, soundproof shield. I sat in lotus pose, covered by a heavy, cozy blanket and watched the snow fall. A reverse snow globe effect. Peaceful didn't begin to describe it. I needed all the peace and happy vibes I could muster right then.

Soon, I felt centered and calm again. I was ready to tuck into my bed for the night when a chime sounded and a small orb of light appeared next to me. I tapped the orb and an image of Ainsley appeared.

"Clay!"

He appeared seconds later as I climbed down from the bus.

"I got it," he said, holding up his phone as proof.

Clay preferred being summoned via text. I dug the little orbs.

Each of us had a different method, which didn't matter to me in the least. Old-fashioned or high-tech, as long as it produced the same result.

"Let's go," I said. "You take us this time."

I'd been teaching him about transporting and, as with manifesting, he picked it up right away. He placed a hand on my shoulder and lowered his head while exhaling. Instantly, we arrived in the cornfield by Ainsley's barn. On our butts.

"Sorry," Clay said. "Gotta work on landings."

"You think?" I asked, brushing off my backside.

Ainsley was pacing in a tight circle around the fallen tree, crushing long-dead cornstalks and husks to powder beneath her feet.

"It's freezing outside," I said. "Isn't there someplace warmer we could meet?"

"There's nowhere else private."

Her eyes were wide and unblinking, and she was shivering from cold. Or anxiety. Couldn't tell. Either way, the girl was freaking out. First, I manifested a shield, like the snow globe I'd been sitting in. This was a globe of warmth though. Next, I produced a mug of chamomile tea.

I pointed at the tree. "Sit. Drink."

As she did, I asked Clay, "You've been following Amber for nearly two weeks. Are you ready to try this on your own?"

"You'll step in if I mess up?"

"You won't mess up, brother." I had tons of confidence in him. He'd be ready to go solo in no time. "But yes, I'm right here."

Clay manifested two rather comfy-looking chairs then looked at me, gave a sheepish grin, and added a third. Gently, he guided Ainsley from the tree trunk to one of the chairs.

"So? What's going on?" he asked as if they'd just run into each other on the street. "You're looking a little stressed."

Words spewed from her mouth like lava from a volcano. She told us everything that had happened from the moment her dad arrived at the lefse table to walking away from Mina's house moments ago.

"Okay, that's what's going on there." Clay gestured toward the barn and the house. He reached over and gently tapped her temple. "What's going on here?"

She stared at the mug of tea still steaming in her hands as if the answers to all of her questions might appear there.

"I don't know what to do. If I leave Mum . . ." She looked up. "*How* can I leave Mum? I've never been without her. At the same time, I really want to go meet Noelle and Noah. And I've got a baby sister on the way."

"What're you afraid of?" Clay asked.

She hesitated before saying, "I don't know."

"Yeah, you do," Clay said. "Spit it out. Stuff is easier to deal with when it's out in the open."

She lowered her gaze to the mug again and after a few shaky breaths said, "If I go, everything will change."

"Don't you think everything already has?" Clay asked.

"Guess that's what I'm afraid of." Ainsley sniffed. "How am I suddenly supposed to be the daughter of three people and a sister to two? I don't know how to do that."

Again, I was struck by how her struggle mimicked my own. I'd been a daughter, a friend, a girlfriend, and a Guide. Now, I was supposed to be a leader? I didn't know how to be a leader. Everything was changing in the magical world, too, and I had no idea if things would get better or worse. All I wanted was . . . I had no idea what I wanted.

Clay sat up and took a breath like he was going to say something, but Ainsley started again before he could.

"I'm angry."

"That's understandable." I nodded in solidarity. I was angry, too.

She stood and thrust the mug into my hands. I sent it away.

"Mum lied to me. For fifteen years, I've thought I was Ainsley Blue. Turns out, I'm Kira Freeman." She ran her hands through her hair and grabbed fistfuls of it. "No. That's Noelle's married name. I don't even know what name is on my birth certificate. And Noelle!" She kicked at a corn husk. "She left me. How could a mother abandon her child? Because she decided she wasn't lesbian?"

"I doubt that had anything to do with it." Clay looked simultaneously pained for her and offended by her comment. "I know lots of gay and lesbian people who are great parents. Better than the ones I got. Don't make assumptions. If you want to know, you gotta ask her. Or your dad; he probably knows."

"People do a lot of unusual things when they're emotional," I said and thought, with shame, of the walkabouts I'd gone on when I felt overwhelmed. And the one Kaf went on for the same reason. "I'm not saying that's why she left you, but keep it in mind when you talk to her. That could be why Judy ran with you, too."

Ainsley shook her head, and something visibly shifted within her. The shift said, *this is too much to deal with right now. I'll tuck it away and think about it later.*

"You know," she said, "everything turned out fine. I mean, look at all that I've gotten to do in my life. All the places I've seen. I've always had everything I needed."

Me, too. I'd gone to Woodstock. I lived in a commune. I got to grant wishes and help make thousands of lives better. I'd had a great life so far and either had or could manifest anything I needed.

"Connections?" Clay asked.

Ainsley and I turned to look at him like synchronized swimmers going for gold.

"What?" Ainsley looked at him with bright eyes and an obviously forced smile.

"When my father found out that I'm gay," Clay said, "he kicked me out."

For the next few minutes, he told Ainsley the same story I'd heard him tell Amber the other night.

"Wow." Ainsley's happy mask was still in place, but her smile drooped appropriately. "I'm so sorry for you. I'm not sure what that has to do with me, though. I've had a great life."

"You have a five-year-old brother," Clay said. "A father who has been searching for you for practically your entire life. How many friends do you have? How many people can you call when you're desperate for someone to talk to?"

"I've got Gabrielle and Bryce," Ainsley said.

I had Mandy and Crissy.

"How many of the friends that you've made over the years are you still in touch with?" Clay continued. "How many of their names do you even remember? How long do you suppose it will take before Gabrielle and Bryce are in that group, too?"

Ainsley looked down at her hands.

"I would have given anything to have someone to go to," Clay continued, a look of pain like a shroud on his face. "And I don't mean the men I ended up with. Just one family member to take me in."

"Your father was your only family?" Ainsley asked.

"No. My father was a sonofabitch who called every person I knew and told them not to speak to me if I called. Because he didn't approve, I had no one." The more upset Clay got, the stronger his accent became. He closed his eyes and exhaled. "My point is that you have a chance to bring more people into your world. Are you really gonna walk away from that? How long are you gonna let Judy keep you away from them?"

"I can't agree with Clay more." Technically, we were interfering with Ainsley's wish. But why should I change my ways now? "I ran away from home a long time ago. What I wouldn't give to change that."

"So? Go back now," Ainsley said.

She assumed I was nineteen, because that's how old I looked. She didn't know it had been nearly fifty years since I'd left home.

"See, that's the thing," I said. "I can't. All of my family are dead. Except for my sister. We're working hard at patching things up, but it's a slow go. My parents and my brother, they're gone. I've got no one else."

"No friends?" Ainsley asked.

"I have a few, but for a long time, I had no one. Trust me, you can't pass up the opportunity to bring people into your world. Especially when they want you in theirs."

Mandy. Crissy. Rita, my surrogate-mom whom I hadn't seen in months. My sister. That was it. They were the only friends and family I had left. If I wasn't the boss, I could try and be friends with some of the Guides. If I thought I had a chance, I could be more than friends with Kaf.

"Well," Ainsley said, mask still in place, "I'll never be alone. I'll always have Mum. She'd never leave me. I understand what you're saying, though. I should go to Oregon."

"You should," Clay said.

"Can you tell me something?" Ainsley asked. "It'll help me make my decision."

"Possibly," he said. "What is it?"

"My parents, Dad and Noelle, they're good people, right? I mean, I'm thinking about getting on a plane, flying across the country, and staying with people I don't even know. They're not going to kidnap me or something, are they?"

Clay looked at me. I took a step back and gestured for him to answer.

"You haven't quite grasped the reality here, Ainsley," he said. "Eddie and Noelle are your parents. Your birthparents. They have every right to take you home. As far as we can tell, yes, they're good people. Noelle messed up, but she and your dad have been trying to fix that for fifteen years. Judy actually did kidnap you. You get that she took you and forced you to live like a fugitive, right?"

By the look on her face, no, she didn't, not completely. She opened her mouth to say something, but Clay was on a rant. He might have overstepped a little, but he was passionate about this, and a passionate Guide was what every charge deserved.

"You weren't nomads," he said. "You weren't exploring the country and having a fun adventure. She disguised you and changed your name and kept you hidden from two people who love you unconditionally."

The struggle was clear on her face. She didn't want to live this way anymore, but she had lived with and loved Judy as her own mother for her entire life.

I stepped in then. "Go to Oregon. You wished for the truth. You'll get it. And I promise, everything will work out as it should."

Chapter 15

Ainsley

W hen I went back inside the loft, Mum wrapped me in the tightest hug ever. She cried and begged me not to go to Portland.

"They're going to tell you all sorts of horrible things about me," she said, desperate. "They're going to try to convince you to live with them."

I peeled her arms from around me, gestured at the futon, and asked her to sit with me. Clay said that if I wanted to know the truth about why Noelle did what she did, I had to ask her. Same was true with Mum. My entire world had turned downside up and outside in. I felt like the rope in a tug-o-war, and I hated it.

"There's something I want to talk to you about before I go."

It must have been the word *go* that set her off again because the crying turned into sobs.

"Mum, come on. I'm only going for a visit. We'll figure something out that will work for everyone. Like, I'll go see them for Thanksgiving or Christmas, maybe a week every summer. They are my family, too, after all. That wouldn't be so bad, would it?"

She wasn't convinced, I could tell by the set of her jaw, but she didn't object.

I took a deep breath. "You've been lying to me about a lot of things for a long time."

"I know. I panicked."

"For fifteen years? You told me my dad was a creep and a cheat, but he sure doesn't seem that way to me. And you kidnapped me? That's why we kept moving. Not to see the country. How could you do that?"

"When I got home that day and Noelle was gone and you were still there." She ran a hand over my hair. "You were such a good baby. And a good toddler. And now, look at how beautiful you are."

"You're not answering my questions. You knew they were looking for me, didn't you?"

"No." She shook her head hard. "No, I didn't know that. I didn't know what to do."

"Did you go to the police? Did you report me as abandoned?"

"That's what they did. They abandoned you. People who would do that . . . They didn't deserve you."

"So you took off with me?

"She left you with me," Mum said for about the tenth time. "You were mine. She gave you to me."

Honestly, she was starting to scare me. She worked so hard all weekend at Lefse Fest. She was ready to drop from exhaustion. Now this. I had a lot of questions, and it looked like I'd have to get the answers from someone else.

I dragged her to the bedroom and told her to go to bed. She lay there, mumbling incoherently, for a few minutes and then fell soundly to sleep. She'd always been able to do that. No matter what was going on, she always fell right to sleep. She'd be better in the morning.

Clay and Desiree were right about one thing. As much as I hoped Gabrielle, Bryce, and I would stay in touch, I couldn't count on that. Less than twenty-four hours ago, Mum was the only forever-person I had in the world. Now, I had a set of parents, a brother, and soon, a sister. A whole family. Something I'd wondered about and wanted my entire life. Not that I ever told Mum that. I always said she was family enough for me. Guess I was a liar, too.

☮

At six in the morning, Dad knocked on our door with our tickets to Portland in his hand. "Ready?"

The dark circles beneath his barely-open eyes said he was as tired as I felt. He probably stayed awake all night, watching to make sure Mum didn't take off with me again.

"I'm ready. I have to say goodbye to Mum."

She locked me in another death-grip hug when I woke her to let her know we were leaving. Again, she begged, over and over, "Don't go, please don't leave me."

I held her hands and stared at her until she calmed down. "I'm not leaving you. I'll be back."

"Call me when you land," she said.

"I will."

"And when you get to the house."

"Mum."

"Please, Ainsley. We've never been away from each other. I'm your mother. I need to know where you are and that you're safe."

"Okay." I didn't want her to freak out again. "I'll call."

"And no matter what she says, remember how much I love you."

Who? Noelle? What would she say? "I'll remember."

I got my backpack with my school stuff and a small duffle bag with clothes.

"Don't worry about bringing much," Dad had said the night before. "We have a computer you can use for school. Your mom has shampoo and a razor and all that other girly stuff for you."

Every time Dad called Noelle *your mom*, I first thought of

Mum. I tried to start associating my *mom* with red and white hair. Probably after I saw her face-to-face it would be easier.

"And she wants to take you shopping to buy you new clothes."

New clothes? I'd never had new clothes before. Not that there was anything wrong with what I had, but we could only afford things from Goodwill or the Salvation Army.

"What about a toothbrush?" Why did they have all this stuff for me? Maybe so I'd have a supply of things for when I came to visit.

"If she forgot, we'll go get one." He smiled. "I can't tell you how excited she is. She's been dreaming of being able to take care of you for so long."

Then why did she leave me? I had so many questions.

I was about to get into the car when Mina came running outside in her well-loved bathrobe, flannel pants, and boots. Another bear hug. My ribs were starting to ache from all these hugs.

"I'm so excited for you." A little sob escaped her. "Do you know how lucky you are that your parents never gave up on you?"

Emotion clogged my throat like a lump of stuck lefse. They never gave up on me.

"Your dad helped me clean up the living room a little last night, so he could sleep on the couch."

"Was that weird? Going all the way into the room?"

"A little," she admitted, wrapping the robe tighter around her. "It was time, though. I heard a quote once that said, 'the depth of your love is not measured by the length of your mourning.' It's way past time to take my life back. I'm going to start cleaning every room until this house is livable again. I'm going to finish the living room today and then move on to the dining room. I'm not going back to work until the main level is clean. Then I'll start upstairs."

"Wow. That's great, Mina. I won't be able to wait until I get back to see it. Send me a picture."

She gave me a confused look and then hugged me again. "Can't tell you how grateful I am that you guys stopped by my gas station that day."

"You sound like we won't see each other again." My eyes stung with that thought. Mina had started to feel like a big sister to me.

"I don't intend to ever lose touch with you." She glanced over my shoulder, at Dad, I assumed. "You never know where life will lead. You have to take advantage of things when the opportunity is before you."

"Ainsley," Dad gently prodded. "We should get going. Don't want to miss our flight."

"You've got my number," Mina said. "Call me. Text me. Send me pictures of your new bedroom."

During the two-hour drive to the airport, Dad told me more about my birthmother. She gave up her physician's assistant job when Noah was born.

"She was excited and terrified," Dad recalled with a smile. "Neither of us had any idea what to do with this little person suddenly living in our home."

He kept glancing over at me so many times, I finally asked, "What?"

"We missed out on so much of your life."

"Have you forgiven her?"

"For not telling me about you right away? Of course. Honestly, it took a few months. I had a hard time with it. We almost didn't stay together. Eventually, I was able to understand her reasons for not telling me and not bringing you with her right away."

"What were they?" I asked, even though I was scared to learn the answer. What if he said it was because she wasn't sure she wanted me?

"She told me," Dad began, "that she wanted to make sure I was the person she thought I was. If after a weekend together we didn't feel that same spark, she would go home and we wouldn't see each other again. She was prepared to raise you on her own if that was the case."

"She wasn't going to tell you about me?"

"That's what upset me the most. Regardless of how I felt about her, you're my daughter. I had a right to be a part of your life." He blew out a breath as though blowing away the old hurt. "I can't imagine she would have ever kept you from me. Knowing her like I do, I don't think she would have. Her intentions were honest. She wanted to make sure that if we stayed together, it was because we loved each other, not out of a sense of obligation. Fortunately, those sparks returned the minute we saw each other again."

"Why did you wait so long to go back for me?"

He sat straight, surprised by my question. "We didn't wait. We took the first flight we could. When we got there, Virginia . . . Judy had already left with you."

But why? That was the question that wouldn't let go of me for the rest of the drive. When we got to the airport, I forced the thoughts aside. I wanted to take it all in and remember everything for my journal. My first time at an airport, going through TSA, walking on board the plane.

"Do you want the aisle or the window?" Dad asked when we got to our seats.

"Window, please," I said. "I've always wondered what cities and trees and cars look like from thousands of feet up. And what clouds look like from inside."

He smiled at my giddiness.

The takeoff scared me at first. The force sucked me back into my seat, and even though I knew planes took off from here every single day, I didn't believe we had enough runway to leave the ground. I was sure we'd career off the end and onto one of the highways circling the airport. Once we were airborne, though, I giggled like a five-year-old.

For the first half-hour of the three-hour flight to Portland, I stared out the window. I'd been through nearly every state on the eastern seaboard from Maine to Florida. Across the southern states, most of the southwestern states, and through many of the Midwest ones. I'd never been through the northern or northwestern states, though, and it felt strange to be seeing them not only from the air but with my dad instead of Mum.

I felt a sudden pulling sensation in my chest, and all I could think of was her. One time in fifth grade, I stayed overnight at a friend's house. I'd never spent a night away from Mum before, and I missed her, but I was so excited to stay at my friend's that it was pretty easy to ignore the feeling. This was different, much more intense. Was this homesickness? Could it happen this fast?

"Would you like something to eat or drink?" Dad asked when the flight attendant stopped by our row.

He showed me the menu, and my stomach rumbled. After all the goodbyes, we left Lake Bellwood a little later than planned and didn't have time to stop for breakfast. I chose a breakfast bagel sandwich, fruit, and yogurt.

"And some coffee, please," I told the attendant.

"You can sleep if you'd like," Dad said. "After you eat, of course."

"And miss all this? No way." I sat taller so I could look over my seatback and around the plane. It was full of people of every kind. Businessmen and women, families with kids, couples old and young, couples without kids, people traveling alone. Were any of them going to meet their family for the first time like I was? "You can sleep if you want."

"And miss this?" He reached out and touched my chin. "No way."

I smiled and sat back. Now that my initial excitement over

the whole flying experience had died down, my nerves flared. Meeting my family was super-exciting, but I had so many conflicting feelings about Noelle. My stomach twisted with nerves over meeting her. I wanted to like her—she was my mother, after all—but honestly, I wasn't sure I'd be able to.

"What are you so deep in thought about?" Dad asked.

"I was thinking about Noelle and Noah. Mum, too. I'm worried about her. She's so sure she'll never see me again, and that you and Noelle will report her to the police or something."

The flight attendant set our breakfasts in front of us, and I immediately took a huge bite of the sandwich. Not the greatest breakfast I'd ever had, but I was so hungry I could have been chewing on cardboard right then and not cared.

Dad stirred the contents of two tiny half-and-half pods into his coffee and took a sip before answering.

"All your mom and I ever wanted was to find you. We had no idea where you were or if you were safe. You are a great girl. Judy did a fine job raising you. Except for dragging you all over the country."

"But I've seen so much during our travels," I objected. "Not many people get to see the things that I've seen."

He frowned. "People usually call that vacation. They go visit a place and return home."

He sounded like Bryce telling me we were fugitives, not adventurers.

"Not everyone," I told Dad. "That's one of the things I learned. There are a lot of people who don't have a permanent home. They live in motels or in their cars or on the streets. I've always had a bed to sleep on." I laughed. "Or a futon, at least."

His frown reached his eyes then.

"Why are you looking at me that way?" I asked.

"You could have had so much more in your life. Judy is an intelligent woman. She was the manager of a financial department at a large company when you were born."

"She was? So, what, she's an accountant or something?"

"Not simply an accountant, she has an MBA from a prestigious college."

"Huh. She never told me that. She said she loved working at diners and being with people. I can't imagine her sitting at a desk crunching numbers."

He turned stone-cold serious. "Ainsley, I'm not sure you fully understand. It's fine if she wanted to work in a diner, but the lifestyle you and Judy lived, the moving so often, that isn't normal or healthy."

I didn't answer, but I did understand. I got a sampling of normal during our year in Holly Lake. I liked it. A lot. I never felt lonely thanks to Gabrielle and the other friends I made. And Bryce made me feel excited for the future, instead of worried that it would only bring another move.

Despite my plan to stay awake and take in my whole first flight experience, once I had a full belly, I fell asleep. The next thing I knew, Dad was rubbing my shoulder and telling me that we were almost to Portland.

"I thought you'd want to experience the landing for your journal." He handed me my glasses. "I slipped these off when you fell asleep."

The flight attendant instructed us to return our seats to their full, upright position. Don't quite get how six inches of recline would make a difference, but okay. I put my glasses back on and watched the world get bigger again as we descended into Portland. Big patches of forest became clusters of houses. As the plane got closer and closer to the ground, I grabbed Dad's hand, sure that not only wasn't a runway long enough to take off from, it wasn't long enough to stop on, either. The plane touched the tarmac with a little squeak of the wheels, and then the pilot hit the brakes. The force threw me forward a little, but soon, the plane slowed and was rolling along easily, heading for the gate.

I let go of Dad's hand and laughed, embarrassed.

"Landings still make me nervous," he admitted and patted my knee.

When I saw everyone else taking out their cellphones, I turned mine back on to send Mum a quick text and found one from her waiting.

Did you land yet? I miss you already. Did everything go okay?

Just landed at Portland International. Everything went fine. I miss you, too.

She responded instantly. *If you want to come back, say the word. If you want me to come get you, I will.*

Everything's fine, Mum. Stop worrying. I'll call you later.

It was raining softly and a little on the cool side in Portland. Not all that different from Minnesota.

"Do you want anything before we go home?" Dad asked when we got to his car.

Before we go home. Like I'd been away visiting friends or something. I cracked my car window open to let some air in. That same claustrophobic welcoming sensation from in the bedroom in Mina's loft came over me. *Don't get attached,* the sensation screamed in my head. *This is only a visit.*

And then what? It was pretty much a guarantee, now that Dad had found us, Mum would want to run again as soon as I got back to her.

But you know how to find the rest of your family now, the sensation said. *Relax, Ainsley. Enjoy this. Take advantage of the opportunity. Besides, your dad will be keeping close track of you now.*

Then Desiree's voice was in my head. *Peace, girl. Live in the now.*

Okay, I told the sensation and Desiree. *I'm good.*

"Can we drive around for a little bit?" I asked. "Just so I can get a feel for the area?"

"Sure," Dad said. "We'll go past the hospital where I work first. Then, I'll show you where we shop, where Noah goes to school. Stuff like that."

"That sounds good." Truth was, the closer the time came for me to meet Noelle, the more nervous I was getting.

"It's only ten o'clock here, but it's noon in Minnesota. I'm sure your mom has lunch planned, but we could grab a snack."

"Ice cream," I said immediately.

"That sounds good. I know the perfect place."

An old fashioned ice cream parlor was within walking distance from the hospital where Dad worked. We laughed after we both said, "mint chocolate chip," when the man behind the counter asked if we knew what we wanted. I noticed when Dad put the change back into his wallet, he flattened any folds and creases and kept the bills in numerical order, largest to smallest. I did the same thing.

Dad's phone rang as we were finishing our double-scoop cones. "It's your mom . . . Hi, honey. We stopped for a little snack over by the hospital... Yes, the ice cream shop. We're leaving now."

He hung up, laughing.

"What's funny?" I asked.

"She sounds nervous. She never gets nervous."

"Well, let's get . . . Let's go, then." I almost said let's get home.

It took another half hour to get from Dad's hospital to the house.

"This is our street." He'd been narrating the entire trip. *That's the park where Noah loves to play. That's where I take my dry cleaning. That's where Mom gets her hair cut.*

The street was a two-lane winding road that had an out-in-the-country feel to it. There were so many trees. All covered in leaves with fall hues—reds, oranges, yellows, and even a few greens still scattered throughout.

Finally, he took a left and went down what I at first thought was another single-lane road, but soon realized was our driveway. At the end of it stood a house like I'd never seen before. It wasn't huge, but it was really nice, covered with stone and wood siding and tons of windows. The driveway ended in a circle so you could either pull into the garage or follow it around and go back down the drive. Huge pine trees towered over the house while smaller pines and evergreen bushes filled the beds surrounding it.

"So." My mouth had gone dry. "This is it?"

"This is it." Dad held my hand, the warmth comforted me. "Are you ready?"

Chapter 16

Desiree

Less than a year ago, Kaf assigned Mandy's wish to me. I was bored with being a Guide at that point. All I saw was that others were getting what they wanted, while I would never get my own wish. I'd become bitter and sent my charges on unnecessarily difficult journeys. I'd lost focus of the fact that granting wishes meant I was helping people. Thankfully, it didn't take long for me to realized their journeys were already hard enough. They wouldn't have asked for life-changing wishes if they were content.

I watched in the big window in my cabin as Ainsley was about to be welcomed by her family, and that sickening pang of jealousy flared up in me again.

What was wrong with me? I was doing what I wanted to do, living in a place I wanted to be. Why did I still feel so unsettled? I had to figure that out. I didn't want to risk taking my frustrations out on the Guides the way I had my charges.

"Rasta, let's go for a hike."

By a hike, you mean be gone for a long time. Many days?

"That's what I was thinking."

I thought you wanted to take care of the Guides and the problems here.

"When you're flying on an airplane, they always tell you that in the case of an emergency you should put on your own oxygen mask first. That way, you'll have enough oxygen pumping into your lungs and will be able to help the other passengers."

You feel like you need oxygen?

"Yes. I need to breathe and think for a while. I'm not sure I trust myself to make good choices right now. I won't be able to take care of the Guides until I figure some things out." I manifested my favorite hiking sweater from a shelf inside Gypsy V. "Let's go."

I fear that if you leave now, all the passengers will be dead by the time you return.

"I thought dogs only want to make their mistresses happy."

Too much thinking can make a problem worse. Talking with another person can make a solution obvious.

"You're saying I should talk to Kaf again."

The problem is large. You shouldn't take care of it by yourself.

When Kaf returned to the magical world, Adellika had asked if he could share her room with her.

"I'm not comfortable with that," I'd said. "The lodge is for the Guides."

She glared at me. "He is my brother."

"He isn't part of our world anymore," I'd told her. "He can't stay in the Lodge, but you may provide a visitor's home for him."

So, she manifested a cabin on the far side of Mystic Lodge. I'd seen it from a distance but hadn't gone there.

"Guess I should go and welcome him to the neighborhood." I looked at Rasta. "Do you want to walk to Kaf's cabin with me?"

I do not like him. He upsets you. Do you need to be protected from him?

From Kaf? Not physically. "No. I just thought you might like to walk."

Not this time. I will go to the bus.

As Rasta trotted away, I thought of simply transporting to

Kaf's front door. It was a beautiful clear and crisp night, though. I wasn't going to get to hike, but a walk might help me think.

There was no beaten trail to Kaf's cabin, so I manifested a pair of snowshoes. As I walked around the Lodge and wound my way around Ponderosa pines and boulders, I thought of Ainsley and how her family was about to become bigger by three, soon four, people.

The only family I had left was my sister. Carol and I were bonding again, but it wasn't like I could show up at family gatherings. How was she supposed to explain to her husband that I was the same pesky kid-sister that he knew in high school? I could put a charm on him to accept and not tell, but that didn't seem right.

Kaf's cabin was only about a hundred yards away now. The closer I got, the stronger a single thought became in my head.

You have no family left from the past, but you could have a family in the future.

I imagined being with Kaf. That's what I wanted. What I had wanted for years. We could manifest a bigger cabin to live in and convert Gypsy V into my office. If we brought little genies into the world, would they be born magical, or would we need to give them powers like we did the Guides?

It would take a while, but Rasta would learn to like him. If we restored harmony to the magical world, Adellika would come to like me again, too.

As I got closer to his cabin, I saw that it was small. Probably only a single room. I couldn't imagine it was anything fancy inside. Kaf had lived in a cave in the desert for two hundred years, after all. A fieldstone chimney poked out of the roof, a thin tendril of smoke trailing from it.

I climbed the stairs, and before I knocked, I looked through the window on the door. Like I thought, the cabin was a single room inside. Immediately upon entering was a living room area. To the far right, a huge fireplace made from the same fieldstone as the chimney took up almost the entire wall. A fire roared in the box. That's where I saw them. In front of the fireplace.

Olanna stood inches away from Kaf. She was looking up at him, anguish of some sort clear on her face. They were probably talking about how I was dooming the Guides and the magical world to destruction.

Or, maybe she'd seen reason in my argument. She loved this world, too. She could see how fragile it had become. Maybe she was pleading with him to talk with the Guides and convince them that a little change was okay.

That's what I hoped was going on. But as I watched, Kaf looked down at her with a look of compassion. He said something to her that I couldn't decipher. I could have enchanted the cabin so I could hear. If they were words of love, though, I would crumble to dust right there on the porch. He pulled her tight against him. One arm wrapped around her shoulders, the other hand cradled her head.

When he lowered his cheek to the top of her head, my breath froze in my lungs. The world around me started to fade to black. I was about to faint. I had to go. I needed to be with someone who understood what seeing him with her had just done to me.

I held onto the doorjamb to keep myself from falling and closed my eyes. I envisioned the loft in the faded-red barn, a sign hung from the railing, the words *Mandy's Haven* etched into it. Then I touched my fingers together and vanished.

Chapter 17

Ainsley

We stepped through the front door into an entryway that was nearly as big as the loft back in Minnesota. At the top of a curving stairway that ran along the wall to the left of the door, a little boy with curly reddish-brown hair peeked through the bannisters.

"That must be Noah," I said and looked up at Dad. "When you had hair, was it curly and brown?"

I'd meant it as an honest question, not a tease, but that's how he took it.

He feigned insult and ran his hand over the smooth, shiny surface of his head. "I'll have you know, I look this way by choice."

"That's because there isn't enough of it left to cover his whole head anyway."

The smile froze on my face as I turned to my right. The first thing I noticed was her hair. Just like mine. I'd never, in all of my travels, seen anyone with hair like mine. The next thing was that she wore glasses. Mum had perfect vision. Eddie didn't wear glasses or contacts as far as I could tell. Guess I got Noelle's eyesight as well as her hair color.

She stood at the threshold of the entryway and family room with a hand resting on her big belly.

"Hi, Ainsley," she welcomed cautiously. "I'm Noelle."

I had no idea what to do. What was I supposed to call her? Should I go to her and throw my arms around her? Should I burst into tears of gratitude that I'd finally been reunited with the woman who'd abandoned me fifteen years ago?

"Hi." Kind of lame, but that's all that would come out.

"Sister!" Noah screamed like a ninja announcing he was about to attack. He ran down the stairs, both feet on each step, but so quickly I'd swear he was a video on fast forward. "Hi, sister. Hi," he said breathlessly from the midpoint of the staircase. "I'm, Noah. I'm your brother."

He was working so hard at getting down those stairs, I didn't dare move until he got there. When he finally did, he stopped inches from me and let his head drop back to look up at me.

I took a step back and held my hand out to him. "I'm very happy to meet you."

He slapped his little hand in mine and pumped my arm with all of his strength, which was significant. He pointed at my bangs. "You look like Mommy. Wanna see my room?"

I glanced at Noelle who had a huge smile on her face but, at the same time, looked as nervous as I felt. We should get this part over with.

"I absolutely want to see you room, but you know what?" His face fell from a big grin to a crooked frown. "I need to talk with our mom first."

"Do you want me to stay?" Dad asked quietly. "If not, I'll go upstairs with him so you can have a little privacy."

What to do? I liked having Dad next to me. He'd been right there to support me since I turned and saw him at the lefse table. I honestly wasn't sure how I was going to react to Noelle. Probably better to not have an audience.

"Go ahead," I said. "I'll be fine."

I watched as the two of them climbed the stairs and turned

left. A door clicked shut to the protest of, "But I wanna play with her!"

Noelle laughed. "He's been so excited." She motioned around the corner toward a kitchen with a long counter that reminded me of some of the diners Mum and I had eaten in. "Would you like something to drink? Water, juice, iced tea? I'm making chicken fajitas for lunch."

Making them? Mum never cooked. She said that was one of the benefits of working in diners.

"I'm good. Thanks." I was still standing in the same spot in the entryway.

"Would you like to sit down?" Noelle offered.

I couldn't stop staring at her hair. "We've been sitting all day."

"A walk outside, then? The rain stopped." She let out another anxious-sounding little laugh. "Have to take advantage of that when you can around here."

She was trying. I had to try, too.

"Sure. Okay. A little fresh air sounds good." I pointed at her belly which was enormous and caused her to waddle. "Are you okay to walk?"

"Oh, yes. I'm supposed to walk every day. Doctor's orders."

She led me through a family room that, like the entryway, also soared to the roof. In the corner was a floor-to-ceiling stone fireplace.

"Wow," I said of the fireplace, "that's cool."

She smiled, like a stranger I was passing on the street. "It's supposed to be chilly tonight. We'll light it up."

We went through the family room to a door that opened onto a covered patio with a long L-shaped couch, a few chairs, and a little outdoor kitchen.

"Do you actually cook out here?"

"As often as possible," Noelle said. "We eat out here all the time when it's warm."

I figured we'd sit on the couch, but Noelle kept walking. We crossed the patio and walked on a red-brick pathway that led past a small pond filled with Koi fish, through a clump of trees, and ended at a dock floating on a river. A table, big enough to set a couple of plates and drinks on, and two chairs sat on the dock along with a large plastic box.

How cool. "This might be my new favorite place in the world." I hadn't realized I'd said it out loud until Noelle let out a little gasp, like that was the best news she'd ever heard.

"Sit with me?" She motioned to the chairs. "I'd like it if we could get through the awkward stuff as quickly as possible. So much time has already been wasted."

Couldn't argue with either statement. "Okay."

A short, wooden walkway led out to the dock. It didn't have a railing and was only about two-feet wide. Noelle held a hand out to me.

"Would you mind? I'm not very steady on my feet lately." She indicated her big belly.

"You do look a little off balance."

My hands were sweating. My hands never sweat. I wiped one across my jeans and took her hand.

The connection, like an electric charge, hit me as soon as our hands touched. What had to be a mother's love—warm, compassionate, accepting, and absolutely unconditional—surrounded me. I'd never felt anything like that before. Sure, I felt love from Mum, but not like this. Noelle must have felt it too because she gasped again.

I helped her across the little pier, and before we sat, she wrapped her arms around me and held me as best she could with that belly between us. The tears I felt stinging my eyes had started out in the cornfield with Desiree and Clay when I understood that coming here was the only answer. They threatened, but never fell. Some tiny dam had been holding them back, refusing until this moment to release them.

How long we stood there, holding each other like that, I couldn't say. When we finally pulled away, Noelle ran a finger through my bangs. She didn't say a word, just studied me like she was tattooing every detail of me onto her brain, the way I did with things I wasn't sure I'd get to see again. Finally, she wiped tears off my cheeks and held a hand out to the chairs.

"Sit, please," she said.

I did, and for a long time, neither of us said anything. My eyes darted from my hands to her to a leaf floating past on the river.

"I'm not sure," I started to say, and she jumped at the sound of my voice. "Sorry. I'm not sure what to call you."

She nodded, understanding my dilemma. "What have you been calling Eddie?"

"Dad."

"You can call me Mom if you want."

The look of hope on her face tore at my heart.

"See," I said, "it's been easy to call him dad. Maybe because I've never had a dad or a dad type person in my life." Her look of hope faltered. "I've had a mother person. Until about twenty-four hours ago, I thought she was my mom."

"I know." Noelle's voice croaked with sadness. "I understand how hard this must be for you."

Did she? Could she? I caught myself staring at her, looking for a gesture or mannerism of some kind that linked me to her. I had Eddie's face, yes, but we also shared a preference for mint chocolate chip ice cream and a habit of bouncing our legs when we had something to say but didn't know how. My left leg was bouncing right now. I needed something other than hair, no matter how small, to tie me to Noelle. Some sort of silly something that would prove to me I had come from her.

"I know you heard Eddie's and Virginia's—"

"Judy," I interrupted her.

"I'm sorry?"

"She calls herself Judy."

"Right," Noelle said. "Eddie told me. Sorry, I forgot."

Despite the anger that had to be burning inside Noelle

toward Mum, she didn't show it. What I did see was a shadow of pain on her face and heard a tremor of it in her voice. Pain over the long-ago death of a love? It seemed unintentional on Noelle's part and made her suddenly human to me.

She started again. "I know you heard Eddie's and Judy's sides of things. Maybe it would help to hear mine?"

"Okay." I said.

She got up and opened the plastic, weather-proof box sitting on the corner of the deck. She pulled a gray blanket with white stripes from inside and held it out to me. "The wind is a little chilly."

"Thanks," I said, accepting it from her.

I opened the blanket, made from thin but dense wool, wrapped it around my legs, and tucked it underneath my thighs. She came back around to her chair and opened an identical blanket and covered herself the exact same way I had, with the blanket tucked beneath her thighs.

A little shiver went through me, but I brushed it away. That could be a coincidence. It was chilly. Anyone could cover up that way. Maybe she had watched me cover myself and simply copied me.

She took a breath and then another deeper one. "The baby is crowding pretty much everything inside me right now. It's hard to get a good breath sometimes. Would you do a favor for me? Drag the blanket box over so I can prop my feet up on it? My ankles have started to swell these last couple of weeks. I'm supposed to prop them whenever I sit."

"Sure." I jumped up and positioned the box in front of her.

"Thank you, Ainsley." She settled her feet on the box and let out a sigh. "All right, let's do this. I know you know that Judy and I met in college. We were friends right away and lived together for our last two years there." She smiled. "I remember every detail of the night she told me about her feelings for me."

I had a hard time picturing Mum with a woman. Of course, I couldn't picture her with a man, either. I don't remember her ever going on a date or even out with friends. Had she always been that way?

"Did you feel the same way?" I asked.

"That's where things got a little complicated for me." Noelle's cheeks flushed a little. Was that due to the chilly air or remembering her feelings for Mum? "I thought I felt the same. I was attracted to her. Vir—Judy was a beautiful woman." She tapped her heart. "Inside and out."

My cheeks got warm. Then I got embarrassed because I was embarrassed.

"I guess," Noelle began, "I was testing things out. Figuring out what was the best fit for my life. I was doing that with everything right then. Jobs, clothes, hair, makeup . . ." She looked at me, like a mom trying to teach me something. "That's what you do in your twenties. That's your time to figure out who you are."

I didn't say anything, just bobbed my head in agreement.

"Judy and I had been friends for years." Every time she said *Judy*, she paused first then said it slowly, like it was a foreign word. "We'd been together for a while, and I was struggling so much." She frowned. "I can't tell you how much."

"With what?"

"Everything. I still loved her as my best friend and as a person, but I wasn't in love with her the way she was with me." She stared blankly across the river. "I didn't know how to tell her. I knew once I did, everything would change. I'd lose my best friend and my girlfriend all at once."

"Is that when you went to the conference?"

She nodded and picked at the edge of her blanket. "I had to get away and clear my head for a while. I met your dad and, well, you know."

Noelle seemed like a pretty open person. Not afraid to talk about anything. That was awesome, but I was grateful she stopped where she did. My mind was already showing me pictures I didn't want to see.

"We shared a cab to the airport," Noelle continued. "He said he'd call me, maybe come for a visit. We left it at that with no real plans."

"And then you found out you were pregnant."

I couldn't take my eyes off of her. As she told me about the different events, the emotion on her face kept shifting. Now, she looked ashamed.

"That's how Judy found out what I'd done. She refused to speak to me for almost a week. When I told her I'd leave, she panicked and said no, we'd work it out." Noelle turned toward me. "Meaning we'd figure out a way to raise you together."

And then I saw it. The thing I was looking for. Her glasses had slid down her nose, the way mine always did. To push them up, she reached up with her fingers splayed wide and pushed on the bridge of her glasses with her thumb. That was exactly how I pushed my glasses up. Gabrielle used to tease me about it, said I was making a rude gesture at her. Maybe I was a little desperate. The white bangs should have been enough. That simple, unconscious gesture was the thing I'd been waiting for, though. I decided that I would accept and believe whatever she told me.

"I admit it," she continued, blinking a few times. "I was selfish then. But I was twenty-something, pregnant, and terrified. I knew that if I told Judy the truth, that I didn't have feelings for her anymore, that I'd fallen in love with Eddie, she would kick me out. Eddie didn't know about you either, and I was afraid that if I told him, he'd reject me, too."

"It must have been tough for you," I said, forgiveness starting to trickle in.

"It was." A single tear slid down her cheek. "That's my version. You know the rest."

"Most of it." I had a lot of questions.

She sat forward, as best she could. "What else? What do you want to know?"

It was hard. I felt like we had connected, and I didn't want to risk harming that, but I needed to know the rest.

"I don't understand," I said slowly. "How could you leave me?"

She reached over and grabbed my hand. "She didn't tell you?"

"Tell me what?"

"Judy knew I was coming back."

"For me?"

"Sweetheart, of course. I told her I'd only be gone for the weekend."

"She said she came home to find you were gone and that you'd left me behind."

"That's what you thought? You thought I walked out of our apartment and, what, left you in your crib?" Noelle looked horrified. "God, no. Ainsley, I never would have done that. I asked Vir— *Judy* if she would watch you for a few days. I explained I needed to come out here and be sure of Eddie first. She said she would watch you." Noelle smiled sadly. "She adored you."

I couldn't believe it. Mum lied to me while having a conversation about all the lies she'd told me.

"I'd fallen in love with Eddie through our phone calls and emails," Noelle said. "There's nothing like being face-to-face, though. I needed to make sure he was the person I thought he was, for your sake, too, before I packed us and our things up and moved us across the country."

Us and our things.

"After one day, I knew he was the person I thought he was. I called Judy to let her know that he would be coming to Pennsylvania with me to help me pack all of our things and have them shipped to Oregon. Then we'd bring you here with us. I thought giving her a little warning was the kind thing to do." Noelle took off her glasses and rubbed her eyes. "That decision has haunted me for fifteen years."

"You got there, and she'd already left with me." My heart sank.

"I called everyone I knew. Then I called everyone who knew her." Noelle shook her head, her expression blank like it must have been that day. "No one knew where she was. The two of you had disappeared. We called the police and eventually hired a private investigator. You know the rest from there."

I did. Bryce was right. Mum had kidnapped me.

Chapter 18

Ainsley

It had started to rain again. Just a drizzle, but Noelle . . . Mom looked up at the sky and said, "We should go in. It's going to get heavy in a minute."

As we made our way through the backyard, I looked up at the house. Noah stood waving at me with both hands from one of the windows on the second floor. When I waved back, he jumped up and down and then disappeared.

Mom was right. We'd made it to the Koi pond when the clouds let loose. Dad met us at the door with towels.

"I saw you two coming from Noah's window." He handed one towel to me and wrapped the other around Mom's shoulders. "Are you okay? You didn't get too cold did you?"

She turned to me. "Every woman deserves a man as chivalrous as your father." She turned back to him. "I'm fine. The baby is fine. We were in the rain for approximately ten seconds, not trudging hours through waist-high snow in a raging blizzard." She reached up to kiss him.

My parents were cute together. It made my heart feel good to know I'd come from people who seemed to love each other so much. Too bad I'd missed so many years with them.

"Is it lunchtime yet?" Noah came through the family room, over to me, and leaned his head on my hip. "I'm hungry."

"The chicken is ready," Mom said. "It will take five minutes to fix the vegetables. Why don't you go let Sprite and Pixie out? By the time you're back, lunch will be on the table."

"Okay," he said and took off like a little super-charged jet, arms out to his sides like wings.

"Sprite and Pixie?" I asked.

"The dogs," Dad said.

"Dogs?" My excitement level skyrocketed. "I've always wanted a pet."

Mom and Dad exchanged a look. They felt sorry for me, but that was probably okay. When I thought of the life I'd had versus the life I could have been living, in a beautiful home with parents and a brother and pets, I got angrier and angrier at Mum.

Immediately, I felt guilty. Despite everything, Mum did love me.

"Noah adores those dogs," Mom said, interrupting my thoughts. "I'm sure he'll be happy to introduce you after lunch. Want to help me get it ready?"

Another entry for my journal. *I made lunch with my mom today.* She had the vegetables already cut up, so while she stir-fried them for the fajitas, I cut the chicken into strips.

"Would you like to sit here at the kitchen bar or at the dining room table?" Mom asked.

"Dining room." I'd noticed it when I first came in the front door. Very fancy.

"Wonderful," she said with a smile. "We normally use that room for special occasions."

"Oh, well," I said, "we can sit in here, then."

"Ainsley," she sighed happily and rubbed my shoulder, "I can't think of an occasion that is more special than today."

I tried to swallow the lump that had formed in my throat but couldn't, so I just nodded.

The fajitas were good, but honestly, eating around that table like a family was the best part. Noah talked non-stop about his pre-school and how he was going to be a search-and-rescue hero when he grew up. Dad talked about things at work. Mom discussed events for Noah and appointments she had. Clothes shopping with me was on the list.

When we were done eating, I offered to wash the dishes. Noah was so excited to show me the dogs, though, that Mom shooed us out of the room.

"This way. They're in the muddy room."

"Mudroom," Dad corrected.

Noah took my hand and dragged me through a door in the corner of the kitchen. A washer, dryer, and folding counter lined one wall of the room. Hooks loaded with jackets, trays on the floor filled with shoes, and a bench to sit on were on the other. Next to the bench on the floor lay a giant tan and brown plaid pillow with two tiny black and tan dogs perched on it. They looked like shrunken Dobermans.

"They're so cute," I said. "What are they?"

"Miniature Pinschers," Noah said proudly. "They don't pinch, though."

They were practically identical. If I looked close, I could see that the tan marks on their faces and chests were a little different.

"How do you tell them apart?" I asked.

"Their collars." Noah dropped to the ground next to the pillow. "Sprite's has circles all over it. Pixie's has stripes."

"Good idea. Will they let me pet them?"

"Sure. You gotta sit down, though."

He patted the floor and snuggled close to me when I sat next to him. Sprite stood to investigate me right away. Pixie wasn't quite so sure, preferring to sit and observe until Sprite gave what sounded like an all-clear *ruff*. Then they both pounced on me. I'm not sure who was laughing harder, Noah or me.

"Do they play fetch?" I'd always wanted to play fetch with a dog.

"What's fetch?" Noah asked.

"What's fetch?" I repeated, tickling him so I could hear his great giggle again. "It's when you throw a ball or a stick or a Frisbee and the dog runs to get it and brings it back to you. It's a game."

He shook his head. "They don't know how to do that."

"Well," I said, "we have to teach them."

His eyes went wide. "You and me?"

"You and me." I looked out the window over the washer and dryer. "Only not right now because it's raining."

"And it's naptime." We turned to see Mom leaning against the doorframe. "You four are making an awful lot of noise in here."

"They like Ainsley," Noah announced. "We're gonna teach them fletch."

"Fetch," I corrected.

"Fetch," he said. "It's a game."

"Sounds great," Mom said, "but for now, you need to go lay down."

Noah pouted. "Don't wanna. I'm playing with my sister."

My heart clenched. *I played with my brother today.*

"You know what?" I told him. "I'm kind of tired, too. How about we both lay down for a while, and we can play again later?"

"Take a nap together?" His eyes went wide again.

"Not in the same bed," I laughed.

He stood, grabbed my hand, and pulled me through the mudroom again. "Tuck me in."

"He's very excited that you're here," Mom said. "I hope he's not overwhelming you."

"Are you kidding me?" I called over my shoulder as we passed her in the doorway. "This day is at the top of my Best Days Ever list."

Noah dragged me through the house, informing me of the *no running* rule, and up the stairs. His bedroom was the first one on the left. It was decorated in gray, white, and red. His bedspread had firetrucks, police cars, ambulances, rescue helicopters, and Coast Guard boats all over it. Big plaques with logos from all the different rescue groups covered one wall.

"Cool room," I said.

"Yep," he agreed and started to show me everything.

Mom came in, breathing hard, from carrying that big belly up the stairs I assumed.

"Later, Noah," she said, in that tone moms used, and pointed at his bed.

He hung his head and shuffled his feet to the bathroom attached to his room. His own bathroom. It was easily twice the size of any bathroom in any apartment Mum and I had ever rented. What a lucky kid. When he was done, he dragged himself to his bed, like his legs weighed two tons each, and climbed under the covers. I sat on the edge and tucked his blankets underneath him so tightly he couldn't move his arms.

He lay there, motionless, then started to wiggle his shoulders a little bit, then more and more until his arms burst free from the covers. Then he wrapped them around my neck.

"Promise you'll still be here when I wake up." It wasn't a question but not quite a command either. More a need for reassurance. I totally understood that.

"I promise." I'd never hugged a little kid before. What an awesome feeling. "Door closed?" I asked when I got to the doorway and he nodded. "See you in a little while, buddy."

Across the hall from Noah's room was a bedroom set up for the baby. It was all soft pinks and yellows with birds and hot air balloons and butterflies painted on the walls and hanging from the ceiling. In the white crib, two little stuffed animals, a pig and a duck, waited in the corner for their baby. They made me realize that I'd forgotten Moo Cow and Hound Dog. I always slept with Moo Cow, how could I have left him? On the wall over the crib the words *SOAR* and *DREAM* were painted in an elegant script. What a lucky baby.

"Ready to see your room?" Mom asked as she led me to the end of the hallway.

"Sure." I hadn't expected much. A bed, maybe a chair, a little dresser for my six possessions.

"We can change anything you don't like." She opened the door then, and my jaw literally dropped.

It was like a princess room. The walls were pale gray, almost white, on the bottom half. The top was black wallpaper covered with bouquets of silver flowers surrounded by swirling, silver vines. I couldn't help myself, I had to touch it.

"It's like velvet," I said of the fuzzy paper.

"It's called flocking," Mom said softly.

The bed was huge. The headboard was silver with a padded, hot pink fabric center. Black nightstands flanked either side of the bed. There was a black free-standing mirror in one corner, a black dresser next to it. A silver desk and a hot pink chair in the opposite corner. A black chandelier bejeweled with hot pink crystals hung from the center of the ceiling.

"Fancy guestroom," I said.

"This isn't a guestroom," Mom said. "It's yours."

"Mine?"

"The police had been searching for you for years when they told us that they'd leave the case open, but it wasn't a priority anymore." Anger flashed across her face. "That didn't sit well with us, so we hired a private investigator.

"He called one day to tell us that there was a girl in New Mexico who matched your description. By the time we got there, the girl's school said she hadn't been there in three days, and they hadn't been able to contact the mother." She groaned at the memory.

"I think I remember that," I said. "We'd gone to some community thing, a carnival or whatever, and were having a great time. There were news reporters there with cameras. Mum freaked out when she realized they'd been filming us. We left that night."

Mom took my hand. "We were hugely disappointed but took it as a sign that we would find you. Even though hope would fade sometimes, we never stopped searching. I set up this room for you after the New Mexico sighting."

She had done all of this for me? She set up this bedroom not knowing if I'd ever spend even one night in it?

"If you don't like it—"

"I love it. I love every single thing about it." I spun in a slow circle, trying to take it all in. On the wall across from the door was a window seat with black cushions and hot pink pillows. Another door showed a white bathroom with silver fixtures and pink towels. My own bathroom.

My knees went a little wobbly, and I had to sit down on the bed.

"Are you all right?" Mom sat next to me and put a hand on my back.

My throat tightened and my eyes prickled. "I never expected anything like this."

"It's what you would have had if I'd done the right thing from the start," she said shamefully. "So, did you really want to take a nap?"

A yawn snuck up on me, making me laugh. "I could sleep for an hour."

Mom stood, took the throw pillows off of the bed, and pulled back the fluffy white comforter. "Why don't I tuck you in, then?"

I crawled in and pulled off the Zion National Park fleece to reveal my faded Stone Mountain tank top. Suddenly, everything I brought in my tiny duffle bag seemed cheap, no longer good enough. A twinge of disloyalty to Mum shot through me, but I was still angry at her for lying to me. I tossed the disloyal feelings aside with the fleece that I threw at the black-and-silver striped lounge chair in the corner.

Mom pulled the covers over me and then went to close the window blinds. She came back and sat on the edge of the bed.

As she did, she let out a little groan and put her hand on her belly.

"Are you okay?" I sat straight up.

"I'm fine." She put her hands behind her on the bed and leaned back. Through her shirt, I could see her belly moving like that baby was trying to burst free.

"What's happening?" I asked, horrified by the sight.

The look on Mom's face, though, was total peace. "I was wondering when she was going to turn."

"What are you talking about? Is she coming? Should I get Dad?" I pulled the covers back, ready to run.

Mom shook her head. "She's getting ready. When it gets close to the time for a baby to be born, they somehow know to turn so their heads are down, in the right position for delivery." She looked at me, laughed, and put a soft hand on my cheek. "She's not coming yet, there's still a couple of weeks until her due date."

Mom placed my hand on her belly, and we waited to see if my sister would go alien on her again. She kicked a few times, as though getting comfortable for a nap, too, but nothing more dramatic than that.

"She's happy now," Mom said. "Ready for your tucking?"

I lay back down and realized I was in the most comfortable bed I'd ever lain on in my life, in the most perfect room I could ever imagine. Lucky me.

"I've waited so long to do this." Mom smoothed the blankets over me. Then she placed a kiss on my forehead and whispered against my skin, "I'm so very grateful that you're finally here."

I think she stood in the doorway watching me for a while, but I didn't know for sure. I fell asleep almost immediately.

Chapter 19

Desiree

Mandy wasn't there when I got to her loft, but I knew she'd come soon. The Haven was her safe place, her happy place. Her Gypsy V. I was too numb to care that I was alone, so I climbed into the chair hanging from the rafters. The butt hammock.

That image of Kaf pulling Olanna close. The look on his face. It played over and over and over in my mind.

I'd been close to him at times. So close I could feel the heat radiating from his body. He placed a kiss on my forehead as he wished me happy birthday a few months earlier. But he'd never given me even a friendly hug, let alone a lover's embrace like he'd given Olanna. I'd dreamt of being in his arms for so long. To feel the strength of them, the safety of being enclosed by them. What an idiot I'd been. What a silly, stupid, childish fool.

"Desiree?"

I opened my eyes to see Mandy standing before me, her forehead furrowed in confusion.

"Hey, Mandy. You look nice." She had on the white sundress, jean jacket, and cowgirl boots she bought during the shopping spree she'd gone on with Lexi seven months earlier. Had it only been seven months? How could that be possible? So much had happened. Everything had changed.

"Thanks. Ethan and I went out with Crissy and her new boyfriend."

"Crissy has a new boyfriend?" I didn't know. I'd been out of touch.

"Yeah, he's a friend of Ethan's. Nice guy."

"A Mandy-approved guy?" I joked. Mandy had done everything in her power to get Crissy away from Brad. I couldn't imagine she'd let Crissy anywhere near another guy without making sure he checked all the right boxes first.

"Desiree? What are you doing here?" Her voice was gentle. Guess she could tell I needed gentle right then.

"Everything's such a mess." I wanted to cry, but that required too much effort.

"You need a girls' night. Can you stay?"

"I can't face going back right now," I said.

"You can stay all day tomorrow, too. I've got a ton of homework to get to on Sunday, though."

I laughed. Same old Mandy. Thank the cosmos.

"We need Crissy," Mandy said.

"We definitely need Crissy," I agreed, and then the tears started.

"Oh, wow." Mandy pulled out her phone. "Hey, you'll never guess who's here . . . Yep. Can you come . . .? Plan to spend the night." She nodded and hung up. "It'll take her thirty minutes or so."

"Okay," I sniffed, and the tears fell harder.

"We'll need brownies, too." She held out her hand to me and pulled me out of the chair. She wrapped her arms around me and let me cry, then she led me to the futon. "You don't have to say anything until Crissy gets here. Lay down. Close your eyes. I'll go make brownies."

Mandy's cat, Brulée, snuggled in next to me. Between the soft futon mattress, the warm blanket, and the purring cat, I fell asleep in no time.

☙

"She looks like crap. What's she doing here?" That had to be Crissy.

"I don't know. I decided to wait until you got here to ask for details."

"Are there any brownies left?" I mumbled.

"Sorry to wake you," Mandy whispered.

"No we're not," Crissy said. "I didn't come all the way out here to watch you sleep. I was saying good night to Lukas when Mandy called."

"He drove you out here," Mandy said. "You got an extra half hour with him."

"Yeah." Crissy sounded disappointed. "I got to hold his hand but missed out on other stuff."

"Um," Mandy warned.

"Don't worry. Nothing big has happened. Yet."

One of them plopped onto the far end of the futon, right on my feet. Had to be Crissy.

"What's going on?" Mandy asked. "You said something about things being a mess."

I pulled my feet out from under Crissy, sat up, and wrapped the blanket around my shoulders like a cape. Then, I held my hand out for the plate of brownies in her lap.

"Don't worry." Crissy handed me the plate. "She made a double batch."

I took a big bite and savored the chocolaty, nutty, non-manifested goodness of the first of many brownies I'd consume.

"I've totally messed up the magical world," I explained. "It's in total crisis mode and is falling apart around me. Oh, and I saw Kaf with one of the Guides."

"Hang on," Mandy said. "Kaf is back?"

"What do you mean *with*?" Crissy asked. "There are many ways to interpret that."

Through the brownie I'd just shoved in my mouth I mumbled, "The kind of *with* you think I mean."

I told them how Adellika was Kaf's sister and that she'd basically been spying for him since I took over three months ago. "She brought him back because she thought I needed help. He claims he'd planned to come back all along, but since I moved us from the desert to the mountains, he couldn't find us."

"Did you need help?" Mandy asked.

"Not *his* help. I was starting to figure things out. Most of the Guides had stopped giving me such a hard time. All I needed was their patience and cooperation. Then Kaf showed up, and everything went to hell again."

"If he's causing problems," Mandy said, "why don't you make him leave?"

Crissy gave her a look that said, *think about it.*

"Oh, please." Mandy waved dismissively. "Just because she's in love with him doesn't mean she has to let him hang around and cause problems. They can see each other somewhere else."

"I went to his cabin," I said, trying to get back to the reason I was there. "I wanted to talk to him about working together to try and unite the Guides. Olanna was there."

"She's the one who's in love with him, right?" Mandy asked.

"She's the one," Crissy sneered.

"That doesn't mean Kaf feels the same way." Mandy, ever the voice of silver linings.

"What were they doing?" Crissy asked. "And you can spare the specifics, thanks."

"He was hugging her," I blurted and put my hands over my eyes, as though that would stop the image from showing up in my mind again.

"Hugging?" Crissy asked. "That's it?"

"It was the way he was holding her and the look on his face. I didn't stick around to see what else might happen."

"You don't actually know what was going on between them, then," Mandy said. "You're assuming."

"You are." Crissy nodded. "You need to find out the facts."

"And the truth is," Mandy said, too wisely for her sixteen years, "if he does want to be with Olanna, there's not much you can do about it."

"Bull." Crissy slapped her hands down on the futon cushion and turned toward me. "Do you love him?"

"What are you talking about? That's not—"

"Stop." Crissy held up a hand to me. "You've run away, again, and are sitting under a blanket shoveling one brownie after another into your mouth. You're either high and have the munchies or you're in love. Considering what you just told us, I'm going with in love."

"She's right," Mandy agreed. "We know you as well as you know us, Desiree. You've been moony over Kaf since the day we met."

"Moony?" Crissy rolled her eyes.

"I don't know what you're talking about," I said.

"What's going on then?" Mandy asked. "Yes, the magical world is having issues, but that's because its leader is the one in crisis mode."

"I'm not in crisis." I shoved another brownie into my mouth.

"Of course you are." Crissy said and leaned over and snatched the plate from me. "You told us you were happy when you got to go back to the human world. You had a plan to go to college and help Rita run her soup kitchens. Then Kaf tricked you into going back."

They both stared at me. Probably waiting for me to spew a breakthrough, heartfelt confession of some kind.

"What do you want me to say?" I asked.

"Tell us the truth," Crissy answered. "What do you want?"

"I don't know." My tears started again, but not as dramatically.

"Yes, you do," Mandy said. "You're just afraid to say it."

This was why I came to them. Crissy ripped off the bandage, then Mandy soothed the sting so I could deal with it.

They both sat back and waited, neither of them saying a thing. The silence in the room pressed and pressed until I couldn't take another second.

"I want Kaf!" I slapped my hands over my mouth. That was the first time I'd said the words out loud. And it felt amazing. Like I'd whipped off a too-tight bra and could breathe again. "Yes, I love him. I've been in love with him for years."

"Well, what are you waiting for?" Crissy asked. "He's back in your world. You said he planned all along to come back, and I'm willing to bet it wasn't for the genies. Don't let this Olanna chick get in your way. If you want him, then damn, girl, go for it. We've seen that guy. Hot doesn't even begin to describe him."

"More importantly," Mandy scowled, "we know how you look at him and talk about him. You have to tell him."

I laughed. "Tell him?"

"I thought you were this independent, go for what you want, liberated hippie babe," Crissy said. "Maybe he's one of those big, tough shy-babies. You could be alone for a long time if you're going to wait for him to work up the courage to make the first move."

"Shy-baby?" Mandy asked. "And you picked on me for moony?"

What was I afraid of? Rejection. Humiliating myself. After all these years of imagining what it would be like to be with him, what if I was wrong and he'd never had any romantic feelings for me? What if we got together and it turned out that an independent, liberated hippie babe couldn't make it with a traditional, set-in-his-ways dude? The dream would be dead.

I'd never been afraid to put myself out there and do what needed to be done for my charges. The same held true for friends. I always put their needs above my own. But, to stand in front of Kaf and tell him I loved him? I wasn't sure there was enough magic in the world to make me brave enough to do that.

Spending Saturday with Mandy and Crissy was far out. Exactly what I needed. I listened while they gossiped about some of the kids in school. They told me about the colleges they'd decided on for next fall. Mandy had already been accepted to the best culinary school in Minnesota. Crissy was waiting for word from a local college where she could study photography and journalism. Of course we talked about boys—Ethan, Lukas, and Kaf.

Mandy gave us manicures. Then we made an amazing lunch of lentil stew and rustic bread. I understood why Mandy liked cooking. There was something Zen about chopping vegetables.

"Now what?" Mandy asked, ever the tour guide.

"We don't have to do anything," I said. "We can just hang out."

"You have to go back to the genie world in the morning," Crissy reminded me. "There has to be something you'd like to do here that you can't do there."

I thought for a minute. "A movie. I haven't seen a movie at a theater since I was in high school."

"Really?" Crissy asked. "Get ready to have your mind blown. Things have changed in forty-five years."

I transported us into town, and we went to a romantic comedy about a surfer dude and a snowboarding chick.

"Love at opposite ends of the water spectrum," Crissy joked.

After stopping for garlic cheese bread, I took us home. We tucked into our spots in the Haven for the night—Mandy and Crissy on the futon, me in the hanging chair.

"Face your fears," Crissy whispered in the darkness.

"Everything's going to be fine," Mandy assured.

I fell asleep feeling comforted and cared for. It was still dark outside when I woke up. By the light of the moon, I watched Mandy and Crissy sleep. They lay in opposite directions on the futon, their feet in each other's faces. How could two people change my life so much? I couldn't imagine ever having better friends.

I drifted off again and woke to Crissy saying, "Geeze, Desiree, can you turn down the lights?"

I'd been able to cloak the wish auroras while awake, but I couldn't maintain it once I fell asleep. Now, the auroras hovered below the hanging chair and filled the Haven with light.

"Sorry." I dimmed them again. "Incoming wishes."

There'd be hell to pay when I got back to Mystic Lodge. Not only had a hundred wishes come in, someone had been summoning me repeatedly. Probably Olanna. She'd have to wait until I was ready to deal with her.

"You two need to get back to your lives," I said, unfolding my stiff legs. "I'll get going."

"Not before breakfast," Mandy said.

"You are part of our lives," Crissy reminded me. "You need us, we're here. That's how friendship works."

This was exactly one of the things I felt most strongly about. The Guides needed connections to the human world other than their charges. Not only was it important to get away for a while, it was important to remember where we came from and know what was happening in our charges' world.

While Mandy grilled thick slices of French toast, fried a pound of bacon, and scrambled some eggs for us, I thought back on all that we'd talked about. Something was still poking at me. It wasn't Kaf. They were right, I had to work up the courage to tell him how I felt. I couldn't keep going this way. If he said no, then at least I could move on.

"Thank you for everything," I said, as the three of us stood in a group hug.

"Always," Mandy said. "Anytime."

"Go get your man," Crissy ordered. "Send us a selfie of your first date."

I released the hug, placed my hands in Namaste, and disappeared.

Chapter 20

Ainsley

On my second day in Portland, Mom took me shopping and bought me new clothes and shoes and anything else I could possibly need. The back of her SUV was crammed with bags. Dad had taken time off from work, so the four of us explored Portland and did all sorts of family things together. We went to the zoo and a super-cool museum. We gathered in the family room and watched movies every night. Noah and I worked on teaching the dogs to fetch. That would take a while, though, as neither dog seemed interested. After a few days, I felt like I'd known them all my entire life.

I texted or talked to Bryce and Gabrielle every day. They wanted to hear all about my family and new home. Gabrielle squealed over the pictures of my bedroom. Bryce laughed at the ones of Pixie and Sprite. They both told me over and over how happy they were for me.

Dad had to get back to work on Thursday. "Especially since it's a short week next week."

"Why is it a short week?" Mom asked.

"Turkey! Smashed 'tatoes! Pun'kin pie!" Noah hollered with delight and punched the air with each item.

Mom groaned. "Thanksgiving. I completely forgot. Too much excitement around here. Okay, definitely time for us to get back to our normal routines."

For me, that meant a lot of sitting in my beautiful room at my desk and studying. Between moving from Colorado to Minnesota, making lefse, and hanging out with my family, I'd fallen behind on schoolwork and had a lot of catching up to do. Noah insisted he should be able to stay home and do preschool online. I convinced him it was better to be with friends. It was. I missed being with people my own age and almost asked Mom to enroll me at the local high school. I'd be going back to Mum soon, though, so no sense in that.

At the end of the school day, we did things like going to Noah's soccer practices and running errands. I finally had the family, home, and life I'd dreamed of—when I dared to dream. Everything was perfect, almost too perfect.

My favorite thing about my new home, other than my bedroom, was that dock floating on the river. Especially at night, the gentle rocking of the dock and sloshing water soothed me. I liked to lay there and stare up at the stars or talk to Bryce or Gabrielle.

That's also where I went when the nightmare woke me up.

The first night I'd had it was after I'd been there for almost a week. It came every night around two-thirty or three and was always the same. In the dream, I'd be standing in the middle of the cornfield by Mina's house. It looked the same as it had when I'd been there, row after row of hacked-off stalks and picked-clean cobs scattered about. Nothing resembled even the hint of life. The wind blew biting cold, and sleety bits of snow skittered across the ground.

To my right, Mina's house and the barn seemed miles away. The Portland house, to my left, was the closest shelter from the weather, but with every step I took toward it, the house got farther away. In front of me, far in the distance, I saw Mom and Dad. Mum was behind me, just as far away. Like with the house, every step toward one of them sent them away ten steps. I called and called for them to come to me, but no one took even one step toward me. I'd never felt so completely alone. I'd never felt such a pull in so many directions.

Every night, I woke with a start, my heart hammering my ribs. I'd look around the bedroom that was familiar yet still strange, and it would take a few seconds for me to remember where I was. Then I'd go out to the dock and stare at the sky. Unless it was raining, in which case I'd sob into my pillow until I fell back to sleep.

I was pretty sure I knew what had brought the dream on. Mum had started calling me five, ten, sometimes fifteen times a day. Like the nightmare, the conversation was the same every time.

"When are you coming home?" she'd ask.

"I told you, Mum. I want to be here when the baby's born. That might not be for a few weeks."

"You can't be away from me for that long. You need to come home. It's Thanksgiving this week. We've never been apart for Thanksgiving."

In my most soothing voice, I'd assure her, "I promise I'll come back. You have to stop worrying."

But what would happen if I never went back? Mum wasn't exactly the most stable person. I had always thought her frantic, pack-your-things episodes was her being quirky. I understood the truth now. If I never went back, would Mum end up like Mina, living with all of my stuff around her, right where I'd last used it? I didn't *really* think that would happen. Besides, I was going back. But how was she while I was gone? Was she sleeping? Eating? Washing her clothes?

"I heard you on the phone a lot today," Mom said at dinner. "Who were you talking to? You should be focusing on school."

"It was Mum," I answered.

Mom stiffened.

Dad sighed and his shoulders slumped. "Ainsley—"

"Can we talk about this after . . ." I tilted my head at Noah, meaning after he went to bed.

Mom nodded. "Good idea."

A few hours later, we all settled in the family room by the fireplace. Mom and I on the couch. Dad in a recliner across from me.

"I'm a little worried about her," I told them. "She misses me. She wants to know when I'm coming back."

Neither of them responded. Instead, they gave each other looks that I didn't understand. While lying on the dock the night before, I thought about Mum's phone calls and the life that I now had with Mom and Dad. I'd come up with a plan and felt sure it was the right solution.

"So, I've been thinking we could treat this as a custody arrangement. Like people do in divorces. Mum could move here and get a job. Obviously she's not picky about where she lives or works. That way, I can be with all of you."

Dad cleared his throat and let out a sigh. "Part of being a parent is doing what's best for your child. That often means making some hard decisions."

I nodded. This would be hard for them, I understood that. After all those years apart, they wanted me here with them. That's why I figured Mum could move here.

"We understand how close you and Judy became over the years." Dad glanced at Mom and back to me. "While we respect the time and thought you put into this, your plan can't happen."

My heart and jaw dropped. "Why not?"

"Ainsley," Mom said, and with that one word, I knew she was on his side. "Virginia . . . Judy has no legal rights to you. She's not your mother. She's not even your adoptive mother. We can't allow you to live with her anymore."

"In fact," Dad began, "we're not comfortable with you being around her at all."

Mom nodded. "We'd prefer you not even talk on the phone with her anymore."

Not even talk to her? How could they ask that?

I shook my head. "That's completely unfair. Mum never once hurt me. She's always taken good care of me."

"She kidnapped you, sweetheart," Mom said. "You've lived your life on the run for fifteen years. There have to be consequences for that."

"What does that mean?" I asked, panic rising.

"Remember the test we had done?" Dad asked.

A DNA test to prove that I was their daughter. Mom and I stopped at Dad's hospital the day we went clothes shopping. It was a simple thing. The nurse rubbed a cotton swab around the inside of my cheek for ten seconds or so to collect some of my cells. That was it.

"The results came back. You are definitely our daughter." Mom touched her white bangs. "As if we had any doubt."

"It also means that the police have proof that Judy kidnapped you," Dad said gently.

"What does *that* mean?" I sat on the edge of the couch, trying to stay calm. Then the dots connected. "Wait. They're not going to . . . You can't let them arrest her."

"That's out of our hands," Dad explained. "What happens next is up to the police. They're not looking at only kidnapping charges, though. Judy has broken many laws. She bought fake IDs, Social Security Numbers, and birth certificates. She hasn't paid taxes in fifteen years. You need to prepare yourself. She could go to prison."

Prison? Mum couldn't go to prison.

"You guys won't press charges though, right?" I was starting to hyperventilate. "I mean, if you don't, maybe the police will go easier. Right?"

Mom and Dad glanced at each other.

"We won't press charges," Mom promised and placed a calming hand on my knee. "But we also won't let you be alone with her. Like your dad said, part of being a parent is making unpopular decisions. We won't risk anything happening to you again."

"Happening to me?" I yelled, pushed her hand off my leg, and shot to my feet. "She would never hurt me. She loves me. She did what she thought was best because you left me."

Mom flinched, and I immediately regretted my words. I dropped back onto the couch.

"I'm sorry. I didn't mean it that way."

She nodded her acceptance.

"It's possible she could avoid prison," Dad said, "but the alternative isn't much better."

"What?" I put my hands over my face. I couldn't believe what I was hearing.

"They will evaluate her," he explained. "If she's not mentally fit, she could go to a psychiatric hospital instead of prison. I don't know that for sure, I'm only guessing, but it might be an option."

He was right. That wasn't any better. Locked up was locked up. For someone used to taking off at a moment's notice and doing anything she wanted, that would kill her.

"Listen," Dad said. "We'd like for you to talk to a counselor."

I laughed and stared at the flames crackling in the fireplace. "A shrink? I'm fine. I don't need counseling."

"Maybe you don't," Dad said. "But to ease our minds, would you be willing to meet with someone a couple of times? We've got a topnotch psychiatrist at the hospital, and she's happy to meet with you. If she says you're okay, we'll let it go."

"Ainsley," Mom added, "you have to agree that you've been through an awful lot. Particularly in the last month. Leaving your friends in Colorado. Finding out about us. And now . . . We understand how huge this news about Judy is. That alone would shake anyone up."

No doubt. But I couldn't simply walk away from Mum.

"What about, what do they call it, supervised visitation?" I asked. "You can't really expect me to never see her again."

Dad fidgeted. "Why don't we leave that out there for now? I'd rather not make decisions on the future until you've talked with the doctor, and the police and hospital have made some decisions about Judy."

I agreed, and my anger at them slowly backed off. I understood that if Mum broke the law, she had to be punished, but I hated everything about it.

On the fourth straight night of having the same horrible dream, the night we'd had our discussion about Mum going to prison, I shrugged my new fleece bathrobe on over my new flannel pajama pants and T-shirt, and stepped into the fuzzy slippers Mom bought me. I went outside, hoping the night air would help like it had on other nights.

Using the flashlight app on my phone, I made my way across the backyard, past the Koi pond, and through the clump of trees. When I got to the dock and looked down at my phone to turn off the light, I saw Bryce's and Gabrielle's faces on my wallpaper. I sent Bryce a text.

Staring at the stars. Looking for meteors. Wishing you were here next to me.

The text didn't wake him, which was fine. I just wanted him to know I was thinking about him. He responded first thing in the morning.

Why are you star-gazing and texting when you should be sleeping?

Bad dreams.

I'm sorry. Hope you sleep better tonight.

Doubt it. I've had the same awful dream every night for the last week.

If it happens again, call me.

Not at three in the morning.

Yes. Promise me. No one should suffer through nightmares alone. Call me. Seriously. I mean it.

Okay, okay. If I have it again, I promise to call you.

"You look tired," Mom said at breakfast. "Aren't you sleeping well?"

"I'm fine." I rubbed my chin. "Getting used to my new bedroom, I guess."

She narrowed her eyes at me. "You have a tell."

"I have a what?"

"A tell. A physical tic that indicates you're hiding something," she explained as she pulled a pumpkin-pecan muffin out of the microwave for me. She'd gone pumpkin-pecan crazy getting ready for Thanksgiving in two days—muffins, pie, bread... The house smelled amazing.

"What's my tell?"

"Same as mine." She smiled. "You rub your chin. What's going on?"

I buttered the huge pumpkin-pecan muffin she set in front of me on the breakfast bar. The flavors blended perfectly, and I closed my eyes so nothing could disrupt the experience. Warm, homemade muffins. None of the supposedly-homemade muffins at any of the diners Mum and I stopped at were this good. Mum had never made homemade anything. It's like I'd stepped through a portal that shot me into a polar-opposite existence.

"Just getting used to my . . . to all of this."

"Your new home? Is that what you were going to say?" She leaned across the counter, the best she could with my sister in the way, and took my hand in hers. "This *is* your home. Until you're ready to live on your own."

A jolt went through me like a static shock on a dry winter day. That was the second part of my wish. To *have a real home that I never have to leave until I'm ready to. Please. Amen. Thank you.*

Nothing special happened to commemorate the event. Shouldn't bells sound? Shouldn't the rain stop and the sun's rays burst through? Shouldn't Desiree show up with a confetti cannon? Had I reached my *satisfying conclusion*, as Desiree called it, or not? Probably not. I still didn't feel satisfied.

Dad had made an appointment for me with the psychiatrist for that day. I didn't want to admit it to my parents, but I was glad to have someone to talk to. The first thing I told her about was the nightmares.

"You're in a field," Dr. Kagan said, "with your parents and two homes on either side of you. What do you think that means?"

"It's pretty obvious when you say it like that. I'm trapped in the middle of everything I wished for." I told her about the wish I'd made, but not the Desiree and Clay granting it part. "Do you suppose it means anything special that in the dream I'm closest to the house here in Portland?"

"It could," Dr. Kagan said with a shrug. "Or it could simply be that you're closest to it because you literally are closest to it right now."

We talked a long time about Mum and how my life had been with her.

"Since you've been with Judy from the time you were a baby," Dr. Kagan explained, "and you've never known any other parent, it's understandable that you want everyone to feel the same way about her that you do."

"Understandable? Am I supposed to hate her?"

"You're not *supposed* to anything," Dr. Kagan answered. "Surely you see that Judy is not a mentally balanced person, though. Anyone who was would have reported a baby as abandoned, if that's what she believed had happened, not run with her for fifteen years."

"I get it. She needs some help. Does that mean it's not okay for me to be upset that they want to send her to prison?"

"If she had done this to another child," Dr. Kagan began, "or if you'd heard on the news about someone doing this, would you feel the same way?"

I left Dr. Kagan's office with a different perspective. She was right about the *another child* thing—I would have felt differently.

The doctor gave me a list of relaxation tricks to prevent the nightmare from coming back, and I tried every one of them that night. I took a warm bath before bedtime and had a cup of chamomile tea to get me good and sleepy. I kept the lights in my room low and stayed off of the computer and my phone. I read a book to keep my brain quiet. Once the lights were out, I listened to the rain on the roof and thought of all the things I was grateful for as I drifted to sleep. Still, at three-twenty-three I sat straight up in bed and burst into tears. Fortunately, the rain had stopped, because I really needed the dock.

"Hello?" Bryce's voice was a groggy, husky whisper.

"I shouldn't have called," I said as I stared at the cloud-patched sky.

"You had to. I made you promise." He still sounded husky but less groggy. "Tell me about it."

I told him every detail from the blowing snow to the funhouse expansion of the cornfield and no one coming to me, no matter how long and loud I screamed.

"Not much is scarier than a cornfield," Bryce said. "You do see the symbolism, right?"

"That I'm not sure where I belong?" I told him what Dr. Kagan and I had talked about. Tears formed in my eyes but didn't fall.

"They're sending you to a shrink?"

"Yeah. She makes sense. I'll probably see her again."

Then I told him about how Mum could end up in jail.

"I agree with everyone," Bryce said. "Your mum needs help. But if the decision was yours, who would you want to be with? I know how you feel about your mum, but your life in Portland sounds pretty sweet."

"It is. It's getting better here every day, but sometimes I still feel like an outsider."

"What do you mean?" His voice was deep and soothing, like a warm blanket on a cold, damp night. I heard rustling sounds and imagined him rolling onto his side in bed, his head propped on his hand.

"Like when Mom asks me what kind of salad dressing I want

or what my favorite dessert is. Moms should know that. Mum does."

"That's not Noelle's fault," Bryce said.

"Um, it kind of is," I said. "She left me."

"But she was coming back. I agree, she could have brought you with her right away, but that didn't give Judy the right to take you. So that's a negative point for each."

"You're keeping score?"

"Aren't you trying to figure out where you belong?"

I stood from the dock, wrapped one of the blankets from the box around me, and crawled into a chair.

"It's not that simple, Bryce." I was getting frustrated. "This isn't a decision that can be made with tally marks."

"Okay, but in reality, there isn't a decision to make. Your parents are your parents. Your mum might care a lot about you—"

"She loves me." I was starting to regret that I'd called him. "Everything she's ever done was to keep me safe."

"But you didn't need to be kept safe from your parents."

Desiree swore to me that they were good people, and I believed her. Honestly, though, there was this little spot in me that kept wondering if what Mom told me was the truth. Had she *really* wanted me? Had she sincerely wanted to be with Dad, or did she go to him simply because he was the father?

"What are you thinking?" Bryce asked.

"Wondering if they're telling me the truth," I said, "or if this is another bunch of lies."

"I can't imagine anyone searching for someone for fifteen years only to lie to them once they found them."

"I know." I did. It was hard to trust them completely now that I knew my whole life had been one lie after another. "All I've ever known is my mum. Regardless of how we ended up together, she raised me as her own child. What am I supposed to do? Give her a hug, say thanks, and walk away?"

"You know you kind of have to, right?" His voice was doing that blanket thing again.

"Yeah. But I don't know how." I stared at the sky. The clouds had cleared away, and I could see the stars. "Can you see the sky from where you are?"

"Please hold." I heard the sound of a door opening, footsteps, and then another door opening. "Now I can."

"Did you go outside?"

"I did. I'm lying on our picnic table. What am I looking for?"

I scanned the sky until I found something familiar. "The Big Dipper."

"I see it."

"Stare straight at it," I said. "Pretend I'm next to you and put your right hand at your side. Palm up."

"Okay."

I turned my left one palm down. "I'm holding your hand."

After a minute of staring at the stars he said, "I like holding your hand. Are you feeling better?"

"A little."

"If you have any more nightmares, you should call. I'll hold your hand again."

"Promise." A yawn sneaked up on me then, a big, gasping one.

"You ready for bed?"

"Yeah. Walk me to my room?"

I heard doors opening and closing in Holly Lake, Colorado as I walked down the path, past the pond, through the family room, and up the stairs to my bedroom.

"Telephones are a pretty cool invention," I said as I climbed under my covers again.

"They are. But it would be better if you were here. Then I could kiss you goodnight."

"That would be better," I mumbled, suddenly exhausted. "Thank you, Bryce Dalton."

"You're welcome, Ainsley Blue. It's after midnight. Happy Thanksgiving."

I smiled and felt all warm inside. "Happy Thanksgiving. I'll talk to you later."

I woke hours later to Mom stroking my bangs. I peeked one eye open to see her with that look moms get when they're in love with their children.

"It's nearly ten o'clock," she said. "I tried to wake you two hours ago, but you were out cold." She motioned to my bedside table. "I found your phone clutched in your hand. Were you talking to someone?"

I stretched, feeling better than I had in days. "Bryce."

"Who's Bryce?" She actually winked.

"He lives in Colorado. He's the first boy I ever kissed." A waking-up yawn hit me. "He was almost my first date."

Her smile turned to a frown. "I'm sorry, sweetie."

I didn't even have to tell her why he hadn't been my first date. Maybe she knew me better than I thought. Salad dressing and dessert are nothing compared to knowing someone's heart.

Chapter 21

Desiree

Mandy and Crissy were right. I had to let Kaf know how I felt about him. But first, I had to get things in the magical world under control. I still wasn't sure how to do that. I needed to think, so I went to the woods but not on walkabout this time. In fact, I could see Gypsy V and Mystic Lodge from my perch on the mountainside.

Rasta, brilliant dog that he was, had also been right. Thinking would only get me so far. I needed to talk this out with someone who understood both the magical world and the human world.

"What's going on?" Clay asked when he appeared alongside me on the mountain.

"I'd like your opinion on some changes I want to make."

I explained Kaf's rules and how I thought they needed to be tweaked.

"You've got advisors to help you with this stuff." He fidgeted, uncomfortable both sitting on the rocky ledge and with the topic of discussion. "Why're you asking me?"

"I need to figure out what will both serve the Guides and benefit our charges at the same time. You just left the human world, so you're the most in-touch with it."

"You don't need me to tell you about that," Clay countered.

"From what I hear, you slip into the human world a lot. You got friends there. And it sounds to me like you know what you want to do about the rules."

I stared down into the valley at the Lodge. Guides, like bitty bugs from this distance, wandered the grounds. "They're so divided. I've changed so much, and I'm afraid to make things worse."

"They're divided because of that Kaf guy, not because you changed some rules. He used to be the Wish Master, right?"

I nodded.

"So if he's a used-to-be, why's he here?"

A cold wind gusted and blew snow at us. I manifested a globe of warmth, and at the same time, Clay held out his hands, producing two big mugs. He handed one to me. Hot cocoa, very soothing.

"Kaf returned to give me more instruction on my job."

"Good excuse, but one or both of you aren't being honest," Clay said in his blunt yet respectful way. "If he handed everything over to you, left, then came back, I'd say he didn't really want to leave in the first place. What's your side of it? Why would you even want him here?"

I was about to say, "Because I need his help." But I didn't just spend two days with Mandy and Crissy to keep hiding the truth. "He's here because I'm in love with him." Admitting it out loud made it so real. I felt a little giddy. "I need to tell him."

Clay blinked. He stared silently at the valley below and waited for me to say more.

"What?" I asked.

"Why else?"

He didn't even react to my proclamation of love. I expected a *congratulations* or an, *aw, how nice.* "He can help me with the Guides who are upset with me."

He shook his head and pulled his legs up to sit crisscross on the cliff. "I don't think so. You told him that the Guides needed to get on board with your plans or get out."

I scowled. "You make me sound like a tyrant."

"My point is you know how you want things to be. So, why do you want him here?"

My brain spun as I stared at the mug in my hands. "Seems like you know something I don't. Can you give me a clue?"

Clay turned to face me. "All you'd have to do is tap your fingers and send him away. But you let him stay even though he's messing things up. Makes me think maybe you're letting him mess stuff up on purpose."

"Why would I do that?" Something uncomfortable squirmed in my belly.

"I've got this friend; he's had a lot of jobs. Every time he gets a new one, he's all excited about it, right? He's like super-employee for the first week or so, then he gets bored. He starts coming in late and doing stuff wrong. Pretty soon the boss tells him, thanks but no thanks, hit the road."

"You think I'm trying to get fired?" That was crazy talk.

"I heard you served your time as Guide and got early parole."

I laughed out loud. "That's an interesting way to put it. Yes, Kaf released me from my indenture five years early. He said being a Guide had been part of my wish, to have a second chance at life. After forty-five years, he said it was time, that I could move forward or go back to my 1969 life."

Rita had offered to lend me money for college and the opportunity to run one of her soup kitchens in the future. I'm sure the offer was still available if I wanted it.

"Moving forward was the right choice," I said. "Things were finally coming together for me."

"Then Kaf forced you to take over as Wish Mistress."

"Not forced. He did trick me, though." My face flushed hotly.

"If you needed to be tricked, maybe you didn't really want to come back here."

The mountains felt like they were closing in around me, and

that squirming thing in my gut got worse. I got to my feet and tried to take a deep breath.

"All I've ever wanted was to help people," I explained. "I felt like that's what I was doing when I was working in the soup kitchen. There was so much potential there."

"You don't help people here?"

"I do, but not the way I used to. Now, my job is to make it possible for the Guides to help others." I stared down into the valley at the Lodge and admitted sadly, "I don't want to be the Wish Mistress. I never did."

"Then why'd you say yes?"

"To save my friend, Dara. Kaf used her. He said in order for her to live, she had to serve me. Not just become a Guide for fifty years, but serve *me*. I couldn't let her die, of course I said yes. Being in the human world for those few weeks made me see everything I didn't like about the magical world when I returned. So, since I was in charge, I started making changes." I blinked, feeling like a failure. "That hasn't gone so well, though."

"You're not indentured again, are you?" Clay asked. "If you seriously don't want to do the job, can't you give it to someone else?"

"I can. All I have to do is find a suitable replacement. Olanna would take it. I could hand things over to her right now and hit the road."

"Why don't you?"

"Because I'm not sure Olanna is suitable."

I gave him a cheesy smile, and he laughed.

"Seriously," he prodded, "why stay?"

I sat back down and let my legs dangle over the mountain. "Because I still feel like I can make some changes that will help everyone. Like new Guides apprenticing before taking on wishes."

"Speaking of that, I could apprentice with one of the other Guides. Why're you teaching me?"

"Because I miss being with the charges."

Once again, Clay said nothing, just sipped his cocoa and waited.

Finally, the full and honest truth hit me. "I want to be a Guide again."

Clay raised his mug to me. "There it is."

A feeling of peace settled over me. I had the answer I'd been searching for. I knew what I wanted. Now, how to make it happen?

Chapter 22

Ainsley

Mom had been feeling little pains for the last couple of days. Every time any of us asked, she said they were nothing, pre-contractions so normal they had a name. Braxton Hicks. I told her that sounded like a cool name for the hero in a romantic movie.

"Only if he comes to save me from labor," Mom said, wincing through another one. "It's probably all that Thanksgiving cooking. I should have taken it easy this year, but I was so excited, it being your first year with us."

Turned out they were actual contractions. Her water burst while she was making lunch. As she called Dad, who got home from work in record time, I mopped the kitchen floor then ran upstairs to get her prepacked bag from her bedroom closet.

On the way to the hospital, a hard contraction hit her. She leaned her head back against the car seat, her face a grimace of pain, and let out a long, hissing breath through her teeth. When it passed, she left her head resting on the seat, looking exhausted already. How many of those would she have before the baby was born?

"Here's the plan," Dad began while pulling to a stop at a light. "You're pre-registered so we don't need to mess with any of that. Once you're all tucked into your room, I'll run and pick up Noah from preschool. Ainsley, you'll stay with your mom."

Me? Stay with a woman in labor? Was he crazy? "What do I have to do?"

"I'll be back in plenty of time for the main event," Dad promised. "All you have to do is hold her hand when the contractions hit and help her breathe through them." He did a few of the same kind of hard hissing breaths Mom had done. "She knows what to do. Your job is to remind her."

I looked at Mom, who was clearly lost in a quiet meditative zone, and swallowed the lump in my throat.

"Okay." I swallowed again as sweat soaked the armpits of my shirt. "I can do that."

"You can." Dad locked eyes with me in the rearview mirror. "I don't have a single doubt."

His confidence helped, but it didn't make the sweating stop. By the time we were settled into Mom's room, I was soaked and the contractions were coming stronger and more frequently.

"You're sure you'll be back in time?" How long did babies take to be born?

"Noah's school is only twenty minutes from here," Dad said. "Our original plan was for our sitter to pick him up and stay with him. But you're here now."

"So, I should go pick him up, and you stay with Mom." Never mind the fact that I wouldn't be able to get my driver's license for four more months.

"Nice try." And then, as if reading my thoughts, he added, "Remind me to sign you up for driving lessons."

He gave me a hug and kiss on the forehead and assured me, again, that everything would be fine. Then he went to Mom and sat on the edge of the bed. He clutched one of her hands in one of his and swept away the hair sticking to her sweaty face with the other. I couldn't hear what he said to her, but whatever it was, it soothed her. She closed her eyes and rested against the mattress, which was raised into a sitting position.

"She might want to walk a little." Dad tossed his keys from hand-to-hand. "That sometimes helps speed things along. She's got some meditation music in her bag. Ask her if she'd like you to turn it on."

"Okay." I pushed him toward the door. "Leave already, so you can come back."

Half an hour later, just as Dad must have been on his way back with Noah, Mom let out a shriek.

"What's wrong?" I jumped to my feet and rushed to her side.

She breathed—*hiss, hiss, hiss*—and then gasped, "Super-strong contraction."

Until that moment, she'd been trying to reassure me with each pain that everything was fine. I was pretty sure soothing my concerns was no longer on her radar and her only thought was getting this baby out.

"That was a big one," our nurse said as she entered the room.

"How do you know?" I asked.

"That belt around her belly?" She meant the monitor that measured Mom's and the baby's vital signs. "It passes information to the monitor next to her bed which sends it to my computer at the nurses' station. I can watch what's going on with all my moms from there. Let's check your progress."

She'd done this checking thing when we first got there.

"What exactly are you checking?" I asked.

"The opening to your mom's cervix. As labor progresses, the opening gets bigger." She snapped on rubber gloves and reached between Mom's legs. Her eyebrows arched. "Are you starting to feel like you want to push?"

Mom nodded and hissed.

I shook my head and freaked. "What? No, Dad's not back yet."

The nurse chuckled. "Babies wait for no one. She's at nine centimeters. That was fast, but it happens." She went to a cabinet in the corner and pulled out a gown, cap, mask, and booties.

"Put these on. I'll call her doctor, and we'll get this show on the road."

I must have looked as panicked as I felt. For a few seconds, Mom somehow forgot about her pain and focused on me.

"I'm proud to have you in the room with us," she said. "Not what we had planned, but not a lot in our relationship has gone according to plan, has it?"

I shook my head.

Another contraction hit. I held her hand and reminded her to breathe. No more time for chatting. Once the contraction ended, I put on the things the nurse gave me and called Dad.

"She's coming," I said. "It's time for Mom to start pushing. Where are you?"

"Damn. I've got Noah, but there's a huge accident on the highway. We're at an absolute standstill. I have no idea when we'll get there."

They were trusting me. With the birth of their second, no, their third child, they were trusting me. I could do this.

"I'm on it, Dad."

"I know you are. I need you to do something."

"What?"

"Take a video?"

Eww. "Are you serious?"

"There's a camera in her bag and a tripod. We already talked about this, so Mom knows it'll be happening. Ask the nurse where you can set it up."

Who would they show that video to? I had visions of family and friends gathering for game night and then watching my little sister come into the world. Did they do that for Noah? For me? Would I want to see my own birth?

I got dressed and started the camera recording. One nurse attached leg holders to the sides of the bed and strapped Mom's legs to them. Then she removed the lower third of the mattress—for easier access to the important parts, I assumed—and tucked it under the bed. Meanwhile, a second nurse prepared a tray of surgical instruments and a table to put the baby on once she was here.

A woman in pink scrubs with bobbed auburn hair walked in.

"Hello, Noelle." She glanced between Mom's legs from across the room and arched an eyebrow. "Well, don't wait for me."

"Hi, Dr. Doyle," Mom panted. "She's not waiting. I have to push."

Dr. Doyle rushed to the end of the bed. One nurse stood at the doctor's side, the other at Mom's side. They told me to stand at the head of the bed and talk to Mom.

"Let's do this," Dr. Doyle said.

I called Dad's number and only had time to engage the speaker phone when another massive contraction struck. Mom reached for my hand, so I set the phone on the bedside table. I heard Dad say "Hello" and Noah ask what was happening. Mom took my hand and squeezed, my knuckles pressing painfully together. I almost cried out, but my pain was nothing compared to what she must have been going through.

She pushed hard three times, her face sweaty and red with the effort, and the doctor told her to stop pushing.

"Why stop?" I shoved my glasses up on my nose. "Is something wrong?"

"Nothing at all," the nurse at Mom's side assured me. "Dr. Doyle has to clear the baby's mouth of amniotic fluid."

The nurse had barely finished the explanation when the doctor told Mom to push again.

"Hard, Noelle. Give it all you've got."

I leaned in close and said, "You're amazing, Mom. You're doing so great."

"Big push, Noelle. Come on." The doctor's voice was stern but encouraging. "One shoulder is out. Come on, one more."

"You can do it, Mom."

She nodded, did the *hiss* breathing with me to regain her strength, and then gave one last push. Mom's face immediately relaxed and her whole body went limp. As Mom gasped to catch her breath, my sister took her first one. Dr. Doyle set a slimy, squirmy, pink baby on my mom's belly. She had our red hair but not our white bangs. And she was not happy. Each cry seemed to get louder and more insistent. *It's cold! It's cold! Put me back*, they seemed to say.

She was so tiny. At the same time, I couldn't believe something that big had come out of my mother.

"Would you like to cut the cord?" The doctor handed me a pair of scissors.

I looked at Mom, and she nodded. "Bring her into the world with me."

It took me two tries; the umbilical cord was tougher than I expected. Once she was free, they took the baby to the little table off to the side and cleaned her up. The nurse waved me over to watch the process. My sister didn't stop crying even for a moment while they sucked stuff out of her mouth and nose. They weighed her and measured her—eight pounds seven ounces and twenty-two inches long—and cleaned all the goo off of her.

Once both Mom and the baby were clean, they covered Mom with three blankets—she was shivering hard from the exertion she'd gone through—and rolled her to the room she'd be in for the next thirty-six or so hours.

The nurse placed the fussy little bundle in Mom's arm so she could breastfeed. The baby started sucking immediately. How did she know? I mean, were all babies preprogrammed with this knowledge?

"This was one of the most amazing experiences I've ever had." I couldn't wait to add it to my journal.

Mom smiled wearily. "Me, too." She placed her free hand on mine. "My two girls."

I stared in awe between my mother and my sister. Mom had been so calm through the whole thing. Had she been this way with me? Or did she freak out because she was a new mom? Had she loved me as instantly as she obviously did this baby?

When Dad and Noah walked in, about ten minutes later, Dad went immediately to Mom and kissed her. His smile filled his face as he looked at their new daughter. Noah climbed into my lap to get a better look.

"Another ginger," he said disgustedly.

We all burst out laughing.

"What's wrong with gingers?" I asked.

"Nothing, I guess." He patted his own dark head. "I like mine better."

"She needs a name," Mom said.

"You don't have a name picked out yet?" That surprised me. "Isn't that one of the things you obsess over while pregnant?"

"It didn't seem right to choose a name for her," Mom said. "We wanted to meet her first to see what fit."

"What about Ginger?" I joked as the baby squawked angrily. "Or maybe something fierier, like Cayenne or Caliente?"

"I like Ginger," Dad said.

"No, Dad, I wasn't serious."

"We'd never considered it," Mom said thoughtfully, "but it's perfect. Ginger Kira Freeman."

Kira. The name Mom gave me when I was born. That was kinda cool.

We sat and watched as the newest member of our family staked her claim in the world. Every time Mom tried to stop feeding her, she complained. I could already tell she was going to be a feisty kid. Finally, she drifted off to sleep, and Mom handed her to Dad. He held her for a few minutes and then offered her to me.

"Oh, no," I protested. "Not yet. She's too new. And I'm still a little freaked out by this whole experience."

Life had been perfectly normal when we woke up this morning. Now, normal was completely different.

"Okay, later then," Dad said. "Let's head home so Mom and Ginger can get some rest."

"I wanna look at her some more," Noah said. "Just a couple more minutes. Please?"

Dad looked to Mom, and she gave a tired nod.

"Just a couple more." Dad handed little Ginger back to Mom. "You can only look. No climbing on the bed."

Rescue Hero Noah gave a little salute. "Sir, yes, sir."

"Come with me." Dad led me into the hall where he wrapped me in a huge hug. "I'm so grateful you were here. I can't thank you enough for putting me on speaker phone so I could at least hear the birth. Although it was hard to concentrate on driving."

"I felt bad that you weren't here."

"I did, too. Not at all the way we had planned for things to go."

"So, speaking of things not going as planned, is it hard to change a name?"

"As in a legal name change?" He looked at me, confused.

Hearing the name *Kira* reminded me that *Ainsley* wasn't who I was intended to be. Mum bought a birth certificate with that name on it. After all these years, I was Ainsley, but now, it didn't seem quite right.

"In the past two weeks everything has changed for me," I said. "Some of it has been not so good. A lot of it is great. I always thought I knew who I was and where I came from, but none of it was true. Now that I know, I'd like to start fresh. I want my legal name to be Ainsley Kira Blue Freeman."

A blend of all my names. I honestly hadn't thought of it until the whole naming of the baby discussion. It felt right, though.

I couldn't tell from his reaction what Dad thought of it. I knew Mum wouldn't be happy. She'd say I was denying my true self or something, but the opposite was true. I was claiming myself.

"I'll check into the process." He stretched and yawned

suddenly. "Don't know why I'm tired. I didn't do anything here. Let's get your brother and head home."

Chapter 23

Ainsley

We'd left for the hospital so quickly, I forgot my phone. When we got home, I found a message waiting for me.

"Hey, girly, it's Mina. I've got some big news. Huge news. I've got to tell you about it before I burst, so call me. Soon. I'm sitting here waiting."

I smiled as I flopped down on my bed and hit redial.

"Ainsley?"

"What's going on?"

Mina blew out a shaky breath. "God, I hope I'm doing the right thing."

"You're freaking me out. What are you doing?"

"I told you I was going to clean up the house."

"Right. How'd it go?"

"So well that before I realized it, I hadn't been to the gas station in ten days." She groaned, embarrassed. "I sort of got into a zone and the cleaning turned into packing. My family's stuff has been lying around for eight years. I decided it was time to let it all go. I threw away a ton of stuff. I donated another ton. I kept some things that I'm not ready to part with yet. It was quite cathartic."

"That's great, Mina." I couldn't even come close to identifying with that. Everything Mum and I owned fit into the Volvo and U-Haul.

"I put everything I wanted to keep into storage."

"As in, not in your house? Why?"

"Yeah. I'm going on a trip."

"A trip?" I sat up, excited for her. "That's awesome. Where are you going?"

"Before my brother reported for duty, he spent a few days in Boston. He told me about the narrow streets and old buildings and the harbor. It all sounded so charming." The more she spoke, the more excited she started to sound. "Since then, I've wanted to go there and be around all that history. So, I'm going to Boston. From there, I don't know. Europe maybe. The Eiffel Tower sounds like something I should see."

"Wow, Mina. This is so cool." The world was such a big place. She missed so much by never leaving Lake Bellwood.

"That comment you made that day, asking how could I consider the people here to be good friends if they never came to check on me after my family died. That shook me up. I love it here, I always will, but I want more, and I need more people in my world."

"Are you going to sell your house?"

"No. Not now at least. I'm not sure where life will lead me, so I'm going to hang on to it for a while. I've got money. I've been saving for years, and I got a life insurance payment when my family died. I don't have a boyfriend. I'm pretty free. Who knows what's next for me?"

"Who knows?" I was happy for her sudden traveler spirit and happy that I had helped her find it.

"I'm going to rent my house to a family from a town about twenty miles away. Theirs burned down last year and the five of them have been crammed in a two-bedroom apartment all this time." She paused. "There's another reason I called. When I told Judy I was leaving, she got kind of upset."

"Upset how?" Cold dread filled my veins.

"Look, I don't want to upset you, too. Your dad told me, the night he stayed here, that you wouldn't be coming back. I think Judy is figuring that out."

A wave of embarrassment washed over me. How could I have been so naïve to believe that Mom and Dad would let me go back to the woman who had taken me from them?

"You're where you're supposed to be, Ainsley," Mina continued. "I thought you might want to know what's happening with her."

"I won't be living with her again, you're right. But, I still care about her."

"I think she's having a breakdown of some kind. Hank called one day to find out if I was okay, since I hadn't been to the station in so long, and to see if I knew what was going on with her. He said she shows up to work but gets half of the orders wrong. He finds her staring into space doing nothing. She yells at the customers if they have a complaint."

That, the yelling, wasn't normal. Mum loved being around the customers.

"I see the lights on in the loft all night. She looks horrible. I don't think she's sleeping or eating. I asked if she'd act as landlord for me and keep an eye on things while I'm gone. Now, I'm thinking that's not such a good idea." Mina let out a sigh. "Anyway, I thought you'd want to know."

"I'll give her a call." But what would I say? I'd promised her I'd be back, and that wasn't going to happen.

Mina and I chatted about traveling for a little longer. Now that she'd made the decision, she was ready to go and go and go. I made her promise to stay in touch because traveling alone could be dangerous. She assured me she would investigate places thoroughly before staying anywhere and promised to send pictures and emails often.

"If you ever head northwest . . ."

"I promise," she said. "I'll stop by. I'd love to meet your mom and little brother."

"And baby sister. That's where I was when you called."

I told her about Ginger, and how I was right by Mom's side through the whole thing.

"That's amazing, Ainsley." I could hear the smile in her voice.

We said goodbye, but not the never-see-you-again kind. In the short time we'd known each other, we'd pretty much become sisters. We were bonded forever now.

I tried to call Mum. She didn't pick up, so I left a message.

"I assume you're working or sleeping. I talked to Mina and she told me you're not doing so well. I'm worried about you." I debated about saying the next thing and decided it would be all right. "Call me if you want. If I don't answer right away, it's because the baby was born today, and I might be helping with stuff around here. Ginger. She's cute and feisty."

I said goodbye, awkwardly, hoping everything was all right.

☮

Being the uber-prepared mother that she was, Mom had everything ready for Ginger's arrival. The nursery was fully stocked with diapers and wipes and little pink clothes. Everything was so well-organized, Dad, Noah, and I had nothing to do but wait for the thirty-six-hour hospital stay to be done.

The night before they were to come home, the three of us gathered at the kitchen bar when Dad and Noah came home with burgers, fries, and mint-chocolate-chip shakes.

"Don't tell Mom," Dad said. "She'll kill me if she knows I fed us fast food. One night of takeout won't kill us."

"I won't tell her," Noah said. He stuck a fry in his mouth and then sucked ketchup out of one of the little packets.

"Noah, eww." I made a face at him.

"What?" he said through a mouthful. "I love kepech."

"Ketchup," I corrected and squirted some on his plate then demonstrated the proper way to apply ketchup to fries. He continued with his own disgusting method. Mom was big on table manners. He'd never get away with that if she was here, so Dad and I let it go.

"It feels weird around here," Noah said a minute later.

"What do you mean?" Dad asked.

"It's weird that Mommy isn't here." His voice quivered a little. "She's always here. Who's going to tuck me in?"

"Dad and I tucked you in last night," I reminded him. He'd been so excited about the baby he didn't even think about Mom not being here. "We'll do it again. And we'll call Mommy so she can say goodnight."

He leaned over and hugged me, smearing his hamburger-greasy face all over my cheek. "I'm so happy I have a sister."

"You have two sisters now," Dad reminded him.

"You're the middle of a sister sandwich," I teased.

Noah didn't find that funny.

I stayed up late that night watching Netflix on my computer. I also tried to call Mum a couple times. She hadn't called me back, and I was worried that she'd gone off the grid again. If that was the case, who knew when, or if, I'd hear from her again.

The next morning, Dad and I dropped a protesting Noah off at preschool.

"It's not fair," he said. "Ainsley gets to stay home with Ginger. Why can't I?"

Dad looked at me with an amused grin. "You're officially brother and sister. Sibling rivalry has set in."

"You know what you can do?" I knelt down in front of Noah.

"What?" he asked with a scowl and a pout.

"You can make a picture for Ginger. Her very first one. Make it the best one you've ever made. We'll hang it on the wall by her crib."

It was the funniest thing I'd ever seen, watching him try to keep pouting while simultaneously fighting off the grin trying to bust loose on his face.

"Can it be a fire truck?"

"Of course it can. No one knows fire trucks better than my brother."

"Okay." He lifted his chin, trying to maintain his five-year-old cool factor. "I'll be driving it and saving Ginger because our house is burning down."

"There's a comforting image." Dad gave Noah a squeeze and a pat on the shoulder. "Okay, bud. You've got a big project. Better get busy."

Noah nodded and ran off to the art corner. His teacher assured us she'd keep him busy and they'd have a Noah is a Big Brother celebration at the end of the day.

"You're pretty amazing," Dad said, putting his arm around my shoulders. "Are you sure you've never done this big sister thing before?"

"It's easy with Noah. He's a cool kid." If only I could have been with him from the start.

On the way home, Mom rode in the backseat with Ginger. Then Dad carried her in her car seat through the house, showing her every room.

"She can only clearly see about eighteen inches away right now," Mom told me as Dad paused at the door that led to the backyard.

"Does he know that?"

"I'm not sure. Let's not ruin his fun, though."

We followed him up the stairs, to all the other rooms, and finally to the nursery. He pulled Ginger out of the car seat and turned toward me.

"Are you ready to hold her now?"

I'd been watching how Mom and Dad and the nurses did it. They were gentle but not like she was made of glass. Still, my mouth went dry and my hands sweaty.

"I've never held a baby before."

Mom pointed at the rocker by the windows. "Sit down. It's surprising how heavy nine pounds can get when you're not used to it. The muscles in her neck are very weak, so you need to support her head."

I sat, and Mom put a pillow in my lap. Dad set Ginger in my arms on top of the pillow. This little person had been inside my mom's belly a little over two days ago. Now that she was here, she was everything and nothing that I had expected. I'd never felt such instant and overwhelming love for anyone before.

I held a baby for the first time today. My sister.

My little red-headed sister lay there and studied me. She was within eighteen inches, so I think she could see me. Her big blue eyes narrowed and widened. She looked like total innocence and total wisdom at the same time. It's like the secrets of the universe were trapped behind those eyes.

Foolish girl, they seemed to say. *I have you now.*

"You sure do."

"What?" Mom asked.

"She's sucking me in with her baby ways. I am helpless within her tracking beam." At that moment, Ginger started to cry. "What did I do?"

"Nothing," Mom assured. "She's probably hungry. I'll feed her, and then we'll let her check out her crib."

☽

Late the next afternoon, after Mom had finished feeding Ginger, she put her in her crib.

"I'm exhausted," she said. "I'm going to go lay down for a while. Ginger isn't asleep yet. She's a little gassy. Do you remember what to do?"

For the last twenty-four hours, my world had been baby boot camp. I wasn't anywhere near as fast as Mom, but I could change a diaper. I could do that walk-and-bounce thing. The stand-and-sway thing. I could change her clothes without worrying I was going to break her little arms and legs. I knew how to wrap her in a blanket so she looked like a baby burrito.

I stood at attention. "Ma'am, yes, ma'am."

"Your brother is wearing off on you." She weaved her way toward her bedroom. "If I'm not awake in an hour, come get me."

Ginger wasn't at all happy. Her little tummy was bothering her like crazy, and the only thing that helped was to hold her close while walking around the house.

"I know," I soothed, looking down at her little pinched face. At least she wasn't crying. "Your life was fine, wasn't it? You had everything you needed. A comfy home that was warm and snug. Now, you're someplace completely new, and even though you belong here, you're not sure how you fit in." I nodded. "We've got a lot in common."

The similarities between my life and this baby's were not lost on me.

"I'm adjusting to this place, too," I told her. "How about we figure it out together."

The doorbell rang then.

"Oh!" I made an excited face. "There's someone at the door. Let's go see who it is."

We walked through the family room and foyer to the front door. The last thing I expected to see was a Volvo with a U-Haul attached to it in the driveway and Mum standing at the front door.

Chapter 24

Desiree

I don't know what made me think I'd be able to sneak back into the magical world from the mountainside. Even transporting directly into Gypsy V didn't work. Olanna must have set up an alert of some kind, because the moment I turned a light on in my bus, she appeared. *Inside* my bus.

"No." I pointed to the door. "That's pushing things too far. I don't barge into your home. You're not allowed to come into mine like that."

I touched my fingers together and cast a charm to prevent something like that from ever happening again. I'd never bothered with that before because the only person to ever enter my home without asking was Kaf. And I didn't mind if he showed up unannounced.

"Come out and talk to me, then." She descended the bus stairs and the second I stepped onto the ground, she let me have it. "This has to stop, Desiree. You can't keep disappearing like this. Don't you care at all about what happens here?"

"On the contrary, that's actually why I was away." I remained as calm as she was agitated. "I'll explain it all soon, but what I will tell you is that I was soul searching. Trying to figure out the right answers for everyone. Including me."

"And you had to run away to do that?" she asked. "You are a poor excuse for a leader. Why Kaf ever chose you, I'll never understand. The best thing you could do for our world is step down and let someone else be in charge."

"I saw you."

She sighed, irritated that I'd interrupted her rant. "You saw me doing what?"

"I saw you with Kaf at his cabin. It appears he has chosen you."

Crissy's voice sounded in my head. *What the hell are you doing? Fight!*

I expected a smug look from Olanna. An elevation of that too-long neck. A smirk that said she always knew she was better than this raggedy little hippie girl standing before her. Instead, she looked away. It was dark, so I couldn't be sure, but it looked like she was blushing. Her moment of humility, or whatever that was, passed seconds later.

"How arrogant of you to assume he had even considered you. That's why you ran, isn't it? You saw him with me and couldn't accept it."

Always on the attack. She couldn't even accept victory with grace. I was tired of fighting with her.

"Olanna, why are you here? It's the middle of the night, and you're here harassing me. Why do you have to constantly torment—" Out of nowhere, something I'd never considered occurred to me. Something that had become clear to me during Robin's wish. "Bullies attack when they're unhappy about something. You are probably the least happy person I've ever met. Why is that?"

"You think I would tell *you* my worries?" Olanna scoffed, finally raising that neck to its full height.

I saw the pain in her eyes, though. I'd gotten close to a raw nerve. Enough of this. I wasn't going to fight with her anymore.

"I'm going to sit on top of my bus and take in the stillness of the night before I go to bed. Would you like to join me?"

She made a little *tsk* sound and turned away.

"Olanna, please. Just for a few minutes."

I could barely believe it when she accepted and followed me up the ladder. I manifested two large pillows for us to sit on. Then, I held out my hand, manifested a cup of tea, and offered it to her. She couldn't have looked more shocked. She accepted my peace offering, and I manifested another for myself.

"If the situation was reversed," I began, "if you were the one disappearing all the time, I would feel the same way you do. Believe it or not, I want only what's best for everyone, and I agree with some of the things you've said."

She sipped the tea and sighed contentedly. It was good tea. "You said you agree with me. What exactly do you agree with?"

"That we need someone who will be a better leader. If I tell you something, will you, for the good of our world, keep it to yourself for a little while? A day. Two at most."

She narrowed her eyes and then gave a nod.

"I'm not scattered and wandering because I can't do the job."

She laughed, a condescending sound.

"It's because I don't *want* to do *this* job."

That silenced her.

"I disappeared for these last two days because I needed to figure out why I've been so unhappy since coming back. I needed to come to a decision, and to do that, I had to consult with the people who know me best in this world."

"Those girls?" she asked. "Mandy and Crissy?"

Mandy and Crissy were like folktale legends around here— the two girls who caused the shakeup of the magical world.

I nodded.

"And did they help you come to a conclusion?" Olanna asked.

If I told her everything and she let it slip, our world would slide into absolute chaos. The Guides couldn't take much more.

"They did help. And, I promise, I'll tell everyone my decision soon. I have a plan and need to talk with Kaf about it. He's the only one that can help us come together again."

Olanna frowned. She thought I was going to confide everything to her.

"I will tell you this," I said. "You might get your wish."

☮

I found Indira waiting for me at the little office cabin early the next morning.

"Groovy that you waited until morning," I said. "I got both barrels from Olanna last night."

"Olanna's wrath is more than enough for anyone," Indira said with a knowing shake of her head. "Where were you, Desiree?"

"Come on in." I opened the cabin door and Rasta burst in ahead of us. He wasn't happy I'd left either. He punished me with silence, though, which was worse than getting yelled at. "I left to figure out what to do about . . . everything. Since you're here, I'd like to bounce some thoughts off of you."

"This sounds big."

"I'm not the right leader for the Guides. We all know that."

"You tried," Indira said, "but I'm glad you're finally acknowledging the truth."

It stung a little that she agreed so quickly. I'd hoped for a little *no, you're doing a fine job.* But this wasn't about making me feel better.

"To some, this will look like a failure," I admitted. "If I would have followed my instincts and said no to Kaf when he asked me to be the leader, this disaster wouldn't have happened."

"Disaster isn't the right word," Indira said softly. "In a few short months you've implemented some great things. Clay is fantastic."

Rasta, still mute, rested his head on my lap. A peace offering.

Only Mandy and Crissy knew better than this dog how much I'd been struggling.

"Well then," Indira scooted to the edge of her chair, ready for business, "what are your thoughts? You'll need a replacement."

"Would you like the job?" I wanted her to say yes so badly. She'd be perfect. Besides, I wasn't sure my second choice would be interested.

"Thank you, but no," Indira stated simply but graciously. "I am perfectly content with my life as it is. I have the freedom to come and go, and I get to help a lot of people."

"You do take off a lot," I noted. "Where do you go? What do you do?" I winked at her. "You got a guy tucked away somewhere?"

"No," Indira said simply.

"A girl?"

She smiled. "We're not talking about me right now."

I squinted at her. Despite all the time I'd spent with Indira, I didn't know much about her. Once I wasn't her boss anymore, that could change. Far out.

☮

I'd spoken to Kaf tens of thousands of times in the nearly forty-six years that I'd known him. "Why am I so nervous?"

Because you care.

I looked down at Rasta, sitting on the floor by my chair in the little cabin. "Glad you're talking to me again."

You couldn't have taken me with you? I would like to meet your friends.

"I'm sorry." I scratched his ears. "Next time, I promise you can come with me. We'll go see Rita, my surrogate mom. She'll want to meet her grand-dog."

Kaf is almost here. I can smell him.

I knew what he meant. I always thought that sweet/spicy/bitter/sour thing was the green and orange smoke that hovered around him. Turned out, the smoke was his barrier to the incoming wishes like the little auroras were for me. The scent was pure Kaf.

"Desiree."

He filled the doorway. Not just with his physical presence but with his aura and attitude as well. With each second that passed, my heart beat a little faster.

"Come on in," I said, my throat dry. "I need to talk to you about some things."

He came in and sat in one of the two chairs I'd set out for the Guides. When I took the one next to him, instead of my Wish Mistress chair, he looked quizzically at me.

"I've come to a conclusion."

"That is why you ran away again?"

His words were scolding, but the tone wasn't. He seemed more concerned than angry. I'd been running since the first of August, 1969. That was the day Glenn, Marsha, her boyfriend Stan, and I took off on our road trip. First Woodstock, then the commune. As a Guide, I had moved Gypsy V from country to country. When Kaf released me from my duties, I immediately headed for San Antonio. Now, I couldn't seem to get myself to stay in the magical world for more than a few days at a time.

"It's long past time for me to stop running." I searched for a sign that he felt something being this close to me, too. That maybe his heart was racing as much as mine. He fidgeted, anxiously clasping and unclasping his hands. Was that because of me or because he wanted to move on to something else? Like Olanna. I couldn't be sure. "I've come to a conclusion. I don't want to be the Wish Mistress. You didn't sentence me to a set term, so I am stepping down as soon as my replacement agrees to step up."

His jaw muscles tensed and released as he swallowed. "Who will be your replacement?"

"You, I hope." I kept talking so he couldn't object without hearing my proposal. "The Guides prefer you as their leader.

Regardless of my feelings about the way you ran certain things, the magical world has held together well for over two hundred years."

"Fairly well," he amended.

"*Fairly* well?" Was this an admission of some sort?

"For these last few weeks, I have had the opportunity to be among the Guides as a human." He looked down at his now-still hands resting on his thighs. "As you have pointed out, half of them prefer your ways. Many of them have felt free to tell me of their dissatisfaction with the way I did things."

Was this a compromise? Was he capable of that?

"What are you saying?" I wanted him to stay. I needed him to stay. It would be torture to live in the magical world without Kaf. "Will you come back as the Wish Master? If you don't, I'll have to resort to my third choice."

"And who would that be?"

"Olanna. Indira already said no."

He frowned. "Does this mean I was not your first?"

I know he hadn't meant that as a euphemism, but a flush ran over my entire body.

"You're . . . controversial. I wanted a replacement everyone could agree with. Everyone likes Indira."

"Still, I am not sure it is possible to make everyone happy. If she had agreed to take over, someone would have been upset."

"Then, like I said before, maybe it's time for those who don't really want to be here to leave. In a humane way. Everyone here has served our world. They deserve to move on to a life that they'll be happy with."

He looked at me for a long moment. A little too long. "We have details to work out before I can resume my post."

"Is that a yes? Are you accepting my offer?"

"Tell me something first." He looked sideways, almost sheepishly at me, and his voice was gentler than I'd ever heard it. "What do you want, Desiree? Will you return to the human world? I assume that Rita would be happy to have you back. You could, of course, take your beloved bus."

"I want to stay here as a Guide."

He spun to face me. For a moment, a few seconds at most, relief filled his eyes and a smile ghosted his lips. His shoulders dropped as he exhaled.

What did that mean? Hope fluttered in my belly.

"I wasn't happy before Mandy's wish," I said. "It was childish, but I was jealous that everyone was getting what they wanted and I wasn't. These last charges who've come to me—Mandy, Crissy, Robin, and now Ainsley—have shown me that everything I ever wanted is right here."

I looked him squarely in the eye, praying he understood what *everything* meant. It took all my willpower to not throw myself into his arms and tell him my true feelings.

He met my gaze, various muscles flexing as his chest heaved. He felt the same way, didn't he? He loved me, too. Didn't he?

"Yes." His voice cracked and he cleared his throat. "I accept your offer and will return and serve the Guides as their leader again."

Relief burst from my heart and flooded me. I'd still be able to see him. I could still fight for him.

I blinked and had to look away. "Then, let's decide on the new rules and summon everyone to the commons area."

Chapter 25

Ainsley

Mum's smile faltered when she saw the baby in my arms. I told her, in one of the many messages I left, that Ginger had arrived. Guess there's nothing like seeing the real thing.

"Mum. What are you doing here?"

I reached out one arm to give her a quick hug while holding tight to Ginger with the other. I closed the door and stepped outside. I wanted to invite her in but wasn't sure what Mom and Dad would think of that.

"I'm here for you," she said. "You said that once the baby was born, you'd come back."

"Wait," I sat on the step, but Ginger started fussing, so I stood again and walked out to the driveway with her. "You packed everything up. Did you let Mina know you were leaving?"

"I left a note," Mum said with a shrug. Her standard goodbye. I couldn't remember a time when she'd ever told anyone face-to-face that we were leaving.

"She told me she was hoping you'd take care of things for her while she's gone."

"I never said I'd do that. That's not what I signed on for."

What had she signed on for? There were maybe a dozen

things, souvenirs mostly, in those eighteen boxes in the U-Haul that she never got rid of. To my knowledge, the only person she'd ever committed to was me.

"Did you at least let Hank know you were leaving?"

"It's not like I would have given two weeks or anything. I left my uniform on his desk."

She had always been . . . free spirited. I'd never considered her to be irresponsible though. Until now.

"You can't do that. People count on you."

"No one is irreplaceable, Ainsley."

"Mina is going to have to scramble to find someone to keep an eye on her house. The other servers at the diner are going to have to rearrange their schedules to fill your shifts."

"Why are you lecturing me? I told you, no one is going to miss me. They'll be fine."

It hit me at that moment, I did more parenting of her than she did of me. I was the one who worried about things like money being safely deposited into a bank rather than stored in a box under her bed. I took care of things like laundry and worried about whether we were eating well enough. I never realized how much help she needed just to get through life.

She'd always been jittery, but I'd never seen her like this. She paced constantly, like she was lost in a maze and every few steps led her to a roadblock. Her eyes were wild like she was strung out on something. There was no sense trying to reason with her right now.

"So, should we make a plan?" She laughed, a sound tainted with hysteria. "I'm not big on plans, but we could try one this time. Where should we go? How about Seattle? We've never been there. Go get your stuff. Let's go to Seattle."

Dr. Kagan had talked to me about this, about what to do if I ever saw Mum again. Actually, we were going to get deeper into that at my next session, so I wasn't as fully prepared as I should be.

"You might feel a pull to go with her," Dr. Kagan had said.

I did. Almost like an addict wanting a hit.

"She might make you feel sorry for her, and you'll feel responsible for her," Dr. Kagan had warned me.

I did. Because I knew I could calm her down if I tried hard enough.

"You're not responsible for her, Ainsley." Dr. Kagan had stated.

Mum's wild eyes were darting from me to the baby to the house. Ginger started to cry, probably sensing my anxiety.

"Nice place," Mum said. "You probably had a good time here. Sorry I can't provide anything like this for you."

She could have. Dad told me she'd had a high-paying financial position. We could have had a nice, normal life.

"I can't leave," I told her.

She looked at Ginger. "Oh, right. Babysitting. How long will they be gone? If it's not long, go put her in her crib. She'll be fine until they get back."

"What?" I hugged Ginger a little closer to me. Would she seriously leave a newborn alone? Something had snapped in her mind. She was scaring me. "No, I mean I'm not leaving *here*. These are my parents. I have a little brother and a baby sister. I want to be a part of their lives."

Her shoulders dropped. Her arms went limp at her sides. The color drained from her face.

"They've poisoned you against me. You lied. You said they didn't say anything bad about me but they have. Haven't they?"

"Virginia?"

I spun to see Mom at the front door, and I felt instantly relieved and guilty. She had her cell phone in one hand and a horrified expression on her face.

"What's going on here?" Mom nodded at the car and U-Haul and gestured for me to come to her. "Ainsley, bring Ginger to me, please."

As I got closer, I could hear Dad's voice calling out from the phone, "Noelle? What's wrong? Noelle!"

She lifted the phone to her ear. "I need you to come home. Virginia is here."

"It's okay, Mom." I set Ginger in her arms. "She's not going to do anything."

Behind me, Mum started laughing. The awful, hysterical sound was getting worse.

"You call her *Mom* now? That sure didn't take long. What exactly did they do to my sweet girl?"

"Ainsley, look at her." Mom stared, disbelieving, at the woman she used to love. "I barely recognize her. She looks psychotic."

"Let me talk to her," I said. "Let me try to calm her down."

"I don't want you to be alone with her." Mom looked sad, scared, and concerned all at once. "Please, come inside with me."

"I can't do that. I can't leave her out here."

"Well, she can't come in the house."

"I'll be right here on the driveway." I looked at Mum again as she paced and mumbled to herself. A little shiver of something, fear maybe, shot up my spine. "What do you think she's going to do? Kidnap me?"

I was trying to break the ice, but even before I saw the stone-cold expression on Mom's face, I knew it wasn't funny.

"I'm not going anywhere, I swear. You can watch us the whole time. It'll be okay."

No matter what Mum had done—all the poor decisions and now the crazy behavior—I couldn't abandon her.

Mom held out her arm for a hug. Careful to not crush Ginger, I went to her. She held on to me like she was never going to see me again.

"Please, sweetheart." Her voice caught. "Don't you see how potentially dangerous she is?"

"I'm not going anywhere. I don't want to leave."

I didn't. This was the house I wanted to live in for as long as I possibly could. My wish house.

Mom frowned and then nodded toward a dining room

window. "I'm going to sit right there until your father gets home. I've got my phone. If I see you get into that car, I'm calling the police and reporting a kidnapping."

"Fair enough."

Mom went inside, and I sat on the bench by the front door.

Dr. Kagan had suggested that I start thinking of this woman before me as *Judy*, instead of *Mum*, to sever the connection. As much as that hurt my heart, she was right.

For thirty minutes, I repeated over and over to Judy that I wasn't going with her this time, so she should go to Seattle if that's what she wanted to do. She paced and picked at the sleeve of her ragged sweatshirt. She kept mumbling to herself. That concerned me, but didn't bother me until I heard her say, "*Mina* will be fine. *Mina* has *friends* who will watch her house."

There was venom laced into the words *Mina* and *friends*. Like me, Mum . . . Judy had no friends. The closest had been in Holly Lake since that's where we'd lived the longest. If Gabrielle had never put my picture on the website, we'd still be there. I think Judy had gotten tired of running, too. The fact that she'd hung a calendar on the refrigerator, that she *bought* a calendar, was a clear sign to me that she had started to consider Holly Lake our home, not someplace we were visiting.

I jumped when I heard the garage door start to open. Dad's silver Audi appeared a second later and pulled directly into the garage.

"Go inside." His voice echoed in the garage. "Go find Mommy and Ginger."

"Who is that lady?" Noah asked.

"I'll tell you later. Go inside." Dad's voice was firm, and the tone was one Noah wouldn't dare argue with. He came out to the driveway and stood, protectively, next to me. "Virginia . . . Sorry. Judy, what's going on? What are you doing here?"

"Ainsley's been here long enough," she snapped. "Everyone got to know her. It's time for her to come home now."

"This is her home, Judy," Dad stated in that same firm tone.

"You know that. This has always been her home. We've just been waiting for her to come take her place in it."

"You can't have her." Angry tears pooled in Judy's eyes. "You gave her to me. She's mine."

Dad turned toward the window where Mom stood with Ginger and gave her a thumbs down.

"We can talk about this," Dad said, soothing now, "but you need to calm down."

"I don't need to do anything," she screamed. "All I need is for my daughter to come home with me."

"She's not your daughter," Dad corrected.

I went to her and wrapped my arms around her. Her entire body was shaking. "Please, you're scaring me."

"Scared?" She pushed out of my arms. "You want to know scared? Imagine your daughter being taken from you and never knowing if you'll see her again."

"Exactly," Mom said, standing next to Dad. She wasn't holding Ginger anymore. She must have tucked her into the cradle in the family room. "Imagine feeling the way you're feeling right now for fifteen years."

"You gave her to me," Mum insisted again, although without quite so much anger. The quiet, steely resolve was almost scarier.

"I left her in your care," Mom said. "I was back three days later, like I told you I would be, and you were gone." She looked at me. "Worst mistake I ever made. I should have taken you with me."

Dad put a supportive arm around her.

"You never should have left at all." Judy's words were heavy with anger and hurt. "Do you remember how much I loved you? I forgave you." She jutted her chin at Dad. "You getting pregnant was a happy accident. I was willing to raise her with you." She smiled and seemed to be thinking back fifteen years at the life the three of us could have had together. "We would have been such a happy family."

"Virginia," Mom said, "I'm sorry. I was young and more than

a little stupid at the time. I didn't handle things the right way. We should have talked before I went to that conference. I should have told you how I felt and how confused I was. I'm so sorry that I hurt you."

A police car and ambulance pulled up the driveway. The police car stopped behind the U-Haul. The ambulance in front of the Volvo.

I spun toward Mom and Dad. I could tell, by the looks on their faces, that's what the thumbs down had been. A signal to Mom that things weren't going to go well. Call the authorities.

"Virginia Rosen?" the police officer asked when he got close to her.

"I don't know who that is. My name is Judy Blue." Her frantic eyes landed in turn on everyone, last and longest on Mom. "What's going on?"

"Ms. Blue," the officer said, obviously trying to not agitate her further, "we need to ask you a few questions about Kira Elizabeth Lancaster."

My breath caught. Was that my birth name?

"I don't know who that is either." The color drained from Judy's face. "I have nothing to say. I haven't done anything wrong." She darted for the car. "Ainsley, come on. It's time to go."

The officer went to her, and she yelled for him to stay away. He grabbed ahold of her and positioned her arms behind her. She went limp, like a protestor, and tried to slide out of his grip.

"Stop, please." I'd never felt so helpless. "Don't hurt her."

Mom was behind me then, her hands on my shoulders. "They're not going to hurt her, sweetheart."

The officer pulled Judy up to stand. As she thrashed and objected, one of the two paramedics came over and injected something into her arm. Within seconds, she was slumping, her head flopping to the side. She looked over my shoulder at Mom.

"I never loved anyone like I loved you." Her words slurred. "You broke my world and shattered my heart."

The other paramedic rolled a stretcher over and they eased her on to it. They covered her with a blanket, strapped her down, and put her in the back of the ambulance.

The officer came over to Dad.

"We'll take her to the hospital, Eddie," he said. "They'll check her over in the ER first, and then she'll most likely be admitted to the psychiatric ward for a thorough evaluation."

"She's not crazy," I insisted.

Even to me, my protest sounded weak. I wanted to defend her. To say she'd taken good care of me over the years. I was fine. And if I was fine, how could she have done anything wrong?

But Mom's words rang out in my head. *I was back three days later, like I told you I would be, and you were gone. Worst mistake I've ever made.*

She hadn't abandoned me. She left me in the care of her best friend. She'd always planned to come back for me.

I turned away from the ambulance and fell sobbing into Mom's arms. She held me and stroked my hair and assured me over and over that everything would be okay. I turned my head to watch the ambulance and the police car pull away.

"She'll be okay," Mom soothed. "They'll take good care of her. She'll be okay. We'll work all of this out."

"Whoa!" Noah came running, full speed, out of the house. "Ambulance. That's so cool."

He would have chased it all the way to the hospital if Dad hadn't snatched him up, mid-run. In the same firm voice he had used minutes before, Dad said, "Get back in the house, Noah. We'll be right in."

Noah started to protest but then hung his head when Dad pointed and went back inside.

When I couldn't see the ambulance anymore, I pulled away from Mom and faced my parents.

"She needs help. Promise me she'll get the best."

"Don't worry," Dad said. "They're taking her to the hospital where I work. From there, she'll get top-notch care."

"Can I go see her?" I wrapped my arms around myself, suddenly shivering and damp from the misting rain. Not sure when that had started.

"They'll have to evaluate her and determine exactly what kind of care she needs," Mom said. "Let's go inside."

She put an arm around me and led me to the family room where Ginger was sound asleep in her cradle. Mom settled me on the couch, wrapped a blanket around my shaking legs, and turned on the gas fireplace.

"I'm going to check on Noah," Dad said. "I'll turn on a movie or something to keep him entertained for a while. I'll be right back."

"Bring Ainsley a sweater when you come back, will you?" Mom asked.

While Dad did that, Mom made me some hot apple cider. Despite the blanket and the fire, I couldn't stop shaking. In my head, I knew that what Mum . . . Judy had done was wrong. Our entire fifteen years together had been a lie, but I still loved her. Dr. Kagan had warned me it would take a while for that feeling to go away. If it ever did.

Dad told me to lean forward and tucked a thick sweater around me when I did. Mom handed me a mug of cider and sat next to me on the couch, one hand on my knee. "Tell us what's going on."

I told them everything I could about Judy. Some of it, like recounting all of the traveling we'd done together, was stuff I'd already told them. Some, like her changing our appearance every now and then, was new. I told them about my under-the-stars phone call with Bryce a few nights earlier and how I was thinking that a shared-custody, divorce-style arrangement might work. I didn't think that anymore. I understood how messed up Judy was. Then I told them what Dr. Kagan said about needing time.

"I know you guys, Noah, and Ginger are my family," I said.

"Please believe me, I don't ever want to be away from you again."

"Would you like to keep seeing Dr. Kagan?" Dad asked.

"I think it would be a good idea," Mom encouraged. "You take all the time you need. We're not going anywhere either."

I nodded and started crying. For the life I missed out on for fifteen years. For the life I didn't have anymore. Most of all, I cried for Judy and wished that one day she would be happy and healthy again.

Chapter 26

Desiree

T he buzz in the commons area was part anticipation, part grumble. I'd let Olanna and Indira spread the word that big changes were about to occur. Because I trusted Indira completely, I told her what Kaf and I had come up with. She approved of everything. Because I didn't trust Olanna to back us up, I told her only that there would be changes.

The Guides had gathered in record time. Despite half of them not liking me—hopefully, that would get better once I was a Guide again and began working on my social skills—they were extremely curious about this announcement.

I hopped up onto the kitchen bar and placed my fingers together. The chime, indicating I was ready to begin, sounded, and the buzz quieted.

"I've got a lot to say," I began. "Some of you will be very happy. Others, maybe not so much. Either way, please keep an open mind and let me say everything before you bombard me with questions or protests. Agreed?"

A soft mumble indicated they did. Ironic that I got them all to agree on something just as I was stepping down.

"There have been a lot of changes made since I took over. Some of them good, some not so much." I motioned to Indira,

Kaf, and Olanna who were standing together in front of me. "We've had many discussions and did a lot of negotiating. This is what we've decided.

"First, we will remain here at Mystic Lodge." Despite their promise, a few grumbles sounded. "New rules are easier to adjust to in a new place. Second, you are no longer bound by the contract you agreed to with Kaf. Most of you agreed to a fifty-year indenture, like I did. From this moment, any agreements are null and void. If you want to stay forever, you can. If you've decided you've done all you care to do here, you are free to leave and move on to whatever life will make you happy."

I knew a few of the older Guides had no family left and were ready to go to wherever and whatever came after life in this realm. I would help them move on peacefully and with dignity.

"Some of you have friends and family in the human world," I continued. "If you would like to see them, you will be allowed to. It's not right for you to never be with the people who mean the most to you." I looked at Adellika and she nodded humbly. When the Guides found out that she was Kaf's sister, many didn't take it well and protested how unfair it was. "Those people will be bound by silence. They can't tell anyone about us or our world. If they break this agreement, their memories of you will be wiped and you will not be allowed to see them again. We have to maintain our privacy. I'm sure you can imagine what could happen if people found out we can grant wishes."

Murmurs of agreement sounded at that.

"Next," I said, "time off."

"We're getting vacation time?" one of the Guides called out.

"Will we get medical benefits, too?" another joked.

"A bonus package for Guides." I smiled. "I like it. Here's the thing, we can't just leave anytime we want."

That got some grumbles.

"I know, I know." I held my hands up in surrender. "I'm guiltiest of that. It won't happen again. We still need to figure out the details for this, but it's only fair that you get time off to do your own thing."

So far, so good. Everything I'd mentioned was for their benefit, nothing they could have objection to. The next two things worried me.

"As we've already discussed, Guides will no longer be only female. All people, regardless of gender, race, sexual orientation, and so on will be welcome here. Like with any job in the human world. As much as I hate it, segregation might be necessary. Separate floors in the Lodge or another lodge altogether. We'll figure it out. Trust me, any Guide, whether male, female, or other who causes problems here will be removed. If you can't live with this rule, you are free to leave."

After the drama of bringing Clay into our world, I was pleasantly surprised that there were only a few objections. Maybe the protests really had been about all of the changes and not him. I looked at Clay, standing off to the side with Amber, and gave him a wink. I knew he'd fit in well.

I took a breath and Bob Dylan's, "The Times They Are A-Changin'," played in my head. Now, for the big news.

"One last thing, and then you can ask questions. Effective immediately, I am no longer your leader."

This created a stew of groans and applause. I held up my hand and needed to sound a gong to quiet them this time.

"This is not a position I should ever have been placed in." Agreements and protests. "I've decided that I want to return to my place with all of you as a Guide. I will work with charges and apprentice new Guides like I have Clay."

"Who's gonna run the place?" someone called out.

I turned to Kaf and motioned for him to join me.

"Kaf has agreed to return."

The uproar was instantaneous. I waited, silently, for the celebrating and objections to die down. Finally, with powers restored, Kaf clapped his hands together. The shock wave through the commons silenced everyone.

"I agree with all of the changes Desiree told you about," he began. "As she has pointed out, the human world changes constantly. To truly help our charges, we must change as well."

"One thing won't change," I said. "Indira will still be Kaf's second in command."

"Actually," Kaf said, "that is not true."

What? She wasn't leaving was she? As much as I wanted Kaf here, I wanted Indira, too. I'd been looking forward to becoming better friends with her. She told me she was happy with her life. What happened?

"Indira will be third in the hierarchy," Kaf stated. "Desiree will be my second."

Me? Was he kidding? We never talked about this.

"As has been made abundantly clear to me, at least half of you prefer the changes Desiree has made." He looked me dead in the eye. Emotion smoldered there and made my breath catch. "It only makes sense that she be my second."

I narrowed my eyes at him and whispered, "I told you, I want to be a Guide again. Don't you think it would have been a good idea to ask me first?"

Kaf ignored me. "You may all return to your duties. You will be able to find me in the small cabin Desiree has been using as an office."

He stumbled a little on the word office. Kaf didn't like thinking of the magical world as a business, but that's what it was. We had customers. We offered them a service. Our employer was the universe.

Many of the Guides came up to Kaf with questions. He responded by holding up a hand.

"Not now," he said. "You may come to me later. I have to talk with Desiree first."

He took me by the arm and led me outside, across the patio, and to the cabin.

I jerked my arm out of his grasp. "I don't appreciate being ignored. Or led around like a dog. I thought we had already agreed to everything. You made me look foolish by altering my words moments after I said them."

"Making you look foolish was not my intention." The smoldering look had grown even more intense. "I should have talked to you about it first, but I have come to a decision."

"A decision about what?"

That look on his face, a mixture of emotions, freaked me out.

"About you, Desiree," he blurted. He clearly was struggling with something major as he glanced toward the windows. Guides were hovering outside like moths drawn to light. He placed his palms together, and the window blackened.

"They can hear what we're saying," I said. "Olanna does an enchantment to amplify our voices."

He placed his hands together again. "Now, they cannot."

"Kaf, what's going on?"

"There is something I need to say to you."

He lowered his eyes. Was he nervous? Kaf *never* got nervous.

"I have wanted to say this for a long time, but events needed to happen the way that they did. Your wish needed to complete."

He was mumbling, partly to me, but it seemed mostly to himself. Was he saying that all of this, all that I'd been going through here, was still part of my wish?

As I struggled to understand, Kaf kept muttering about how events had to happen the way they did. That I had to know for certain what I wanted.

"Because if you did not know for certain, what I want would not matter," he said and looked into my eyes. My heart nearly stopped when he did. "Waiting has been agony."

What was he trying to say? I took a step closer to him, closing the gap to a few inches. I could barely speak. "Kaf, say what you're trying to say."

Chimes sounded in the cabin then.

No. I couldn't leave. She could wait a few minutes.

A pounding came at the door, and I knew it was Clay.

"Desiree," he called. "Ainsley summoned us."

If Kaf didn't say whatever he was trying to say right now, he might never say it. I looked desperately up at him. "I'll be right back."

"Go be a genie." He let out a sigh and gently brushed strands of hair from my eyes. "I will be right here."

The chimes sounded again as I crossed the cabin. I stepped outside, and Clay reached to place a hand on my shoulder and take me to Ainsley's side. Charges always came first, but this time, I didn't have to be the one to go.

"You're ready," I told Clay. "Go take care of our girl. Tell her everything is working out exactly as it should."

When Clay disappeared, I turned back, placed my hand on the knob, and froze.

Chapter 27

Ainsley

Before the flatbed truck came to take the Volvo and U-Haul away, I grabbed my seven boxes from inside the trailer. Dad said we'd put them in the storage area in the basement until I decided how much of it I wanted to keep. The rest of it would be held by the police until the decision on what would happen with Judy was made.

Dad picked up a couple of the boxes to bring downstairs, and I stopped him.

"Hang on."

I opened the box with my pillows and blanket. Until that moment, I never realized how threadbare that blanket was. Compared to what I now had, everything from my life so far seemed threadbare. The blanket wasn't what I wanted, though. Lying safely underneath it were my stuffed puppy, which was about the same size as Ginger, and a small stuffed cow.

"Hi, guys." I clutched them over my heart as I closed the box again. "Okay, you can take it."

"Oh my god," Mom gasped from behind me. "You still have your cow?"

"He's my favorite. Why are you crying?"

"He was the first thing I ever bought for you." She

wiped at the tears on her face but more immediately fell. "I found him in a little gift section of an ice cream parlor. I used to get wicked cravings for mint chocolate chip sundaes with hot fudge and whipped cream when I was pregnant. Haven't had a single scoop of the stuff since you were born. Anyway, I'd settled into my favorite corner table one day and was about to take the first bite when I saw him staring at me."

I smiled at her memory and my heart filled. "I thought he'd be a good nap-buddy for Ginger. Moo Cow is very good at napping."

Judy must have been in a frantic state when she packed this time. Three of my ghost fiddle glasses had broken. It had taken me so long to find them; they'd be hard to replace. Or so I thought. Mom had a small collection of crystal glasses she'd gotten from a great-aunt.

"See if any of them will work," she told me. "You can have them all if you want. I'm not much of a crystal person."

I set up the fiddle on the dining room table and found one from Mom's collection that was perfect.

"We'll go on a scavenger hunt to all the antique shops and second-hand stores around Portland and find more." She nodded at the mostly complete fiddle. "Play for us."

"It's been weeks. I'm a little out of practice." I was in the middle of the theme from *Harry Potter* when the phone rang.

"Keep going," Dad said. "Ginger loves it."

She'd made a noise that almost sounded like a laugh when I started playing. After a minute or so, she fell soundly asleep in Mom's arms with a smile on her tiny face.

"Maybe we'll set that up in her room," Mom whispered. "You can play her to sleep."

After I finished, I did a pinky-promise with Noah that I'd teach him how to play it. Mom brought Ginger up to her bed, and Dad asked Noah to go play with Sprite and Pixie outside.

"I need to talk with your sister for a minute." Once Noah had left, Dad motioned for me to follow him to the family room. "That was my police officer friend."

"News about Judy?" I stuttered on her name whenever I said it out loud. It still didn't feel right to call her that.

"You know that I requested the best team we have at my hospital to evaluate her."

"Have they come to a decision?"

I'd learned to read Dad's expressions, and knew I wasn't going to like the answer. Then again, the only answer I would have been happy with was that she was going free to start a new life.

"She's not going to prison," Dad said. "Not yet, at least. They're sending her to a mental health hospital for treatment. The staff there is topnotch. Understand, though, she could be there for a long time."

It was fair, I knew that. But my heart was absolutely broken that she would be locked up.

That night in bed, I thought of how things had turned out and wondered if I'd really gotten what I'd wished for. I tossed from my right side to my back. A few seconds later, I flipped to my left side and stared out my window at the stars and moon peeking through the clouds. Finally, I threw back my covers, pulled on my robe and slippers, grabbed the stone Desiree had given me, and turned on my phone's flashlight app.

When I got to the dock, I placed my thumb on the peace sign and waited. A good thirty seconds passed. It had never taken them this long. Did that mean my wish was officially over? I knew the truth about everything and had a home that I never had to leave, and now, I was on my own?

I put my thumb on the peace sign again. I needed to talk to them.

It had started to rain, a gentle but steady drizzle. My robe was getting pretty wet, and I started to shiver. I wrapped a blanket from the big plastic box on the dock around my shoulders.

"I was about to give up on you," I said when Clay arrived a few seconds later.

"Sorry, I went for Desiree, but she said I should come myself."

He put his arms in Superman pose, but let them drop when I didn't laugh. He looked up at the rain falling on us and snapped his fingers. An invisible roof formed over the dock. If I would've stuck my hand out beyond the dock perimeter, it would have gotten wet.

"So," Clay said, "what's going on?"

"Is this it? Is my wish done?" I asked. "Is this the way it's supposed to end? I'm happy to be here with Mom and Dad. I don't ever want to leave them again."

"But?" Clay prompted.

"But they're going to lock Judy up in a psych ward for who knows how long." I blinked. "She's a good woman. She did a bad thing, but she's not a bad person. Why can't anyone see that?"

"Is that what they think? That she's a bad person?" He waited for me to respond, but my emotion-clogged throat wouldn't let me. "I don't think they do. I think they see someone who needs help, and that's what they're giving her. You get that, right?"

"Shouldn't wishes end happily?" I choked on a sob.

"Listen," Clay began, motioning for me to sit in the dock chairs with him, "as far as I can tell, you got what you wished for. You learned the truth. You get to live in a killer home with your real family. Desiree taught me that when our wishes end, our new lives begin. Your wish got you where you want to be. You get to live the life you wanted. You're gonna have to deal with stuff without magic from here on out."

I listened to the rain falling on the invisible roof and thought of my first fifteen years. "My time with Judy, that wasn't much of a life, was it?"

Clay shrugged. "I don't know about that. Every experience

makes us who we are. Would I do the last two years of my life over again? It wasn't one I'd wish for. Pardon the pun." He nudged my knee with his, and I smiled. "But if I hadn't gone through what I did, I wouldn't be sitting here with you right now."

"She did a good job with me, right? I mean, I'm not a totally messed up person, am I?"

"Not totally." He joked and then turned serious when I didn't smile. "We're all a little messed up. You are a very understanding person. You've got a good heart, and you care a lot about people. I don't think I've ever met anyone who lives in the moment the way you do. That's a damn good quality to have."

Ironically, I learned to live in the moment because of Judy's habit of never returning to a place.

"You are totally you, and she helped with that," Clay said. "I'm proud that you were my first charge."

I leaned over and threw my arms around him then. "Thank you, Clay. Everything will work out like it's supposed to, right?"

"That's what Desiree told me to tell you. Hold on to that, and you'll be fine."

I nodded. "I'm going to miss her."

"Judy or Desiree?"

I laughed. "Both. But I meant Judy."

"Of course, you'll miss her," he agreed. "You know what, though? Even though my dad was a complete jerk, I still miss him sometimes. Not that I ever want to see him again. I'm done with him. Some people aren't meant to be in our lives forever, I guess."

"Will I ever see Judy again?"

"I can't answer that," Clay said. "None of us know what lies ahead. That's why your way, living in the present, is a pretty good plan."

"Speaking of plans." I sniffed and pushed my glasses up. "I want to enroll at the high school here. Going to school in my bedroom is a little lonely. I need to start making some connections."

"See," he winked, "I told you, you'll be fine."

Clay disappeared then. I didn't expect to ever see him again, and that was okay. He wasn't one that was meant to be in my life forever. There were two people who would be, though. That is, if I had anything to say about it. I'd call Gabrielle tomorrow. She'd want to talk for hours. For now, I pulled my phone out of my bathrobe pocket.

"Another nightmare?" Bryce asked in his husky, sleepy voice.

"No. Hope it's okay," my voice cracked, "I need to talk to someone about what happened."

I heard the rustling of sheets, he was probably sitting up. "Yeah, that's cool. You know I'm always here. What's going on?"

Chapter 28

Desiree

I placed my hand on the knob, and froze. It had taken nearly fifty years, but my wish was about to come to its satisfying conclusion. I'd been saved from dying in that roadside ditch and was getting my second chance at life. I was a genie, doing exactly what I'd always wanted to do. There was only one thing missing.

On the other side of the door, Kaf was waiting for me. But what if what he wanted to tell me wasn't what I wanted to hear? If he didn't feel the same way about me, I would shatter into a million-zillion pieces and have to spend the rest of my life putting the bits back together.

I needed a minute, so I tapped my fingers and transported myself to the top of my bus. The cool metal beneath my hands, and the strength of her shell supporting my weight, grounded me. I tried to take comfort in the fact that no matter what happened with Kaf, I still had my home, my friends, and my charges.

In the dusting of snow on Gypsy V's roof, I found a Zen circle —put there by the universe, I assumed. A reminder that until I passed on to whatever came after this existence, my journey wasn't finished. I wanted nothing more than to travel the rest of my life path with Kaf. I'd been alone for a long time. I didn't want to be alone anymore.

I placed my hand on the circle, and the scene from that night in Kaf's cabin burst into my brain.

Look at them, the universe told me. *Really look.*

I couldn't. What if my heart couldn't handle what I saw?

Trust me.

I peeked, but only with one eye and quickly slammed it shut again. Not yet, not ready. I asked the universe for strength, and a sudden gust of freezing wind hit me like a wall. Very funny, universe. I got it; I'd hit a wall, or been hit by a wall in this case, and my journey would not move forward until I faced this fear. So, I opened both eyes.

Kaf and Olanna were together in the middle of his cabin, less than a foot separating them. A fire roared in the fireplace. She said something to him, her hands clutched together at her chest. He said something in reply. She covered her face with her hands, and her shoulders started to shake. She leaned forward, resting her forehead against his chest. His arms went around her. The look on his face, one of compassion. Not passion.

"He wasn't holding her like a lover. He was comforting her." My heart swelled and filled with hope.

What are you doing up there?

I looked down to see Rasta staring up at me. I touched my fingers together and appeared next to him on the ground.

"Assuring myself that I'm about to do the right thing."

You're going to tell Kaf how you feel?

I put an arm around my beloved dog and leaned against him. "I am."

Is there room for both of us, or will you send me away?

Not a question I expected him to ask.

"You and me, Rasta my boy, come as a set." I pointed across the lake to the Lodge. "You know how many Guides are in there?"

Yes.

"In my world I have room for you, Kaf, Indira, Mandy, Crissy, Rita, all those Guides, all of the charges I've guided, all of the Guides and charges yet to come, and I still have room for more."

That's a lot of people.

"Isn't it groovy?"

As long as I don't have to go away, Kaf is welcome.

"All right, then." I slapped my hands on the ground. "I better go do this."

It was a beautiful night. Moonlight glinted off of the fresh layer of snow like a billion scattered crystals. The air was crisp and clean, and while I could have transported to the cabin, I didn't want to miss out on this, so I walked, Rasta at my side.

"Do you want to wait outside, or go into the Lodge to be with the Guides?" I asked him when we got to the cabin.

Guides, he thought and trotted off.

I opened the door and exhaled. Kaf was still there, standing by the window facing the lake. The familiar orange and green smoke once again hovered at his feet, making it appear that he was levitating.

"You were watching me?" I asked.

"I was."

"You waited for me."

He turned to face me, his expression soft. "I told you I would."

"Tell me something else. Honestly, why did you ask me to be the Wish Mistress? You knew I wasn't the right person for the job. Olanna would have been a better choice."

He flinched slightly at Olanna's name. "I needed to get you back to our world."

Needed to? The magical world didn't need me. It was doing fine. Was it that he wanted me here?

"But why make me the Wish Mistress? Why not a Guide again?"

He stepped closer to me "You are a runner, Desiree. When

you left and went to San Antonio, you were not happy with the magical world and all of my chauvinistic—as you have called them—rules."

"No, I wasn't happy." But the rules weren't the only reason. It was too hard being so close to him and not being able to be with him.

"If you had come back as a Guide to the same conditions that you were displeased with before, you would have left again." He took another step closer. We were less than two feet apart. "If I was able to get you back, I could not let you leave again."

Because he wanted me? Was that why?

"The only way I could think to keep you here was to make you responsible for this world." He shook his head. "I am not good at this. Finding the strength to tell you what I have wanted to has taken much longer than I anticipated. It has been more than two hundred years since I last expressed true emotions."

I'm damaged after almost fifty years. I had told Rasta. *Can you imagine how lonely and broken Kaf must feel after two hundred?*

My heart hammered against my ribs. What the hell was wrong with me? It was torture for him to say as much as he had. Was I, or was I not, an independent, go for what I wanted, liberated hippie babe?

"Kaf, I—"

"I wrote this while I was away." He held out his hand, and an envelope appeared. "Please, read it."

I opened the envelope and found a page handwritten in Kaf's neat script. While I sat in one of the chairs to read, he returned to the window, his back to me.

Desiree,

I cannot remember when, but at some point I began to notice things about you. Small details that I am not sure even you are aware of. It is difficult for me to express feelings, my words do not always come together as I intend. Instead, I hope that my observations will speak for me.

Did you know that your eyes are the color of a perfect, cloudless sky?

Did you know that when you smile, a small dimple appears on the left side of your mouth?

Did you know that when you concentrate hard, you bite your bottom lip?

Every spring, after you have been in the sun for the first time, freckles sprinkle across your nose and cheeks.

When you dance, especially to Van Morrison, you seem to slip into a spiritual realm.

When you sit atop your bus to meditate, or simply appreciate your surroundings, a look of such serenity comes over you that my breath catches.

If I could have my own wish come true, it would be for you to be mine. I wish to hold you. To place my lips to yours. I do not know if you have similar feelings, but I cannot keep this to myself any longer. I must take the chance and let you know that I love you, Desiree. I have for years, and if you will have me, faults and all, I will be yours for the rest of time.

Kaf

I read the letter three times, trying to convince myself that it was meant for me. I gasped each time I came to the words *I love you, Desiree*. Still, I couldn't believe this was really happening. I folded the page and held it to my heart as I crossed the room, stopping mere inches from him.

"I know how to make wishes come true." I placed my hand on his arm, and as we connected skin-to-skin, electricity coursed through me. He turned and looked down at me. "I love you, too, Kaf. I have for years. And if you will have me, faults and all, I will be yours for the rest of time."

I stood on tiptoe and reached up to put my arms around his neck. He put his arms around me and held me against him the way I'd dreamed of for so long. I placed my lips to his, and our first kiss was soft, filled with hope, and a little shy. Our second was firm, sure, and a little desperate. All the words we hadn't been able to say to each other came through loud and clear in our kisses and caresses. The emptiness in my soul from being alone for so long, vanished as surely as if I'd tapped my fingers and sent it away. His hands on my back, my arms, and my face made me feel both desired and secure. I never wanted to stop kissing him. At the same time, I had to pull away to reassure myself that this wasn't a dream.

"When you returned to the human world, to San Antonio," he said, nearly breathless, "you asked me to provide a birth certificate. Do you remember the surname I put on it?"

"Inaba. It's your name, isn't it?"

"It is." He brushed another kiss across my mouth. "I would like for us to be together forever. I would like to share my name with you."

I trembled with the emotions rushing through me. "I'd like that, too."

He smiled and trailed a finger down my face. "One day, I will ask you properly. In the meantime, I would like to court you."

"Court me?" Who knew Kaf would be so full of surprises? "I've never been courted. I think I'd like that."

Contentedly doing what I wanted, where I wanted to do it. Finally, finally, finally with the guy I wanted.

Wish granted.

About the Author

Mystery and fantasy author Shawn McGuire loves creating characters and places her fans want to return to again and again. She started writing after seeing the first Star Wars movie (that's episode IV) as a kid. She couldn't wait for the next installment to come out so wrote her own. Sadly, those notebooks are long lost, but her desire to tell a tale is as strong now as it was then. She lives in Wisconsin near the beautiful Mississippi River and when not writing or reading, she might be baking, crafting, going for a long walk, or nibbling really dark chocolate.